WORDS ALONE ARE CERTAIN GOOD

Trenton McKay Judson

Published by Pen & Leaf Press

penandleafpress.com

ISBN: 978-1-959743-02-6

For New Orleans.

And, for Adam,

Even though you've been called home, I've felt you and heard you in every year of my life since. Thank you for sending me so many brothers to learn from, especially Chester, Kirby, Preston, Ray, Jeremy, Johnny, and Amir.

Contents

…Of old the world on dreaming fed;
Grey Truth is now her painted toy;
Yet still she turns her restless head:
But O, sick children of the world,
Of all the many changing things
In dreary dancing past us whirled,
To the cracked tune that Chronos sings,
Words alone are certain good.
Where are now the warring kings,
Word be-mockers? - By the Rood,
Where are now the warring kings?
An idle word is now their glory,
By the stammering schoolboy said,
Reading some entangled story:
The kings of the old time are dead;
The wandering earth herself may be
Only a sudden flaming word,
In clanging space a moment heard,
Troubling the endless reverie.
Then nowise worship dusty deeds,
Nor seek, for this is also sooth,
To hunger fiercely after truth,
Lest all thy toiling only breeds
New dreams, new dreams; there is no truth
Saving in thine own heart…

Dream, dream, for this is also sooth.

-W.B. Yeats.

Chapter One

"Aw! The madness of the life," she said, words curled over her lips. She pushed the cigarette smoke slow and thick out of the bottom of her mouth and it wrapped around her neck and rose behind her head like a halo of a saint in a medieval painting. It made you wonder, the way she always made you wonder, if what she said came from the rye on her breath or from the prayers she said in the stillness before she slept or even if it came from your own mind and somehow you put those words on the air for her. Or maybe it was simply the end of a long southern summer, the end of the sweat and hot air, the end of the dry throat and itchy skin, the end of the heat you couldn't escape.

She stood there hunched in the darkness of cloud cover with her pearly white dentures and her petite and fragile frame which was pushed into a tight red dress and said it again.

"Aw! The madness of the life."

Mama was fond of saying stuff like that, attaching "the" to things that didn't need it, like Jim's Liquor Store. She would say "Let's Go to *the* Jim's store," which Kirby and me were always getting roped into, and if you went one place with Mama it meant the whole day, because once you went to *the* Jim's store then you had to go to *the* Whitney Bank, and then *the* Kim's Market place for *the* green olives, and if you went the whole day with Mama, when you were finally about to go home, you were sure to stop by Papa's grave. And even though it was wet, and we were tired, we still walked with her.

The spray of rain dripped off the trees until it shot through my veins as an icicle. It burned cold under my skin and covered my eyes like justice, murkier than sap that drips through the cracks of the maple and angry like the rise of darkness over a levee.

The memories of what happened played over and over again in my mind.

Sometimes, I imagine myself as a bird, a brown pelican. I spread open my thick feathers and glide out over the Atlantic until I can't see land anymore. Out over the sea, there are endless possibilities and so I don't feel so alone. The cool sea air brushes through my body while I glide and dive between the splashes of water below. I carry nothing from the land with me and only blink when the air gets so cool that my eyes need shelter. I rise up and skip through the clouds, letting the white picture show flip through my mind as light memories of a life I can all but see and never touch. If I could tell you what it all meant, I might call it freedom, but something always pulls me back.

And so, I fly, getting sucked into the Gulf of Mexico, while I head north toward the great continent. It's there I run into the big yawning jaws of the Mississippi, that special place where the wandering tides of sea reach into the river and the mouth puckers at the kiss of fresh water and salt. And passed the skeeters and the floating sticks and the steamboats and long-lipped catfish, I find the zigzag of wooden boardwalks where young boys fish with their little sisters and the rope railings lead nowhere in particular but turn through the endless water grasses and wind struck waves of the marsh.

And as I make it down the neck of that marsh and watch the row boats paddle the wide throat of the Mississippi until they feel like they can't paddle anymore, I run right into the port, which is the heart, the throbbing and pulsing center where boats and cars and people of purpose ferry the dreams and laments of the crescent city from and to the entire world. The chambers of the heart are vast. There is the Quarter and the Garden District and Treme and the Lower Ninth Ward and they move in and out of the heart, pushing people through and then taking them back again, but never stopping, never dying, not even in the last breath of light.

As I hover over the heart I see down the ribcage of side streets and corner cafes, and deep into the belly of the city, which folks like to call Downtown, which doesn't mean much except to say that you've made it, you've made it to the city and to the climate of the city, which is the warmth and acid and energy of all the work getting done to make sure the body doesn't stop. I can see all the tired hands doing the work. It's like a flea circus. They keep working and working and working and when one goes down, another rises to take his or her place. And if you look long enough at them, you aren't sure whether they are real or part of the show. They live in the old places. The places where time slows down and you can hear the chatter, the jaws sawing those fretful notes of love and tears, swinging together like electrons in the same shell.

New Orleans. Where the marsh is always close by, where at any moment your feet might be covered in mud and your knees one inch above water, feet stuck in wet dirt and chest crusted over with abalone. Next to the old oak in Mrs. Walker's yard, and across the street from the peach panels of the Robinson's siding, two doors down from the red brick of Mr. Dottol, the lonely old widower with a sweet tooth for business.

At last, I land on Holt Cemetery, where the grass is never green. The only place in the city where you can bury your dead because what with the city being so far under the sea level, if you bury a body in the wrong spot, they are very fond of popping back up, bloated and full of that special stench that only a half-buried body can provide. If I remember right, they will bury anybody or anything for $450, cash. They say that Holt Cemetery came around because poor folks couldn't afford mausoleums and Holt will bury you for cheap. And the people that built the old places were there, smiling those fleshless grins from underneath the spotty grass and shallow dirt, and one mound, three rows down and three rows up is where they buried my father, Dr. Chester Larsen. I flew down and let my feet grip the chill of the granite. And it's there I see the rock that commemorates my father's life, and it doesn't seem so heavy anymore because a bird sees no more in a tree branch than it does in a telephone pole and no more does it regard the smallest blade of grass than the drop of rain into a river. And yet, a bird sees more in a day than most of us see in a lifetime.

This is one week in the life of a brown pelican, magnified by the poetry of Janus, subtracted from the anger of a monster, and divided by the sage souls that hold my life together like stops while riding on a Delphic train, leaves floating on water, wishes trapped in flesh.

Most of the moments in our lives seem insignificant until we look back on them. We try to order them, put them in some neat narrative that makes sense, but if we look close enough, we can see that the disconnectedness of actual living is even better than the plot we tried to make it into. This is then, a story of a bird.

"Aw! The madness of the life" my mother repeated.

"He was such a good man, don't you know what a good man he was?" she would say, and we would answer, "Yes, Mama, we know," even if we didn't, because it had been so long since we knew Dad. So long since we had heard him tell his stories. He loved to tell stories.

I remember he was strong. He had a large back. He picked his teeth with a toothpick. He had a hairy chest and thick arms. He believed in heritage, that our family had the same blood as the great knights of England. He believed that in our bones was a responsibility to pass on the tradition of chivalry and honor no matter what year it was.

"You are an Englishman," he would tell me. "Then, you are an American. Then, you are a New Orleanian. But above all, you must always be a man of honor."

Of course, it wasn't the chivalry or honor most people know now, which has become opening doors or being polite or some such thing. It was the code of the knights, the true chivalry of acting with honor in all situations and treating every person with that honor, seeing in them the possibility of greatness, of God. He knew all the stories and songs of Arthur, Percival, Guinevere, The Green Knight, Tristan, Lancelot, Merlin, and Vivien. He would summon them in quiet moments: after our meal had settled in at dusk, on the porch as we listened to the ballads of warblers, on a walk through the sticks looking for a wildflower to give to my mother, or before he left for work at the hospital in the morning. My father was a storyteller. That was what I remembered. Being thirteen and told by my father for the last time that I should be a man of honor. And when you are boy and your dad dies you can only remember him as a hero, so I didn't know him as a man, didn't know what faults he had. I had lost that. I had lost a whole side of my life.

From the moment Dad died, Mama changed. The glimmer of her youth was gone, and she became, in a word, desperate. She was spraying on the past with every can of hair dye, every wrinkle cream, every thick layer of makeup pressed on feverishly before she exited her room. My mother never believed in honor. She only believed in herself and her superstitions. When Mama asked me, two days after Dad died, to sit and smoke a pack of cigarettes with her, even though I was thirteen, I did it.

I did a lot of things for Mama. It was hard for me to tell her no and she knew it. I took care of her and Kirby. I had to. The days of wandering the neighborhood on my bike with the other boys were gone. I didn't get to be a child and Mama held that power over me. My Dad told the stories, and my mother lived them. But, even if she had been a good mother, she couldn't have told me how to shave or how to play catch or what to say to the woman I loved.

I had the skin of a man on, but without a father, a man, in many ways, always stays a boy. Even when I graduated from High School, I didn't go. I couldn't leave Kirby with Mama. He wouldn't make it.

But there was Janus. Her name followed me everywhere. It's pronounced Jay-nus, like the Greek god. The only thing I knew about her parents was why they named her Janus, because she looked like a god when she was born, heavenly white skin against scarlet red hair. And that's how I always see her, sculpted by the gods and goddesses of the swamps. But it's more than that too. She's been in the twitch of a vein over my knuckle, in the silence after I exhale but before I catch my next breath. She was in my warm wet nose after a July rainstorm and the scent of spruce and pine and trout. She was the cocktail of yellow crocuses and brown eyelashes and the click-clack of knee-high black boots. Somehow, without even knowing it, she was in the praline and caramel ice cream scoops the first time I realized my dad was really gone. She couldn't have known, could she? But mystery isn't made for us to understand, only to keep us guessing, fruitful, awake.

I needed to leave Mama and Kirby would have to come with me. Janus and me and Kirby. I had to get the strength to leave, even though the soundtrack of my father's words replayed over and over again in my mind.

"Promise me you'll take care of your mother. It's the honorable thing to do. Never forget who you are or where you came from. You are an Englishman. Then, you are an American. Then, you are a New Orleanian. But above all, you must always be a man of honor."

Those were the exact words he said, choking and coughing from the Emphysema and spitting up the last of his dignity into a brown plastic bucket.

I promised him. I wasn't just saying the words, I meant it.

Looking at my father's dull gray headstone, I resented my promise.

Kirby smacked his lips and let his eyes well up. Talking about Dad always riled Kirby and he would get to crying and carrying on all afternoon.

"What's wrong with you, Chubbs?" I asked him.

I had called Kirby "Chubbs" since he was a baby. In retaliation, he called me "Princess."

"Nothing," he would say.

"Damnit! Chubbs, what's wrong?"

So, he told me, the way he had told me so many times, how he was thinking about Dad, how he couldn't stop thinking about him. Then, he asked me what would happen if *he* died and I told him, "Damnit! You aren't going to die, Chubbs. You are going to be just fine!"

"But what if I did?" he asked.

I kept reassuring him he wouldn't, that he couldn't because I needed him, and Mama needed him and Janus needed him and he had too much to do before he left this world.

Mama acted like she didn't hear him. "I'm so alone now," she cried. "Promise me! Promise me you will never put me in a nursing home."

"I won't let you go to one of those places," I told her.

She cried again and added a few more times how alone she really was.

You couldn't help but feel bad for her.

Mama stepped over to the grave next to Dad's. He had bought both of them together so she could be buried with him when she died. Then, she lay on the damn grass next to him and kissed it and cried about being alone and eventually it got too hot, and she was ready for another drink.

We walked her home. Mama with her pea coat and red dress and dark round glasses and pink lipstick. Each step was rehearsed, each shuffle played out. She doused herself in perfume to cover the smell of smoke and always kept a small bottle of Listerine in her purse for the liquor smell. If all else failed, she thrust those hips deeper and deeper into that damn walk until anybody watching her was so dizzy they forgot what hour it was or what kept them breathing air. In the fifteen years since Dad was gone, her pretenses hadn't help her find a replacement, although it wasn't for a lack of looking. A hint of aftershave would perk up her ears like a dog chasing a rabbit. All of it was a production, an attempt to reach some mysterious audience she was always prepared for. I'm not sure she dared to say who that audience was, but I believe it was Father Time. "Halt!" was the name of the play and he wasn't watching. But it didn't stop her from trying. That play ran twenty-four hours a day. We all had revolving roles.

There were times she didn't even like us calling her Mama. "I'm much more like your sister," she said. "You should call me Sally."

She flipped her hair over her shoulder and Kirb rolled his eyes.

Mama went to the kitchen to get a drink. We watched. We didn't know whether she was going to tell us that we were the best sons she ever had or make us check under her bed for phantoms or piss her pants or just go stark mad.

I went to our room to check on Janus. Scraps of paper and napkins were strewn around the room, sowing together the torment of her one ineffable scream.

"How you doing hunny?" I asked.

"I want to tell you something Ernest." She said, in the most casual way. "I want to tell you something, *important.*"

"I'm listening," I said.

She puckered her lips and put on some bright pink lipstick, a shade I had never seen her wear before.

"Why are you putting on makeup this late?"

"I have a job interview tomorrow," she said.

"Okay," I said, puzzled. "What did you want to tell me?"

"I don't like emotion," she said coolly. "I don't want anything to do with it anymore. I don't like touching and I don't like sleeping in the same bed with you and I don't like sex either. I don't like giving any more."

She put down the lipstick tube and picked up the little brush that women use to color their eyelashes. I got a glimpse of her looking at me in the mirror and I noticed that her chin was fighting with the emotion in her throat. Her stare chilled my ribs like a cold ocean swell when you swim out just a little too far. This was the new Janus, the Janus that refused to be hurt.

"If that's how you feel," I said.

I didn't say anything else. I left her to her makeup and her mirrors and her stare.

"I'd like to go outside and look at the stars," Mama professed loudly as I made it to the living room.

Kirb and me took her out on the porch. I'll be damned if she didn't pull one of those mini bottles out of her pocket and throw a couple of pills in the back of her throat before draining all the liquid out with a big sigh.

"Aw!" The madness of the life," she said again, stirring up the stale air. "It doesn't take much to slip away. It's too damn mad and too damn wild and then- What can you do when there's not much left?"

She let that sink into the porch slats and simmer.

"I went to the doctor today," she said all heavy and hot. She might well have put her palm up against her forehead and wriggled on the ground, it was so damn dramatic. She was real fond of painting pictures in your mind of how sorry you were going to be when all the people you loved died, and how much more sorry we were both going to be when *she* died, even though according to her, she'd been dying for years. Mama was always spouting off about how she had a bad heart and bad lungs and bad blood and a bad constitution, all of which was sending her inevitably downward, and she didn't do much living in the meantime, not outside of talking about dying, and what kind of living is that anyhow?

"What'd he say this time?"

"What do you mean *this* time?" She hissed. "He said my heart was failing me and that it is only a matter of God's will until I croak."

Mama twisted off the top of another mini bottle.

"What does that mean?" Kirb asked.

"It means die Chubbs." I told him. "She is telling us that's she's dying."

I wanted to add 'again," but thought better of it.

Kirb's head twitched, and his face turned red and sad, as it was wont to do when anybody mentioned death or dying or even heartbreak.

"And I should tell you boys you need treat this with the delicacy that it requires."

She titled her chin and pulled a cigarette out of her silver cigarette case and lit it.

"You know I would give my left arm. I'd have my left arm cut off right here and now if I could have just one more conversation with my mother. Y'all don't know how lucky you have it."

She puffed on her cigarette with all the theatrical gestures of a royal person at court and in the dark I could see the haunting shine of cataracts in her eyes, like a falcon hovering above its nest, scanning the shadows for prey.

"What was grandma like?" I asked.

"And to think," she said, "Your Mama's right here and all you can say is what did he say *this time*."

I soaked that in and got to feeling sorry for her. I didn't want to, but I couldn't help it.

My grandfather and grandmother had died the same day. Mama was only seventeen when it happened. They were both drunk. They had gotten in a fight and my grandmother went into the garage and put a hose in the exhaust of their '68 Ford and turned it on. What she didn't know, what she couldn't have known is that my grandfather had passed out by one of the heating vents and the monoxide pushed through and killed him too. I never knew them. Mama was still a girl when it happened. She was the one who found them. If she got enough drink in her, she would recount every detail, even the smell of the garage and the blood coming from my grandfather's mouth. Shortly after, she had met Dad. He was her family's doctor, and he was married to another woman. Because Mama was friends with his daughter Shirley and had no siblings, he asked her to stay with them. He left his family for her three months later. She was seventeen. He was forty-five. We were not allowed to speak of it.

"Okay Mama," I said. "I'm sorry about your heart."

"Did you might die?" Kirb asked.

"I am dying honey. It won't be long," she said. Even the horrible parts of the past were Mama's obsession. The heartbreak moved her voice like a marionette.

Kirb smacked his lips and looked down at his stomach, descending deeper and deeper into his own heartbreak. My blood was getting damn warm and you might even say hot. All the pity became rage. I mean, how dare Mama say something like that to Chubbs? She knew he would take it inside, like he took everything. That he would take it right into his soul and carry it with him, carry it to the place where he put all Mama's empty bottles, all my furies, all the glaring looks and insults behind his back, and all the ghosts in the procession of our families' past. How dare she?!

"Maybe it's that medicine you take so much," I said coolly and pointed at the bottle as she tipped it to her lips. She flared her nostrils and gave me the stare of resentment she had perfected, the one where she put all the hate she felt toward herself and pushed it right onto you by squinting her eyes and shaking her head.

"Maybe it is!" She spat. "Or maybe it's because I have such an ungrateful son and God is fixing to teach him a real good lesson, a lesson about not forgetting where he lays his head at night and who puts food on his table and brought him into this world."

Then she pointed a boney finger my way and said, "Beware! Beware of tomorrow boy! Beware of this week! Beware of this month! Things will catch up to you! And you will wish you would have treated your mother better!"

On every word, there seemed a pointed edge, something I did not yet understand, some far off feeling of what was to come. I shrugged it off. It was a penchant of Mama's to offer threats that made no damn sense to anybody. I think you lose a lot in this life if you spend all your time trying to figure someone else out, 'cause nobody can figure anybody out, not even themselves, but it don't stop some folks from trying.

"You can't count on nothing boy," she continued. "As soon as you start counting on something, the lord sees fit to take it away from you. He is a whimsical one! There ain't no order to what he does, at least that much we can understand. You might walk out of that door and never see your Mama's face again, and then how would you feel? Nobody's safe in this world, Ernest! Not you, not me, not your broth-"

"He's safe! He's safe, as long as he's with me!" I snapped.

"Nobody's safe," she repeated. "Death don't run on Pacific time."

Mama was right, it didn't, but luckily for us *she* did, and so after Mama drank a couple more little bottles and cursed me and cursed the weather and cursed even her dear and precious lord, she went to sleep.

I carried her into her bed, her soft and wrinkled frame light on my arms. I pulled the wool blanket over her chest and tucked the sides under her feet, as she had taught me to do when I was a boy.

Janus was asleep on our bed, hair puffed up with hairspray, arms around a pillow.

Kirby and me said our thanks to whatever cosmic force was up in the sky or out in the grass mulling around like a field mouse.

I went to sleep on the couch, making sure my alarm was at an early enough time of morning we would avoid seeing Mama with one of her monstrous hangovers.

Chapter Two

Kirb and me stepped onto the sidewalk. I had the day off, so I had plans to take Kirb for a walk in the city. Janus had left earlier for her job interview. I was happy she was getting out of the house.

Miss Marlin sat on her porch rocking and playing that damn thirties martini music and cold air crept up my nostrils and into my head. I could hear the Goldsmith's black lab barking at the Robinson's terrier while the clang of a garbage truck jumped across the gravel.

There's something about sidewalks. They aren't like streets or highways or train tracks because they *transport* you rather than take you somewhere and the only other thing I know that can do that is water. In New Orleans, sidewalks are the veins and arteries of movement, winding through Upper and Lower Ninth ward, dipping into Treme, and grinding through the French Quarter before diving under bridges into Downtown. Each step can ferry you away to a riverfront, a cityscape, a friendly front door, or to the banquette and its coterie of bricks, some a dizzy southern red, and some an ordered classic granite, and some big blocks of shattered stone that look like they were cut from underneath the earth by the soil.

"Did you get snacks?" Kirb asked as I picked up a chive stem from a patch next to Mrs. Walker's grass and plopped it in my mouth.

"Mama didn't have anything." I answered.

"Why not?"

"She spent all her money."

"On what?"

"On you-know-what."

"On be-ER?" he asked, and he let the last syllable ride on out into those thick purple clouds that hovered over us like bastions of the blue sky's secrets.

"I don't know why you are so obsessed with beer Chubbs, Mama don't drink nothing but whiskey."

"Why don't we buy a be-ER?" he asked.

"You don't even like beer! I let you try it once and you spit it out like it was the damn devil and you know what happened to Grandma and Grandpa."

I gave him a warning look.

"So, we don't need to go over this again, right?"

He shook his head.

"Are you excited to go on a walk today and finally get out of the house?"

Kirb sighed and dropped his shoulders. "I just don't understand why we can't stay home and watch T.V."

"All you do is stay home!" I exclaimed, pushing the stem to the other side of my mouth, and letting that mild chive spice numb the tip of my tongue.

"We need to get out and enjoy the day! And we are running low on food. Plus, it would do some good for your fat ass to get some exercise. You are starting to look like a hamster!"

His skin flushed like it always did when he got embarrassed, and he smacked his lips in defiance. I put my arm around him.

"Kirby, you aren't fat."

"Ernest," he said, clearing his throat. "Would you never make fun of me?"

I knew then that he was not talking about me calling him fat. I knew he was talking about the other thing, the thing we don't talk about. I told him of course I wouldn't make fun of him, and his eyes softened, but it was not the comfort I wish I could have given him. It was only words, that's all I had to give. Inside him there was a loneliness I couldn't understand, a sorrow so deep and dark that he couldn't tell anyone what it felt like, but you could see it run up his face like hot breath on cold glass.

"What would you do if someone made fun of me?" he asked, meekly.

"I'd kill them!" I said. He nodded at me, taking deeper strides in his walk and holding his head high.

It didn't take long until we were neck deep in the miasma of people. There wasn't a skin color or a nationality or a tongue that you couldn't find congregating around café tables. They drank coffee and chicory and whispered gossip while they exchanged family food recipes, which were always missing an ingredient or two from the real thing.

There were Creoles with their pirouettes of words and slick wisdoms, South Americans with their swagger and big black mustaches, and Good Ol' Southern boys with their tank tops and dull-colored fedoras and everybody in-between and outside the fire. There were ladies in flowery dresses and men slapping hands and boys chasing girls that were chasing little dogs.

This stirred up the buzz, the whine of the car brakes mixed with the chug of the boats and the happy hum of daytime tourists, and there were no lines or dividers like in all the movies, we chased the sun together. The sweet spots of the world are like this, because we see what's similar in each other, and smack dab in the middle of New Orleans, you can find the best of us, and if you stare into the umbrella of the sun and walk amongst the mirth of smiling faces, you'll know: you've made it.

Kirb took off down an alleyway and I followed. We ran, legs kicking behind us, and troubles bouncing out of barreling chests and into building's bricks while time sank into the asphalt and our whole lives were swallowed up by the mouths of cracked out windows.

Alleyways are the essence of New Orleans and so unlike any other city, in that one minute you can be on a street chocked full of rectangular stone walkways and ancient man-high streetlamps like Paris, and in another, you can be surrounded by balconies with hanging ferns and all manner of plants like a square in a small Italian town, and in another you're surrounded by steaming sewer drains and chalk white facades like a busy corner in London.

I stopped to catch my breath as Kirb took a corner and taunted me. It reminded me of being young, as running always does, and how Dad ran around the yard and chased us with his stethoscope while he pretended to be a swamp monster with hairy hands and big ears. But we were men now, even if, simply shadows of men. I was almost twenty-eight and Chubbs twenty-seven.

And just when we thought we knew where we were going, we found ourselves in a place we didn't recognize, and wouldn't you know it? There was Seth Johnson. That's the way it is with the city, it whirls around with its maze of skyscrapers and industrial buildings and glass facades and if you aren't careful, you can get confused, and then, with the breaths getting shorter and shorter, you might panic. Right before you lose all sense of what is, you turn the corner and find somebody else as deep into the city as you are. For if the city has a heart, it is found in familiar faces and so it never stays in one place. It's like your soul, somehow you can't find it until you get good and lost.

We had met Seth five or six years before. We had been out busting our humps in the hot Louisiana sun and saw a man talking to a pecan tree. I can still see its ripe brown pods hovering over him and jumping in the wind.

"Delilah," he had said. "You are one lovely and mad creature!"

I remember telling Kirb that he must have been drunk or on some kind of drugs or something, but Kirb had walked right up to him. Seth welcomed the company and told Kirby how that particular tree reminded him of an old lover. We couldn't help but be charmed by the fellow and as the best of friendships go, you never really know how they get into your circle, but once they do, you can't imagine them being out of it. That's the way it was with Seth Johnson.

Standing in that alleyway I couldn't help but admire him. Seth's proud stare was America's deep south. His angular jaw poked out like a lingering apparition, carrying with it the centuries, the mysterious history which can only be told, which can't be written down or painted or taken by a picture. I guess that's why they call it taking a picture, because you're trying to take something from history and make it your own, but what we forget is, everyone sees that picture in their own way, and so it isn't ours anymore, it isn't even history's, it belongs to whomever looks at it. But that brown half shaven face, rough on the edges, and soft to the touch, smiling with them pearly white teeth was about as close as you could get to being everybody's. His eyes were muddied, but kind, and although you might not understand it, you were drawn to them. He dressed like he was going to church and if he was wearing white, it was the whitest white, and if he was wearing black, it was the blackest black, and you never saw a wrinkle in his pants or shirt.

He liked to wear hats and he was the kind of man that you couldn't see without one, but he didn't wear baseball caps, he wore real fancy hats that you might imagine movie stars in the fifties wore in Los Angeles. Seth was a real southern gentleman, and he took off those fancy hats when he walked through a doorway and tipped them when he walked passed a lady. And he had a way of talking to things, like that pecan tree, and if you didn't know him, you would think he was half-lunatic, but once you did, if he wasn't talking to the birds or the marshes or the insects, you started to miss it. I'm sure glad Kirb stopped and talked to him on that hot and frustrating day because we never would have had such a friend if he hadn't, even though Seth hadn't stopped talking since.

Seth was playing dice and you could hear him hollering "Where's my money boys? Gotta get that money!"

And he shook those dice like a dancer at Mardi Gras, swaying back and forth and back and forth to the not too distant rhythm of the Mississippi, which was somehow everywhere. If you didn't know the sound of Ol' Blue you might think it was an approaching wind or the bellow of a tug boat but eventually its wet scent probed and announced and finally showed us whose city this really was.

Seth threw those dice against the wall and five or six guys around him were silent as death, the whites of their eyes like marbles until the dice stopped turning and they read the numbers.

"Hot damn!" Seth screamed. "Y'all either hate money or love giving it away to me!?"

He bent down and picked up a stack of cash and Kirb had already taken off toward him. Before Seth could stand all the way up Kirb had thrown his arms around him.

"Seth!" He screamed.

"Kirby!" Seth said. "Now, what are you doing down here?" and he took Kirb by the arms and looked at him.

"It's good to see you, where's that brother of yours?" Kirb pointed to where I stood. "Get over here boy!"

"You done playin'?" one of the players asked Seth.

"I'm done son."

"C'mon now. Give me a chance to win my money back."

"I said I'm done."

Seth folded his money carefully and put it in his inside jacket pocket and I could see the men staring at Kirby and my blood was boiling up and I hollered out, "Why don't you take a picture?" And they whipped their heads back to the wall and resumed their game.

"Ernest," Seth said. "You really like to start some shit, you know that? You are a bona fide shit-starter."

"I hate it when people stare," I said.

"Fair enough. So, what y'all doing this far into the city?"

"Kirb and me were just going for a walk before I have to go home and fix the toilet."

"Well, Hell," Seth said, and he paused. When Seth said "Well, Hell," it meant that he was saying I understand, and it was better then if you nodded your head until he decided to move on, because to interrupt a friend in the south when they start a perfectly good sentence with "Well, Hell" is just impolite.

"Well, Hell," he continued. "I'm sure glad to see you boys. There's no better surprise than running into a dear friend."

He gave us a good once over. He had a way of looking into you instead of at you, like he was sizing up the whole horizon of what you were. Once he was satisfied, he surveyed the alley.

"This way to the city!" he exclaimed, and he pointed his swarthy finger and led the way.

"You know," he said. "Walking around makes one think and you might even say gets one to pondering about things. And when I get to pondering about things, I ask myself. What is love? I mean to say, what is the definition of love?"

Seth was very fond of getting to the definition of things, simple things, things we don't think are important because we think we know what they mean. Hope. Faith. Resilience. Grief. And mainly Love. He was always talking about love in one way or another. It was his job. He wrote a very popular relationship column for *The New Orleans Advocate* and although he wasn't a fan of technology, he frequently updated a blog called, "The True Voice of a New Orleanian" which not only celebrated the beauty of the city but also tackled controversial subjects like red lining and police brutality.

Seth loved so many things, and yet he never fell in love, never dated. I think his problem was that he was in love with too much, and worse, he was passionate. Now, passion is a great and fine and even a dandy thing, but his gargantuan level of passion must have scared the women he met in two very distinct ways: the first was shock, they were not used to such passion and second, if they could get past the first, they probably felt as if they couldn't keep up. How could one keep up with a man who loves the song of the birds and the violin outside the café and weeping oaks and rivers and streetlights all with the same passion? So, Seth had turned off subtle attractions and eye wandering that most men have in favor of this passion and love for the city and the short black dresses and slender long legs and pink lips and delicate hands all went unnoticed.

Romantic love to Seth was a battered winter scarf which seemed as if it might explode into dust and bury itself deep in the ground underneath a patch of purple chrysanthemums. He would fall in love with the flowers and spin a grand story about how they trickled down from the elder gods on a crisp winter day.

"It never runs out! Love! We have been talking about it for centuries! And by damn! It never runs out! We can send a man or a woman to the moon, we can fly to anywhere we want to, and we can jump on our computers and talk to people around the world in seconds, but not one person agrees on what it means to love."

He would start in this way, telling us about the paradoxes and riddles of living and giving us his take on what it all meant, but we didn't feel lectured or talked down to, we felt that Seth was trying to express these words *through* us rather than at us. We knew he was educated. From what I understand, he had three or four different degrees in philosophy, English, and journalism. He knew all the great authors and not just the ones they tell you in the big books. Zora Neale Hurston and Turgenev and Pearl Buck and James Baldwin and Gabriel Garcia Marquez. He knew literature and art and music, but he spoke like a man of the people.

"Love is the most talked about subject," he continued. "You can't find a book or a movie or a song or a conversation in a backyard barbecue that can't somehow be traced back to love. They say the ocean and the brain are the two most undiscovered mysteries here on Earth, but I say, Hell."

Then, he paused and puckered his lips a bit.

"Love will always be the greatest of mysteries."

A cloud covered up the sun and let it back out again and we popped right out onto Canal Street where the mysteries of love were hushed by the Gumbo ya-ya of tourists and the clickety-clack of the red and yellow streetcar.

"So, Kirby," Seth said. "How's life been treating you?"

"Just been boring," Kirb said. "Watch T.V. Listen to Mom. Bored."

"Well," Seth pondered. "Mothers are unique."

"They drive us mad" he continued, "and we drive them mad. They give us a lot of stuff we really need, along with a whole batch of things we don't, but I'll tell you both under heaven and earth and in front of this here goddess of a city that there ain't *nothin* like a Mama."

I knew very little about Seth's past. I knew both of his parents had been dead a long time. I guessed he was around fifty, but I never asked him his age. There were rumors. There were always rumors about a single man later in his life with no wife and kids. I had heard that Seth was raised by his father, who used to make him clean the toilet seat with a toothbrush and eat out of a dog dish when he misbehaved. The other rumor was that his mother died during childbirth.

"Yeah," Kirb protested, "But I just don't understand why I always have to do what she says. Do the dishes. Clean my room."

He sighed and put his hands on his hips.

"I wish I could move out. I want to move out with you Seth."

"Ahh Kirby. You can't move out with me."

"Why not?"

"Well," Seth took in a deep breath.

"A man likes his privacy. A man like me needs it. It's how I keep my sanity if there is such a thing as sanity. I don't know if anyone can rightly say either way. But I also know that your brother and your Mama need you at home."

"Kirby!" I exclaimed.

"I just want to move out, have my own place, get drunk." Kirb said.

I gave Kirby the look of death and Seth pretended not to hear it.

"You know, my handsome friend," Seth barreled out. "Life isn't always what you expect it to be."

"But it's so boring," Kirb protested.

"I don't think in the history of the world I've heard 'boring' used as much as it is today." Seth said. "Every damn thing is boring. Movies are boring and people are boring and life is boring. In fact, the word boring is boring too! Say it to yourself. Borrrr inggg. What a terrible way to live! Wise people are never bored."

Here, he got excited and slapped his thigh.

"A wise man or woman is ever ready to accept the unexpected and turn any situation into something they can use. You must find meaning in *all* things. Not just some. Not just the easy ones. In fact, a wise man or woman will look at the things they don't like and find just as much meaning as the things they do like. That's the journey of wisdom. So, whether you like something or not is irrelevant. Whether it's boring or not is irrelevant too. And how about that?"

Kirb looked at the ground and got stuck in the deep briars and thickets of his mind and smacked his lips. He looked at Seth and said, as clear as the afternoon sky in summer, "Did you have this when you were growing up?"

"What's that Kirby?"

"You know, this Down Syndrome thing?"

Right then I wouldn't have been surprised if the asphalt closed up and devoured all three of us, and my eyes teared up and my throat got stuck, and even Seth was quiet for a minute. I bet it was one of five times in his whole life that he actually had to think of what to say.

Seth surveyed the dilapidated buildings, windows broken, rotted wood hanging from their sides. "We all got our challenges," he said. "What every man or woman goes through, no other man or woman can truly understand. But what separates the good men and women from the great men and women is that the great ones *try* to understand, and with all you have been through, I've never seen you be anything but understanding to everyone you meet. This is why I say you are a great man, not fine, not good, but great," and here he grabbed Kirby by the shirt and raised his voice as if he was angry and my blood boiled, but I pushed it down, because I trusted Seth.

"Don't you *never*, NEVER let anybody tell you different!" he hollered.

Kirb nodded his head in agreement, and I heard a faint rumbling, like a storm cloud rolling in off the coast.

"Did you hear that?" I asked.

"I farted," Kirb blurted out, and he pulled the collar of his shirt up over his nose and said "DEFCON 1," and then we, all three of us, laughed and laughed until we washed out the sadness in Kirb's heart.

Chapter Three

We went home and I spent the afternoon getting tied up in the projects of the house with Chubbs. We rigged the toilet pump to work with some rubber bands and then we chased each other around the back yard, chopped it up with Seth on the front stoop, and then tidied up the room real quick before Janus came home.

"Hello," she said cheerfully, and I was a little bit weary because of the talk we had that night before, but I said hello back and I even dared to kiss her cheek. She warmly accepted.

"It's so windy outside! There's talk of a hurricane."

"Really? I hadn't heard. Do they know how big it's going to be?"

"They didn't say, but we can watch it later on the news if you want."

"Sure thing baby."

"I think I'll make us some dinner," she said. "I've had a wonderful day."

Janus had gotten a job. She was going to be waiting tables at Fat Goodies Diner, which had some of the best breakfast in the city. She was only going to be working there three mornings a week, but it was a start, and finally there was something about her that was familiar. She even twisted her hair in her finger, as she had done so often when she felt like there was nothing to worry about except the sun shining on her face. She got so jazzed up she made us some shrimp stew and vegetables and they didn't taste half bad.

"We should all watch a movie together!" Janus said as she pushed her empty plate away.

"We need popcorn, candy, and drinks," Kirb said.

"Alright but that's a lot of food Chubbs and we just ate. Don't you want to think about losing some weight?"

Janus hit me playfully.

"I think you look handsome just the way you are Kirby," she said.

Maybe she was coming back after all. Maybe we were all going to be okay.

"Your brother's not fat!" Mama threw in as she got up and put the dishes in the sink.

"You going to watch a movie with us Mama?"

"Nah. I'm watching my shows," she said. This meant the X-Files. Mama loved the X-Files. She made a big glass of whiskey and then quietly slipped out of the kitchen and into her room.

"When you watch a movie, you need popcorn, candy, and drinks," Kirb said.

He repeated that every time we watched a movie and if you forgot one of those things he would complain through the whole damn thing. "I wish I just had a drink," he'd say or "I don't understand why we just can't have popcorn" or "that movie would have been a lot better if we just had candy." But once he got those three things, it could be the worst movie you ever saw, and he'd still love it.

"Well, I'll get the popcorn together," I said, and I got up and opened up the cupboard. As I pulled out the popcorn box, I saw something slide off the shelf and onto the ground. I picked up two large white pills.

"What the hell are these?" I called out, confused.

Before I knew it, Janus was right next to me.

"Do you know what these are?" I asked and I showed them to her. She snatched them out of my hand.

"Those are yours?"

"No!" she yelled. "It's none of your business!"

"You're my wife and this is our home and so it is my business."

"Give those back to me!"

"I can't," she said, flustered.

"What do you mean 'you can't'?"

"I just can't."

"Well, then, let's get you some help for Christ's sakes."

She turned around defiantly and ate them. I was boiling over and getting real fired up, so I reached over and grabbed her head and tried desperately to pry open her mouth, but I saw her throat swallow and I let her go.

"Goddamnit! Now you have done it!" I hollered. "Now, you have ruined a perfectly good evening and Kirb and me have to sit around while you get that blank look on your face and watch your eyes roll back in your damn head like some sort of braindead zombie."

"What's wrong?" Kirb asked, coming towards us.

"Go to the front room and sit down and watch TV." I told him.

"Why?" Kirb whined. "I wanted to watch a movie and we were going to have popcorn and candy and drinks."

"Well, I'm sorry, but me and my wife are fighting so it's going to have to be another night."

"You just always fight," Kirb said, and he slowly walked out of the kitchen.

"I can't believe you said that to him," Janus protested, and she put her back to me and I could see that big mole on her right shoulder blade, and it irritated me. It irritated me that she wouldn't look me in the face, and it irritated me that I'd never much cared for that stinking mole or for the way she held her head down when we weren't getting along.

"You know I don't lie to my brother Janus."

"I'm your wife."

"I'm aware of that," I said. "You get on these pills and this is exactly what happens, you get numb and when you are numb you don't care who or what you hurt. But the point is babe, that you aren't you."

I sighed.

"Shoot, I know it's been hard, but we have to stay together, we have to do this *together*, and with you all hopped up on whatever the hell you are taking, it's not you and me dealing with it, it's just me, all alone."

I went close to her, close enough for her to feel my breath on her neck, and I took her hands as gently and lovingly as I could.

"And the truth is I need you baby. I need you."

She mulled it over and then she raised those hands of hers, and my hands too, and she threw them both down.

"You don't know anything!" she screamed. "You don't know what it's like!"

It was happening, I had thought. All the silence in all those months of not saying anything had finally come to the surface and was going to be heard.

"You're right," I told her, staring into the kitchen.

"I don't know what that's like."

"She killed him," she sobbed. "She killed him."

Her crying made me nervous, mostly because I didn't know what to do with it. I didn't know how to help her or how to stop her from feeling all that pain. All I could think of to say was, "Can't you even say his name?"

I regretted saying those words. I still do, but they came out, it was like there was nothing I could have done in that moment *but* say them.

She cringed, stopped crying, and yelled out. It was a wild and pathetic scream like a wounded animal in the woods cornered by a hunter. There was something about it that frightened me because there wasn't anything to stop it, it was coming at us all and we had to accept the consequences.

"I'm sorry, I didn't-"

"That's it though! You don't think about what you say Ernest. You are always just pouring out at the mouth and dear God you are *always* right. Nobody can ever tell you that you are wrong because you will just run them through, right to their arteries and veins. You are cold-blooded Ernest Larsen. Cold like a snake. You have no idea what I've been through. How could you?"

There it was.

"Well, at least I'm not all hopped up on pills making my whole damn family feel worse than they already do," I said.

"You are right. You are exactly right! But at least I'm not worthless," she hissed. "You are never going to med school, and you are never going to leave Kirby or your damn Mama and if you would have been a real man you would have stayed with me, he'd still be here."

She leveled me and in some sick way, it made sense. It was an explanation, an illogical one, but an explanation, `nonetheless. That's the thing about death, it drives the sanity right out of you, and you'll believe anything to try and make it go away. They say death is the most natural thing that can happen besides being born, but what I don't get is how unnatural it made me feel, how I felt then, when Janus said that, that maybe it was my fault, that maybe death can be traced back to some single event, and that one man can take it on his shoulders, can bolster the blame with his actions and say to death with bravery, "Here he is," and know that you had handed death someone you loved.

"Well, maybe I'll make it easier on both of us and just kill myself since you have it all figured out." I said. "You aren't some angel, you know? I feel it all too. I mean, sometimes someone just needs to be held, needs to have somebody's arms wrapped around them. Even a man needs to be held sometimes, when the world is cold and there isn't anybody around to help you or there isn't any sky you can look at without thinking of what you've lost. A man needs to be held then, to be touched, and if a wife can't even do that, then what the hell's she good for anyway?"

She looked at me, different than she ever had. She looked at me with hatred.

"Do it! Just like your Grandma and Grandpa. Kill yourself you dumb bastard."

She pushed me. "Go on! What are you waiting for?"

She'd done it. She'd done it mean and perfect and now I was hot, hotter than I'd ever been before. I opened my palm and I hit her as hard as I could. Then I hit her again and I kept on hitting her over and over, even after she was on the ground, screaming and crying and begging for her life.

When I stopped, hands bloodied and shaking, half drunk on anger and ecstasy, I studied her and in the incoherent wails she spit like madness. I pitied her, and more than that I pitied myself. I had broken my honor.

"Goodbye then" I said, voice teetering.

I said it like I was saying the last line of an old movie, and then I went to the bathroom, and I called through the door to Mama's bedroom, searching one last time for any chance of making sense of my life.

"Hel-lo?" she called out.

"Mama, it's your son."

"Ernest is that you?"

"Yes."

"Whatcha you want boy?"

"I need you to take care of Kirby and Janus. I'm going for a walk."

"You are bothering me with that?" She called out, catching herself as she burped. "Sometimes, you don't have no damn sense or recollection, its retarded I tell you."

My jaw dropped. She'd said it. She had said the unutterable word, she'd broken any and all things that remained to make sense. The room was upside down, the carpet hanging from the ceiling and the ceiling drooping into the earth and the windows danced on the rugs and the coat rack clapped a loud and familiar lullaby. There was only one way out.

I took a bottle of Tylenol out of the medicine cabinet. I inspected my face in the mirror and imagined myself crying. I imagined saying that it was over, imagined sternly telling myself "Why don't you just be a man and follow through with it? Follow through with one thing in your whole damn life!"

I took a few deep breaths and then I ate the whole bottle, swallowing it down with sink water. It hurt my throat, but I got them all down. I glanced back in the mirror, and I felt sorry for myself and I was tired of that damn face looking pathetic and causing me problems and my blood boiled.

"You are pathetic!" I told myself. "Quit looking at me you pathetic bastard!"

And I kept telling myself this until I got so boiled over that I stuck my hand through that mirror, and it broke the pathetic face, and what was left of it bled all over my knuckles.

I tried shaking my hand to get rid of the face still left on it, but the blood was stubborn. I knew there was a creek running through the back of the Wilson's yard and it was as good a place as any to wash away my blood and my sins and everything I'd ever wanted.

I walked through the house as fast as I could, not wanting to see Janus or Kirby. As I reached the door, I heard a whistle. I opened the door, and the wind came at me, pushing me back, but I plowed through it, fighting my way outside. I stumbled out the door and I knew I didn't have far to go, but my stomach wasn't keeping the pills down and I was having a hard time standing up. If I could make it to the creek everything would be okay. I kept waiting for the wind to take its breath as it always does between gusts, but it never did. It just kept coming.

I waded into the darkness and could see the moon above the Wilson's oak. It was the bluest moon I've ever seen. My hands were blue, and the sides of my nose were blue and even the outline of my shirt was blue. It was everywhere.

My eyes were heavy. My stomach was turning and my knees weak. I stumbled toward the oak's giant brown arms and the memories of climbing its rough trunk, of sitting atop its mossy digits scanning the whole neighborhood, feeling like a prince: the prince of the live oak, the commander of its grey and green Spanish moss.

I held onto one of its branches and closed my eyes. I let go and fell onto the wet grass. I rolled over and crawled toward the creek. I felt at peace listening to the sad whistle of the wind, which called me away, back to the legend of the oak, back to the prince of the city, lulled to sleep by the chanting of the wind.

Chapter Four

There exists in the world only two types of memories: those we make holier than they are and those we make worse than they are. But, if you don't remember, then you are free from both, or you are bound to both, because you must live through the memories of others.

From what I was told, vomit was found on the railing, the bottom of the steps, and all over the front of my shirt and the tops of my shoes. I had crawled from the tree and fallen face first into the creek. My mouth was in the lip of the water, but my nose was above it. It was a miracle I didn't drowned. The whole right side of my body fell into the creek, while the left side clutched the grass.

Against Janus's wishes, Kirb muscled his way out of the house. Somehow, he knew, in the way he knew things. He ran down to the creek and tried to wake me up. When he couldn't, he pulled me from the water and took my hand. After a good four or five hours Mrs. Walker heard me groaning and came outside to get us. In their separate drunken and pill induced dazes, Mama and Janus had already passed out. Mrs. Walker had to wake them up so they could help carry me into the house.

When my eyes finally opened, I was sprawled out on the couch. Mama was standing over me on one side and Kirb and Janus were sitting on the other.

"He's awake!" Janus said.

I tried to speak. Nothing came out but a weak cough. I felt strange, like I wasn't even a part of my own body. My legs were stiff, my chest burned, and my mind scattered. I couldn't hold onto more than one thought at a time. It as like those kind of dreams where you know what you should do, but you can't, because something is holding you back, and you don't understand what it is, but you still can't move your legs to run away or put your hands to your face to protect yourself.

"Can you move my darling boy?" Mama said. She clenched her hand to her face, like every sane thing she knew hinged upon my answer.

I tried to speak again, but the same weak cough struggled out.

"Let's get him propped up," Janus said and her eyes were full of pity, not of sympathy or love, just good old-fashioned pity. There was something about that pity that made my insides ache.

"Good idea," Mama agreed.

They put their hands on opposite sides of my torso and pulled me up, putting pillows underneath me, and checking around my sides to make sure I was secure, the way you might tie up a mattress in the back of a pickup truck.

When they were positive I wasn't going anywhere, Janus walked over to the window and pulled up the blinds.

"The mayor gave an evacuation order," she said. "There's a hurricane."

She eyed the front yard while I looked closely at her face. Her cheek below her ear was purple, her bottom lip was swollen, and both eyes bruised.

I had done it. I had added that color to her face. I had let down my wife. I had let down Chubbs. I had let down Mama.

"A hurricane," I thought to myself, and I wasn't surprised. I wasn't surprised because it seemed about as awful as anything could be and that was just right, that was just how it was supposed to be right then: goddamn awful. It was fate, I thought.

"We couldn't," Janus paused. "We couldn't just leave you here."

And then she bent her knees like she was going to sit down on the blue recliner chair in front of the window, the chair that must have come with the house, because it had been there so long. But Janus didn't sit down. Something was keeping her from being comfortable. She shuffled her feet a bit, folded her arms, and then got good and sturdy and unbent her knees.

"You can't tell me to leave my home." Mama said. "We will survive this one, just like me and your father survived Hurricane Betsy. We are a strong people, and we don't need a government to tell us what to do. You know, they always tell you the same thing to pack up all of your stuff and leave. Then you get out in the middle of god knows where and then they tell you to come right back home."

Mama took a cotton handkerchief she had been holding and wiped her forehead.

"Anyway, I'm *so* glad you are awake! I've been *so* worried about you. Your brother," she dramatically put the handkerchief up against her mouth. "He stayed by you the whole night. He wouldn't let go of your hand, not even when we moved you. He was *willing* you back to life."

I looked over at Chubbs and he was nodding his head.

"You hurt yourself Ernest," he said. "I just don't understand why you hurt yourself. You might died."

I turned away. I couldn't look him in the eyes and I couldn't look at

Janus anymore either. So, I breathed, and the whole room seemed to breathe with me. We didn't turn on the television to hear about the storm because Mama wouldn't allow it. She didn't want to hear all the fear and paranoia. We didn't talk or cry or say some wonderful thing that people are supposed to say in such times. We just looked out that old living room window, the window that Dad used to stand at and drink his morning coffee, the window where Kirb and I kept an eye on the goings on of the neighborhood, the window that Janus paced in front of when she was nervous, the window that Mama always seemed to find when it was dark outside, peering into the black canvass as if it understood something about her that nothing else could.

We breathed and we waited. We waited for the hurricane to sweep in and destroy the neighborhood. We waited for it to shake up the silence and show us something, anything really, just something different.

I struggled to keep my eyes open. When they closed, I could still hear the whistle. It had never stopped.

It rained large droplets off the gutter, kamikaze drops that spiraled down through the air and exploded into the wood panels of the porch.

I tried to speak again. "Ju-" I cleared my throat. "J-Janus!" I croaked.

She looked briefly in my direction without making eye contact and then looked back out the window.

"You need to rest," she said. Her words were glass on the air, they were cool and crisp and somehow reflected the ceremony of it all, the way she felt she had to speak. She couldn't say what she wanted to say. She couldn't say what I wanted to hear either.

I wanted to be punished. I wanted somebody to tell me what a son of a bitch I had been and how I'd pushed around my wife like some damn coward and then I'd run off and taken some pills and worried them all sick and how now we were all trapped here to die while a hurricane batted the house around like a marble. But I was stuck. We all were.

We listened to the whistle together. We listened to the whistle build. It rose and rose and rose until it wasn't a whistle anymore, it was a grumble, and that grumble shook the skies, and it shook the ground, and what was in between, the houses and the people left over, we trembled. But we didn't say anything, because if you say something, then it's real, and if maybe you keep that something to yourself, you will discover it was all in your head, and wasn't it just too funny the way you thought you'd heard and seen it all.

Then the city blew out the streetlights and the house lights and the clouds sagged down into the horizon. Each cloud reached far into the night and bathed in its soot until they slithered back into the sky with a dusky grey coat. Fields of wheat curled toward the tops of trees and bushes shook like children in frost. The live oak stood like a scarecrow, branches as knotty fingers, pointing to the river, stirring the air with its thick black hands until there was nothing left to see except that damn old terrible moon, that blurry blue lantern, that somehow said, "There isn't much hope left, nope, it's all going away."

The rain came down even harder, each drop pulled with it a shrill cry and as it pelted the roof, it sounded like pebbles were thwacking the tin cover over the porch. It beat down on signs and aluminum siding causing a crushing wail that echoed through the house and into the plates on your knees. And it occurred to me then that there's an illusion a house gives you. It's the same illusion that you had when you hid under the covers as a child. It's the illusion of safety, that the wood and the glass and the siding will protect you from the horrors of nature, that it will keep you and your family nestled away from the hurt and the suffering. But what we don't realize is, that nature is old and powerful and has seen the ruin of cities that were born and died before our history began. It doesn't care about our safe little house. It doesn't care about our warm blankets or brand-new recliner chair. It only cares about its wrath.

So, those horrors of nature, the lightning and the rain and the wind, they came creeping into our house until Kirb cuddled up to me on the couch. I could see the fear mounting in his wide eyes and red cheeks and I wished I could speak and tell him that it was going to be okay, even though I felt everything but okay. The wind and the rain got louder and louder, and the louder it got, the closer Kirb came to me.

Janus was still. The only thing that moved on her was her stomach as she took in deep and metered breaths. Mama sipped her whiskey in her bathrobe, ice rattling in the glass as her hand shook. And in the same way I had felt strange in my own body, my body felt strange in this raucous place, where the city grumbled, and the rain wailed and the sky ran away from the earth and nothing I had known about my life was protected.

When we thought we couldn't imagine another sound, the eerie chatter of the ocean wandered into our ears as a bow skipping against the strings of a cello, it was the long groan of New Orleans as it opened up its rickety mouth and stretched its jaw.

There would be no peace. There would only be the violence of a thousand ferried souls. Souls climbing out of trenches in deep ocean swells, souls haunting the empty streets with their floating figures, souls strewn against the fence in the yard, souls that pull a man in with compassion until he's laid up against that fence himself, sobbing and climbing and clambering on top of one another in a swarm of agony. That's what the chatter told us, that's what we were expecting.

Then, as the chorister in the church of Hurricane Katrina, the wind lifted its giant arms and blew. And it kept on blowing and blowing until the dust came up, until the dust swirled into the air as the rain pelted through the ground like steel and the live oak danced on tiptoe.

Everything that wasn't supposed to move, moved. Roof tiles jumped off of houses, trees bent down to the ground, bicycles tumbled across flower gardens, and rakes flew by telephone poles like rebel witches broomsticks fleeing to the heavens. The live oak laughed as it whirled in and out of the wreckage, back and forth between the ground and sky, one foot in the present and one foot beyond all time.

I looked in desperation in the darkness for Seth, to see if he was pleading with the city. Hoping he was talking to the sky or the ocean, asking them to calm down, to spare the wretched fools that wander in the hearts of evil men. All I could imagine though, was Seth in his bright white suit, whipping around his cane like a mage, conjuring the storm with that mischievous smile on his face, somehow content with the city's will.

He knew all along, I thought. He knew that the city was going to turn upside down and he was just waiting for the wind to tell him so. He didn't warn me because he probably already knew what I would do, and that I deserved to be in the evil of it all. But why not save Kirb? Seth must have also known that Kirb would never leave me.

Then, the storm knocked on our window.

"Thwap!" it said as it sent Janus back.

"What was that?" she said, walking backward.

"Thwap!" The storm repeated. "Thwap! Thwap! Thwap! Thwap! Thwap!" It said until it wasn't it saying anymore, it was demanding it.

Kirby got up from the couch and helped me do the same. The knocking was getting louder, and we were moving farther away from the window.

"THWAP!" The storm knocked one final time until it shattered that old window and sent our porch swing flying through the living room and onto the couch.

The water poured through the window nearly knocking us all down. It immediately reached my kneecaps and with the shield of the house broken, it was quickly rising up my legs.

"The attic!" Mama bellowed and it was a savage cry, a cry as old as nature itself.

We hustled up the stairs and Mama opened the hatch. Kirb and Janus helped lift me up the ladder and before Janus could climb up herself, I pushed out, "Water." Janus nodded and went back down the stairs while Kirb and Mama climbed up. Kirb and me huddled together and Mama stoked up a dusty oil lamp. As soon as she set it down and its orange glow reached out into the corners of the room, Mama wept. She didn't hide it like most people did, she took her stringy unwashed hair and pushed it behind her ears and folded her legs before letting her chin raise. Tears came out of her in those few moments like I had never seen them come before. She could feel the song of death and I'm not sure if she thought that God would judge her for drinking away her life or if maybe, secretly, she didn't believe any of the stuff she said about God and thought that everything would end for her, and all that would be left was the memories of the person she left the world with. But no matter how long you've been alive or how many terrible things she's put you through, you still pity your mother when she cries, you still feel the pangs of her tears, like needles in your stomach.

Once you've held your brother in the dark, locked in an attic, your mother weeping as that grumble in the night, that rush of air past the tiny attic window became like thunder, became like the awful voice of God himself, then the wind never blows warm again, you can only feel its coolness, its longing.

Janus came up the hatch door with a milk jug full of water and a box of saltine crackers.

"These are all I could grab," she said. "It's a whirlwind down there."

She shook the water off her legs.

"The water is all the way up to my stomach now."

She half-smiled. Her red hair was as bright as it had ever been, but the rest of her sunk into the darkness with the anxiety and it hid the tempest of my touch.

I nodded. "Thank you."

Mama had stopped crying. She wouldn't let anyone outside the family see her tears. But it didn't stop her from talking. She went on saying prayers and cursing the devil and filling up her whiskey glass, as she had made sure to grab her bottle on the way up the stairs. Yes, she kept talking and she didn't give a good goddamn if anyone was listening.

"And you've shown your face dear lawd and I see it and I know you and devil be damned, he won't take this Gawd fearing woman. Not today! Goodness is in me lawd! I will find the goodness. I will go toward the light. I will ALWAYS go toward the light. You don't have to worry about me. Him? Oh! He's alright. They are all alright. He didn't mean it lawd. He didn't mean it at all. All I was saying is, that we love you. And if love is being in the beginning, like the word, then love is in the word. I know it. I know it's true. I feeling what I feel because love is in the word. I won't never forget it again. I won't never forget the word. I know that's where the love is. I'll pray more lawd, dear Gawd, dear sweet and precious lawd. I say it not so much for myself, but for my boys. The boys need to live. My boys are both missing things and they need your love to live. But I want to live too. I say this special prayer with the love and the word and the heart in the name of the sweet and lovely and precious lawd Jesus who shines his blessings down on us even in the darkest of hours. I'm just a girl. I'm just a girl lawd. I love you. I love you so much."

Seeing her chanting and swaying and drinking in that dim light of the oil lamp she resembled some hoary shawoman holding together a town after losing all its children to a bloody battle, and despite her mad ramblings, all of us in the attic secretly hoped that maybe God would hear this southern shawoman of the swamps and brings us back our home. But the air was bitter, it had no room for mercy.

It seemed to me then that all mad people were not born mad, that something made them that way, something haunted them, and whether or not it was of their own volition or not was irrelevant because they certainly weren't happy. I wonder if anyone was every mad and happy or if the two could exist in the same flesh at the same time.

The thundering and lightning struck the house with their lusty blows and the wind, its rage unleashed, battered the empty streets with its frustration and shook the house until it roared, "Hear me!" And we couldn't stop the shudder that swept through us all, that felt like it grabbed the tips of your spine and wouldn't let you go. We were all prepared to die. We were all prepared to let the fear get released as the storm took hold of us and sacrificed our bodies on the altar of our attic. And when we had made that bargain, when we were ready for our lives to end, we heard it.

It came like the big burst of a bullfrog in the heat of summer, when sweat comes dripping down your forehead, and you can't keep the sun out of your eyes. You might have thought it was an explosion. Some said it was. I know better. I know that cry, it comes from the darkness, it's an uncontrollable scream of pain, one that I had uttered myself once, in the lobby of the New Orleans Radiology Clinic. When we heard that scream, we thought the city had let out its last pitiful gasp, and that the storm was over.

We bunched together at the window, looking out at the mud, the water dripping dry off houses and cars, the clouds blushing white, and with a great sigh of relief I said, "It's over. Thank God, it's over."

And there was a thought we all had. We thought that because we had been through the storm, because of what we had all lost, that there wasn't going to be anymore suffering, that we had all earned the right to be happy now, that all the dreadful and beastly things would go somewhere else on their eternal rounds and teach someone else the value of living. We hugged and kissed and laughed and thanked God, right up until we heard that ghastly rumble. The beast was not done.

The armor of the city had burst. The levees had fallen. The breastplate cracked until all the unsung melodies and fizzled out dew drops plowed into the city with their frothy chariot, with that angry and foam-choked wave, like the lady on the end of an old Spanish fleet ship.

And as a giant bull charging through the city, the water pushed its horns into park benches and then threw them over tall bushes, stomped beneath lamp posts, crippling them to the ground, rampaged through the sewers splattering their contents onto the streets, and decimated sidewalk cafes with its cruel hot breath. Then, with a loud grunt, the water rammed its way into the side our house, sending shock waves through the attic.

The sun came up over the now blue sky. I rushed over to the hatch and opened it. The stairs were filling up with water.

"We have to get up on the roof," I said.

"Why?" Kirb asked. "I'm tired Ernest. I just want to go to my bed and sleep. Why can't I just sleep?"

I went to him. I gave him a cracker.

"Eat this." I told him. He did. "Do you want some water?" I asked, holding up the milk jug.

"I don't like water," he said. "I prefer milk."

"Well, we don't have any milk buddy and we can't go to bed. But I think there are some old blankets up here and I'll make you a little bed on the roof and you can sleep up there. Wouldn't that be fun? Sleeping on the roof! We've never done that before."

He sighed.

"I just don't understand why I can't sleep in my own bed. I don't want to sleep on the roof."

"Your bed is under water right now Chubbs," I said. "We need to get up on the roof. Can you help me out and be strong for Mama and Janus and go up there with me?"

He nodded and clicked his tongue before smacking his lips and I helped him out the window.

"You're a good boy," Mama said as she climbed out the window to meet him.

"Do you want some help out?" I asked Janus, feeling a little bit more like myself.

She didn't answer. The marks on her face hadn't changed any through the night, in fact, they seemed even larger as she stepped into the light of the day and her red hair was washed out by the sun. I followed her onto the roof and made Kirb a bed with the blankets. It was day, but we hadn't slept all night. Mama sprawled out over most of the bed and so Kirb was only left with a little corner of blanket under his head, but he was too tired to fight her and fell asleep. Mama fell asleep shortly after.

Janus walked to the edge of the roof and peered into the rising waters as their bark crumbled wooden doorsteps and walkways.

She blamed herself for what I had done, I thought. She blamed herself for what happened. I knew in the balmy morning air that stunk of death and the underbelly of the city; she would never forget.

"I'm sorry" I croaked. "I'm so sorry."

She did not move. She stood in the stillness with her back arched, creating a new Janus, one that was comfortable in the madness of a hurricane, could only be comfortable in chaos and turmoil. She narrated the moment.

"Why does the memory of love fade?" she asked. "It's as painful as death, isn't it? It's like you don't even want to speak or to hear them speak, because you fear it will all descend into some guardianship of each other's time, trapped in trying to get back to the first kiss on the beach, but even the memory of that fades."

"We can make new memories," I said.

"No we can't," she said. "You spend your whole life learning other people's truths and the rest of your life unlearning them."

"We can make new memories," I said again, rising on the roof tiles.

"I'd let you hit me again. I'd let you torture me. I'd let you hurt me. I'd do anything. I'd even try to make it work. If only-"

She put her hands in her pockets.

"If only we could change the past."

I heard in her the woman that would weep at the small things: a limping cocker spaniel being picked up by her owner, a photograph of a father and daughter in a frame at the grocery store. It was sour, each breath gasped for the last bit of air. It was also different. She wasn't afraid anymore.

I wished for her eyes. I hoped if I could see into them she might come back to me. Those bluest of eyes that pierced you in the way that one gets pierced by the long blue canvass of a sunny afternoon.

"Let me look at you," I pleaded.

"I can't."

"Please, let me look at you baby."

Her back twitched, repulsed.

"I'm sorry that I failed you," I said. "I'm not an honorable man."

I cried. I cried because I wanted to change it all. I wanted to change Janus. I wanted her to forgive me. I wanted her to know that we could make new memories. We all try to get people to be the way we want them to be because it's as hard as cement in wintertime for us to think that somebody thinks differently than we do. We want them to be our way, to talk like we think they should talk. To think like we think they should think. We don't admit it. It's hard to admit those things, but it doesn't mean they don't happen.

"Don't give up on yourself Ernest." she said, prophetically more than tenderly. "No one can remember when they were born or predict when they will die. But there has to be something worth living for. I know you can find it if you try."

My heart broke and kept breaking. It was one of those times in life when something is so powerful you cannot describe it, not exactly, but you can tell your version of it, the phantom of the story that you greet in your mind when you try *not* to remember it.

Janus jumped off the roof and into the water. I ran to the edge and waited until her head popped up above the brown stew of river and earth.

"Janus!" I yelled. "Janus please!"

She lifted her arms and swam, beating the water back in short and thorny strokes.

"Please come back! I'll do anything. I love you! I'm sorry! I'm sorry!"

I repeated the words. I repeated them until they meant something else.

"I love you! I love you! I love you!" became "Don't leave me! Don't leave me! Don't leave me!" became "I'm sorry. I'm sorry." Became "I love you! I love you! I love you!"

It was a chant. A chant for all of us, a lament of love's escape.

Love is the song of the caged human who whistles while overcoming the madness of the everyday. And if someone knows that you suffer the way they have suffered then they understand true love and they would have understood perfectly the language I chanted. It had all the characteristics of what love should be. How love should be half raucous howling, half spiritual musing, half naked, half in the finest clothes you have ever worn, half Dionysian, half Apollonian, half God, half mortal. How love should express all that has beauty and all that wrenches the soul.

I screamed with all this in me. I screamed and screamed and screamed and with each syllable my heart broke even more than I thought it could. It is the heart that breaks most easily and most often.

And, as I called frantically after her, I watched her disappear into the horizon like my weak voice, falling apart at the end of the muddy pool that once was our block. Repetition is the murderer of fine things.

She left because she had to leave, because it was her nature. There was nothing more to say. I was all alone. There was only the thoughts of life and death, carving twitches into small circles in my stomach.

The unforgiving sun spiraled down from the Milky Way with its bright burning stare and its stifling and monstrous breath, and we could not escape from it. After a few hours of pacing the roof, you could see its ravages in Kirby's swollen face, red eyes, and cracked lips. I woke him and Mama up and told them what had happened to Janus.

"Did she might die?" Kirb asked.

"I think she's going to be okay buddy."

"I knew she would run off when things got tough. She doesn't have the constitution for a marriage."

"Knock it off Mama!"

"I'm hungry! I want some food!" Kirb said as he sat up.

I gave him a handful of crackers.

"I want a grilled cheese sandwich."

"All we have are these."

"I want a grilled cheese sandwich!"

"Kirby, I'm being serious. All we have are these crackers."

He rolled his eyes and shoved a couple crackers in his mouth.

"Your fa-ther," Mama came out hot and heavy, "would have known exactly what to do right now. He always knew what to do."

Her brow furrowed and she seemed to be searching through the terrible water, if you could even call it water anymore, for some sign from my dear old Dad.

"You need to go find help," she said definitively.

"What? How we going to get around? Swim?"

"Use that boat."

She pointed to a small blue boat that was banging against the roof of the Dottol house.

"I'll be damned! A boat! What are the odds? Where the Hell did it even come from?"

"You better get down there," Mama said. "It could get washed away at any moment."

She was right. I lowered myself off the roof and into the water. It was cold and fast. It moved through me as I did my best to find my legs and swim across the street. The boat was light blue and rusted. On the side were scribbled the words "Wet Fantasy."

It was empty. I took its nose and swam it back to where Mama and Kirby were waiting.

"Alright," I said. "Mama, I want you to help Kirby down here and then I'll help you get down once he's in the boat."

"I'm not going on that god-forsaken thing," she said.

"It was your idea to get it in the first place! What are you talking about?"

"You and your brother go get help. I'm staying here."

"Mama, I really don't think it's a good idea to stay here by yourself."

"God told me to stay," she said. "And he told me you had to go. I'm not leaving this house."

I relented and she helped Kirb in the boat and then lowered down the crackers and the milk jug full of water.

"Let me split these up and I'll send some back up your way."

"No! I'm just fine. I can go quite a spell without eating. You get help and come back here as soon as you can. You boys can eat what you have."

"Okay Mama." I said sadly and pushed the boat out into the street.

"Bye Mama!" Kirby yelled happily. "See you soon!"

"Bye darling!" she called out, blowing kisses and waving her hands while she stood on the rooftop with her thin and lonely hair blowing past her neck. Those stiff lips and taut forehead were plastered on her face, the gargoyle of the Larsen legacy. You might have thought that she was out of wits or just plain stupid but there was something about Mama, something bold and furious that refused to give in. She was too stubborn to die, I suppose. She put her fingers on her lower back and leaned her body forward and as I paddled away with my hands. The old battle ax would probably outlive us all, I thought.

The murky water had filled up the streets of our neighborhood. It was filthy. It was full of all our regrets, of the things we had flushed down the toilet and hid under the rugs, of all our fears, and anxieties, and every hateful thing we'd ever thought or fantasized about.

All the beauty of the city was gone. It was ugly and smug. It smelled of sewage and stale water. The houses were turned inside out and buried buildings smashed and gutted the trees, massacring them like statues of what we had once believed was true.

It didn't take long to get to the next block, which was eerily quiet. A fridge floated by with a head of lettuce and a couple of empty soda cans in tow next to a pillow with its guts pulled out. There was a tablecloth in a tree, a coat hanger next to a stop sign, a bookshelf split in half underneath a stoplight.

We made it to the next block, which was just as quiet, and then the next, which was the same. I rowed the streets for hours and we found no sign of anything living.

"I don't want to be on this boat anymore," Kirby said.

"I don't either buddy."

"I just want to go home," he said. "I just might want to go home and see Mama. I miss Mama, Ernest."

"We will see Mama again, I promise," I said.

It seemed he might cry then, but he didn't. His head moved from side to side, as if picking up a frequency. I was baffled.

"Do you hear that?" he asked.

"Hear what?"

"Do you hear that?" he repeated.

I listened. There was something. A stir. A group of people.

"People!" I called out. "It's people!"

I splashed the water as fast I could towards the noise. From far away, it sounded like a group of people saying different things, but as we got closer, I noticed they were actually saying the same thing.

"Let us in! Let us in! Let us in!"

We turned the corner by the old Navy base, and I could see about twenty people calling out to a couple of guards at the guard shack. They were all waist deep in water and looked as tired as we felt. I stopped the boat a few hundred feet away so we could listen to them.

"Dear God!" One of them said. "The base is empty! All we are asking for is somewhere to stay. Let us in!"

"We cannot let you in sir, I'm sorry." The naval guard said in his best attempt at sounding official.

"Can you at least let the children in? The women and the children? We've been out here for two days. We need food. The children need food and a warm place to stay."

"I don't know what to tell you sir."

You could hear in the background the rest of the crowd chanting, "Let us in! Let us in! Let us in!"

You could see most of them were wet. The man talking to the guard had no shirt.

"Can't you see we need this?" The man said. "We aren't asking for anything other than human kindness. Can you give us some water at least? Anything sir, please."

"I have to protect the base, sir."

"From what? WE are people. WE are human beings for crying out loud. You have a whole huge base there where people could get dry and get out of this awful heat. We aren't asking for charity; we are just asking for love."

The man was getting angry.

"You let us in there goddamnit! You let these children in there!"

Two other naval guards with bullet proof vests and machine guns popped out of the guard shack and pointed the guns at the crowd.

"Stand down!" One of them yelled. "Disperse! Stand down or we will shoot!"

The crowd members put their hands up.

"We *will* shoot!"

"Please," the man said. "I'm begging you. Take the children."

"We will shoot! You must disperse!"

I didn't know what was going to happen. Would they rush the guard shack? Would the guards shoot innocent people to protect an empty naval base? They sure seemed ready to.

"Daniel," A thin woman said to the leader. "Daniel. Let it go. Nobody is getting shot today. They will have to remember this."

She held up her child, a boy of no more than three.

"You remember this face. You remember these eyes. They will haunt you. This day will haunt you. Because you could have done something, and you didn't. You could have let your pitiful orders go, and you didn't. You picked your orders over human beings, over children. May God have mercy on your souls!"

I didn't want to stick around any longer. I knew there was too many of them to help, even too many children to put in the boat. I had to protect my family, to protect Kirb. With shame curdling in my throat, I turned the boat around and hurriedly paddled away.

We wandered through the maze for the rest of the afternoon until we came across an abandoned Elementary school and I tied the boat up to an open window with a piece of one of my pant legs. We went through it and up the stairs to a classroom full of old books and wooden desks, with the words "There is no truth saving in thine own heart" written in smeared chalk across the chalkboard. I put two desks together for me and three desks together for Kirby and we did our best to sleep.

Chapter Five

It seems difficult if not impossible to pinpoint the moment of one's consciousness, so I imagine that it is a gradual process to form itself in one's mind. My first memory is falling down the stairs, or rather driving down them with a plastic foot propelled car when I was four, but I'm not sure that I was conscious. I feel conscious looking back at it though and I wonder if consciousness is tied to memory or awareness. Is it the act of simply breathing? Or just the continual waking up to what is "real"? If consciousness *is* memory, then my consciousness is complex because I remember a lot. This has proved in darker times of my life, to be a curse.

When I woke up, I wasn't sure whether it was morning or night, but I felt conscious. I was suddenly aware of everything in the room. I got up and rummaged through the teacher's desk and found only worn-out pencils and notepads. Before me were the remnants of where we taught children the basics of education without teaching them anything about how to live. Nothing about surviving, about how to love, how to eat, how to grow in places you can't count on a calculator. There were simply digits and dusty books of literature, a picture of a tree frog, and the lonely green chalkboard. If only I could look into it and see my future. If only it would tell me where to find Janus or how to save my brother and mother from the colossal spray that had bullied the city.

The sun peeked out of the bottom of the windows, and I placed my hand on Kirby's fore arm. His platinum blonde hair was matted and his mouth open.

"Kirb, let's get up."

He turned over a couple of times before slowly opening his eyes.

"Get up buddy. We are going to go find help."

"I'm hungry."

"Here," I said and gave him a couple of crackers and ate a couple myself.

"I might want some milk and cereal."

"I know. This is all we have for now."

"This sucks" he said.

I handed him the milk jug of water and made him take a few swallows. The water spilled down the front of his orange t-shirt before he put the jug back down and screwed on the cap.

"Before we go, I'm going to find a better paddle."

"I wish you would just find some milk and cereal."

"Ha ha," I said sarcastically.

I scanned the room. The ruler? Too thin. I couldn't use any of the books. The desks didn't come apart. I looked up. Fan blades! Perfect! I pushed the desk underneath the fan and carefully broke off the five wooden planks.

"What are you doing?"

"I told you! I'm getting us a better paddle Chubbs."

"Fine," he said, crumbs falling into his lap as he ate another cracker.

We untied the boat and went back into the foul soup. And as you looked out over the strange and awesome valley of water with building tops poking out like reeds, it felt like you were looking through a fogged-up window with streaks down it. I used one of the fan blades to paddle and it was much easier. I kept the other four on the floor of the boat for backup. We soon lost sight of the school and with it any hope of something I recognized.

Even though I had no idea where to go, I felt free, that there was no impending responsibility, no expectations, only the singular aim of finding shelter.

Confusion was scribbled into the housetops in hopeless shades of white.

Help. Five inside: No food.

Please don't loot. This is all we have. God Bless.

1 dead.

2 dead.

6 dead.

Help.

SOS

God will help us.

Help. Please. Old people.

Keep out. Broken Dreams Inside.

We wandered through this cataclysmic poetry, navigating the watered streets and the drowned cars and trucks, passing coffee tables and cookie tins, telephone poles with low hanging wires and the mausoleums we once called our homes. It was one big St. Louis cemetery. All the pointy roofs and porches were filled with the remains of all the things we had put together over the course of our lives. You could call it stuff, could even wonder how stuff defines us, or how your stuff defines you, and you could call me an idolatrous person lusting after stuff, but those things were *ours*. They helped to shape who we were and most of them would be worthless to anybody but us.

We spend most of our lives filling stuff up. We are born empty and have to fill our brains with knowledge and our bones with growth. We have to fill our stomachs every day to live. We fill our time with people we love. We fill our days with work. We fill our houses with decorations and pictures and furniture. And if one piece of furniture gets old, we replace it, but we never completely get rid of it. It becomes a concept in our mind that we need. We hold onto things, savagely. Once those things are gone it's hard to tell who we are because there's nothing left of who we were. I think what's worse than destroying the world is destroying the record of the world, but not in the way a computer or a book holds a record, more like the way the smell of fried catfish makes you feel like that boy at Carmine's that could barely reach over the counter for the red basket and the frozen mug full of Ironport.

Beyond the treetops that poked out over the swell of water, I heard the faint notes of brass. It is understandable in a case like mine that you would question whether those notes were real or if you had created them as some pathetic mirage of hope. I paddled closer and the notes grew longer, calling to me.

"What is that?" Kirb said, perking up a little.

"I think it's music Chubbs."

"There!" he pointed.

On top of a rooftop of an old church I saw a young boy leaning up against the steeple, tapping his feet and playing the trumpet. His song floated across the water like a treasure. The melody skipped and dipped and dove until its silver wreaths circled their way into the soft part of my throat. I paddled closer and could see his bare feet and swollen hands. His feet had red sores on the sides and the tops of his toes were scabbed over. He must have only been thirteen or fourteen, but he had an old face. It was the wisdom of tragedy and poverty mixed with that special genius of an artist. The small neck with its one vein surging as he blew out air. The hazel skin. The skinny cheeks against his full lips and long curled eyelashes. The wiry but strong hands wrapped tightly around the gold maze of the trumpet. It is natural to know musicians in New Orleans in this way. We respect them. They aren't like the pop stars selling out stadiums or even the indie acts that do the bar circuits. All the ego and agenda are stripped away. Our musicians play music to add something to the day, to thrust flavor into your conversation, to give the moment a celebration.

We steered the boat towards the church, and I tied it carefully to the rain gutter using the double loop Dad had taught us to tie our shoelaces. It was simple, but effective. It would hold the boat in place and be easy to untie.

We stepped onto the steep roof and the boy didn't budge.

"Hello!" I called out, but he kept playing as a proud tuft of black hair reached beyond his temple and said "take me as I am, but take me seriously." He didn't even twitch an eyelash until my shadow jumped on his face.

"Who are you?!" he said, crawling backward.

"Woah! It's okay! We just heard you playing and thought we'd stop and see if you needed any help," I said.

"Oh. Well, I'd love some help. I've been stuck up here for two days now. I've been jumping across these hot roofs trying to find somebody to talk to or at least some leftover food."

"We were stuck at our house for a day, but then we found this boat," I said. "What's your name?"

"Khalil Gabriel. What's your guys?"

"I'm Ernest and this is Kirby."

All the things we said felt eternal.

"What's wrong with your feet?" Kirby blurted out.

"I tried jumping roofs for a while and I got on this really beat up one and couldn't get off it," he said. "These shingles are hell on your feet. I even hit a few staples."

"Ouch! I'm sorry to hear it," I said. "Can I look at them?"

He pointed them up and I saw the extent of his sores. They were going to last at least a few days.

"Looks painful," I said. "Let's try and keep them clean. If we can get you somewhere soon, maybe somebody can fix them up for you."

"Sounds good," he said. "Where are y'all headed?"

"Well, honestly, we aren't sure."

He nodded. "I heard someone talking in one of the houses about people getting shelter in the Superdome. You want to head there?"

"If I had any idea how to get there from here, I would," I said. "I've never felt so lost in my own town."

"It's hard to recognize anything, that's for sure," he said. "But I think if we head north, we should run right into it."

"That sounds great," I said. "I'd love to get off the water. Anything you need to bring?"

"Just my trumpet and my case," he said. "Y'all got any food?"

"Some crackers back in the boat. We are trying to conserve what we can, but you are more than welcome to have a few."

"Perfect," he said. "Anything at this point. I haven't eaten in days."

We climbed into the boat, and I noticed Khalil's skinny legs and his wry smile. I washed his feet carefully and tore some more of my pants off to bind them. He seemed so thin and the bags under his eyes bulged dejectedly. It just didn't fit seeing a boy looked so tired.

The vast water stretched before us. We rowed through the labyrinth of houses, turning and turning and turning, but the only thing that changed was the heat which poured out on the tops of our hands and around our temples. The hunger grew too, came like fierce tides, grumbling low and then piercing into the pelvis before rising up through the chest. We didn't talk about it, but you could see the resignation in Kirb's reddening cheeks and Khalil's dry lips. We didn't make it far fast, and the paddling was exhausting.

We split the last three crackers and mine gave me a sudden burst of energy. I paddled for an hour or so until Khalil took over because he knew the way to a nearby shopping district where we were hoping to find some food before we made it to the Superdome. I tried to stretch as much of my body out as I could by laying my head in Kirb's lap and propping my feet next to where Khalil sat. Kirb looked down at me and shook his head. I winked and he smiled.

New Orleans didn't look so bad in the sky. It was only the light of the sun and the occasional cloud that puttered by with really no aim except to be white and puffy. I heard the caw of a crow, whose shadow waltzed frivolously on the water. The whole of our empire was crushed by that single shadow. I have not known a king. I have not trembled under sword and spear. I have not kneeled before a queen. I have not seen God, only His eye in the spray as it covered all the things we spent our lives making. The crow took another turn over the water- logged neighborhoods, shrinking the graven images and skyscrapers before letting out an untamed cry from his sleek black beak.

I closed my eyes and let the chop of the water rock me into a cat nap before waking again as my ankle brushed up against the side of the boat. Then the wind came again. It wasn't a cool wind, it was full of hot gusts that blew into the follicles of your hair and underneath the top layer of your skin, causing a heat blanket in already hot weather. We took off our shirts and then put them back on and took them off again. It seemed as if Khalil was going to dunk his shirt in the water but after looking over the brown mush for a minute he thought better and picked up the paddle.

I drearily sat up.

Kirb's hair was blowing across his face and his eyes were closed happily, like a kid with his face out the car window.

I shimmied to the front of the boat behind Khalil and folded my arms.

"Did you grow up here?"

He did not answer right away, but I didn't much feel the need for answers right then. Answers were just something else to interrupt the blue sky.

"Yes," Khalil finally said, continuing to paddle.

"Us too. When did you know you liked music?"

He chuckled and wiped his forehead.

"It happened before I can remember anything happening. I used to hum to the sound of anything I could hear: the fridge, the vacuum cleaner, the dryer. It was all music to me. I think I might make an album like that one day. Just things you find around the house, you know? Like one track could be called 'air conditioner' and another track could be 'passing car' and another could be 'sandals on feet'. Do you think people would buy it?"

I nodded. It sounded like a great idea. I wondered if he would add, "ceiling fan oar chopping against water" to his song list or if it was something he would want to forget.

A military helicopter passed over us. I waved frantically.

"We are here!" I yelled. "Over here! Over here! WE ARE HERE!"

"Calm down," Kirb said. "You are being loud."

The helicopter made another pass and I yelled again, but it kept going. Khalil didn't move. I wondered if they would see Mama. I wondered if she was stomach deep in whiskey and running around the roof screaming and praying to God. I hoped she was alright. I hoped she was safe.

"I swear they saw us."

"They did," Khalil answered.

"Then why didn't they stop?"

"It's always the poor goes first."

"What do you mean? They didn't stop because we were poor? They have no idea."

"Oh! Yes, they do," he said and looked back with an ironic smile. "They know exactly who we are."

"I just don't understand why you wouldn't help someone if they needed help," I said.

Kirb wanted to paddle and we let him. I tried to show him, but he stubbornly took the oar from my hands and chopped away at the water. It only worked about half the time, but both Khalil and I were getting tired, and it was good for him to contribute.

"The Great Flood of 1927," Khalil said.

"Excuse me?" I asked, confused.

"Mostly poor people got it then, just like now."

I didn't know what to say.

"Chicago Heat Wave. Sea Island Hurricane. Great Quakes in San Fran. I swear, if we could go back and see the ashes of Krakatoa, we'd see that they landed on the poor houses first. We need a Bessie Smith. We need a 'Backwater Blues'."

For thirteen or fourteen, he spoke like a man.

"I guess I've never really thought about it," I said. "That's damn awful."

"Doesn't matter anyway," he said. "How we gonna change it?"

The suffocated animal clinic jumped up in front of us, its only vestige a white paw clutching over the top of the water. I took a deep breath. In it was the smell of decaying people, the smell of bodies after a few days without soap. The smell of dirt on the hands and knuckles and underneath the nails. There was no pollen, no leaves, no flowers, no uncut grass, nothing to smell but the unclean water and three lost sailors. Some part of my molecules knew it was all gone, some corpuscle in my lungs sensed the loss of oxygen and my exhale sifted longingly for a place to deposit its carbon dioxide.

There is so much around us that we forget what we need until it's gone, I thought. In fact, sometimes New Orleans seemed like an awful place to me, because it was all I had ever known. I kept waiting to leave, wanting to find something different, in the same way I was to trying leave Mama's. I did not love the city before that day as I do now. It was then just a place to live. Taking it away made me love it.

Kirb let out a horrific cry and dropped his oar.

"Ernest!" he cried. "Ernest! What is THAT?!"

I crawled to the front of the boat. Bobbing up and down in the water was a dog with no face. There were only eye sockets and teeth. Somehow the rest of its body was still covered in fur. I picked up the oar and pushed the body over, sending its cruel gaze downward.

"It's just a puppy Chubbs. Come here and look."

Khalil helped him.

"But- I saw. It was awful."

"Things look funny in the water, sometimes," I said.

"Is he dead?"

"Yes."

"Did I might die?"

 He started to cry.

"I don't want to die Ernest," he said. "I don't might want to die. I want to go home Ernest. I want to see Mama. I want to go home. I want- Dad! I want my Dad!"

Neither Khalil nor I answered him. I picked up the oar and paddled calmly, letting Khalil take Kirby to the back of the boat and show him his trumpet. Kirby held it ingenuously as he sniffled through the last of his sobs. Khalil smiled.

We took turns paddling for what seemed like days. The anxiety was everywhere. It was the heat and the small boat and the grumbling stomachs. It was the flies, wings beating the air, vicious wings, thousands upon thousands of wings throbbing until it was all you could hear. Khalil attempted to swat them away, but it did nothing. I picked up one of the oars and swung it violently back and forth, back and forth, but all it did was whip the heat around and before I could put the paddle down, the flies came back. It was also the mosquitoes and Kirb's open mouth, gasping for fresh air and salivating over the dream of cold milk. It was the stench, which overwhelmed your nostrils, seeping deeper into your lungs and tongue and teeth, and with a gust of wind it disappeared and with another, it came again. Mostly, it was the maze, the water and houses and buildings and telephone poles and messages and water and houses and water and heat and skin. Skin itching. Nose itching. Feet itching. Hands itching. You moved because your back hurt, but then your feet hurt, so you moved until your hips hurt. There were no comfortable positions. You longed for an end, any end. And the hunger took the strength out of the paddle and the paddle grew the hunger.

Chapter Six

The sign said "Corner Mart." It was a large convenience store adjacent to a Best Buy. The water had thinned out next to the buildings and it seemed to reach just above the shins. We did not get out of the boat. We stopped a few hundred feet from the parking lot and watched. The store had been hollowed out by water and rage. The shelves had long been raided, but there were a few scavengers skulking through the store's remains for food. Their eyes were bloodshot, sunken. Their lips gawked like goldfish. Their shoulders were raised and foreheads long. They stunk of abnormality, of the swell and desperate hunger, of survival. They were terrifying. Even the children had white lips and swollen throats that gasped not for air, not for compassion, not for play, but for something, anything to eat. It had been days since we had eaten a meal. It changes something in you. It awakes some wild evolutionary part of us, that really never left, but has been tamed by years of surplus and round bellies.

After it has been some time since you have seen someone other than your two boat companions, people are foreign. I can only imagine the shock of the Native Americans when they first saw the Europeans or prisoners that get released and view outside the walls after years of confinement. It had only been a few days, but they were ancient days, full and historic.

A business type in a soiled button up shirt, tie hanging off the side of his neck, was picking up plastic wrappers and squishing them to see if there was a forgotten morsel. His fingernails were black, hands covered in caked mud. A thin woman a few feet from him was crawling underneath the aisles with a cracked yellow smile, while two teenage boys were pulling at a vending machine outside. A group of police officers helped one another carry video game console boxes out of the Best Buy and load them into a large truck. The man in the suit gave up on the wrappers and moved to inspect the microwave and nacho stand, while the woman looking underneath moved to the coolers. A young girl of about eight in a pink Easter dress, spattered with brown handprints, went outside to watch the boys move the vending machine. Once away from the crowd, they excitedly teetered the machine, splashing it in the water while the young girl clapped her hands. The police officers went back into the Best Buy and brought out what looked like a large plasma screen TV in a box while behind them three teenage girls scurried with laptop computers and a handful of DVDs.

There was a large crash. The boys had finally tipped over the vending machine, which had hit the cement and broken the lock. Out spilled snacks, candies, and gum into the Corner Mart's water-logged parking lot. Everybody stopped what they were doing. The police officers dropped the TV, and the teenage girls quickly stashed the laptops in a sunken car's window. The man in the button up ran out, pushed aside by the woman looking in the cooler. All the looters had halted their greedy and speedy scavenger hunt to run over and eat.

Chip bags were ripped open and candy bars were shoved greedily into mouths. One of the officers pushed the woman out of the way and stole a pocket-sized bag of nuts while the young girl ate pieces of a cookie from a pool of dirty water. Other people seemed to come out of nowhere. First one and then ten and then twenty. Food was taken from people's hands before they put it into their mouths and eyes bulged with wrath as they all howled together. My mouth watered and I could see the wildness in the eyes of Kirby and Khalil.

The hunger had become so powerful that it numbed all speech and yet the word repeated itself in us over and over again. "Food," "Food" "Food" the frenzy seemed to echo. It terrified. It waxed and waned until the hairs on your neck stood up. It burned into the ears. Oh! The howling! The horror!

The cackle of laughter. Someone laughed? It was a sour laugh, shrill. It came from the thin woman who had found a half of a Snicker's bar and was licking it like a snow cone on a hot day, its brown melted goo smothering her chin and nose. The crowd swarmed more than they moved, picking up every last crumb from the pool of dark water. They splashed and dashed and dived until everything they could see was gone. And even after that, they probed on hands and knees for more, water dripping from their ferocious mouths.

When they could find no more, they went back to their scavenging. It seemed as if nothing had happened. No one talked or thought it unusual. It was true that many of us had built a thick skin because we were used to living in thin walls that couldn't keep the cold out in a winter's chilled night or the wet heat of a Louisiana summer, but this was something different.

What uncertainties passed through my mind as I cautiously turned the boat away, not wanting to arouse suspicions or fight for water-logged scraps. I was hesitant. Survival had never felt so real. It was even stronger than the idea of Janus or Mama or Kirby or myself. My body was speaking a language I could only understand as greed.

The shadow was cast. It came from the depths and rose into the heavens and you couldn't even see your face in the water because the shadow was so deep, so sinister, so bleak. So, instead of looking down, like one might do to see their shadow on the sidewalk, I looked up to see that tall and lean black cloak that hovered over the city of New Orleans like a single cloud, like a dark and menacing angel. I expected that angel to give me some revelation, some proclamation of a purpose to all this, but not something spoken on top of a mountain, but whispered inches from my ear, intimate and horrifying.

There was no revelation, only the sound of howling of human beings as they tore plastic bags from one another's hands, as they ravaged skin cells and muffled cries for help. All the pleasantries of being human had been stripped away and what was left was the beast.

Although the anxiety of the scene had wiped away all the grumbles of our stomachs, they came back unflinchingly after we left, and we did not speak for a long time. We each battled it in our own way. We did not speak of it, not even Kirb, who quietly clapped his tongue against the top of his mouth as the Corner Mart faded from view.

It wasn't until the sun started to go down that Khalil took his trumpet out of the case. He held it as if it was a piece of art in a museum. He turned it over and over in his hands, which against the dwindling light of the sun gave the trumpet a rouge tint, and it tumbled through pinks and reds and golds before he put it to his lips.

"Is it okay if I play?"

"Backstreet boys?" Kirb asked.

"I don't think I know that one," Khalil answered back and Kirb shook his head in disbelief.

"Backstreet is the best music. Nineties music is the best music," he said.

"Well, if it's the best music, then I will definitely have to learn it.," Khalil said. "I'd like to play something from the heart instead. What do you think?"

Kirb ruefully nodded while Khalil pushed out the first few notes. They came out raw and rusty and I cringed.

He breathed in and gave it a second try. The notes blew, roared even. They became as much a story as something you would hear around a campfire or read in a book. I watched the air, waiting for the music to turn into words, to surround me with every wish and desire and heartache that Khalil had ever experienced. You did not have to know him or to know the neighborhood he was born in to have heard the sadness and joy, how each note was a tear from a tired eye or a drop of blood from a mother's arm or the sweat that had rained down in frantic sprays of hunger and desperation. The notes kept coming. Louder and louder. Louder and louder until I couldn't distinguish what the notes were and what my feelings were. This is greatness, I thought. When a theory or a song or idea becomes so familiar that someone accepts it, takes ownership of it. They were my notes, and they were Kirby's notes and they were the people at the Corner Mart's notes and they were our neighborhoods notes, all part of the Big Easy's mournful promenade.

Kirby swayed aimlessly as the sun retired from trying to kill us all and burned its pink and gold banner of victory, reminding the city that the battle would begin again at close of night. Khalil stood up, his thin and proud figure reaching toward that banner, and he raised his trumpet, blasting out the last of the song. It was so beautiful I wanted to cry. I wasn't sad, it wasn't that at all. It was just so damn beautiful. Do you know what I mean?

When the song was done and sun gone, Khalil put the trumpet back into the case. Neither Kirb nor I said anything, although I held Kirb's hand for a while and let him trace my palm, as he loved to do when he was thinking or just wanted to forget something as arbitrary as thinking.

The night was peaceful. It didn't seem the same place where so much had gone wrong. Khalil put down the oar and kicked up his feet so he could look at the stars. I pulled Kirb down next to me and he grabbed Khalil's hand and we all looked up.

And there were the stars and underneath finally the cool air. I scanned the night sky as if for the first time, and really *saw* the stars for the beauty of their white dust and speckled chaos. How they turned on and off, on and off, waving hello, shucking away the flesh we wore in order to speak to the universal connectedness, to whisper finally that no one can ever be alone.

Kirb and Khalil were silent. We all watched the lull of the big dipper and how it spoke to us, each in our own way. For me, it was the pot that held my past, all the suffering boiling through the good things that I kept remembering to keep sane. For Khalil, it seemed to hold the notes of an unwritable song. For Kirby, it was probably cereal and milk or maybe the blithe spirit of our father who was making us all cereal and milk in the ever-present cosmos.

I've never seen something so still and so unfathomable as the night sky after Hurricane Katrina. For a moment, I forgot the violence of it all and we stayed that way, breathing heavily, hands clasped, music moved to our eyes. We didn't want it to end, even though we knew it would.

"It doesn't feel real," I said.

"Can you tell me?" Khalil asked in a deference for speech I have not heard before or since. "How can we tell? How can we *really* tell the difference between what is real and what is not?"

He let that settle a minute before he added, "What's good about reality anyway? The best of us comes from magic."

"Magic" Kirby repeated, and I said nothing because they were both right.

Magic is what we know subtracted from what is a mystery. Magic was there. It was everywhere. It surrounds us. Some call it God or love or faith or even science. I like to think they are all magic, all one part of the same sacred tree. Like the veil nebula, you can name it God or love of faith or science and I don't know that anyone could prove you wrong.

"What are you thinking about?" Khalil asked, somehow sensing that I had caught on to something.

"I'm thinking about the veil nebula," I said.

"What in the hell is that?" Kirb spouted.

"It is the last of an exploding star. It was discovered in 1784 by William Herschel," I said.

"Sounds bored" Kirb added.

"Can you see it?" Khalil asked.

"Actually, it is one of the more difficult things to see. We would need a special telescope lens with a OIII filter that picks up the exact wavelength of the light."

"Have you ever seen it?"

"I have," I said. "I was in an Astronomy club in High School. We went out as far as we could away from the city and pointed our telescopes to the sky. The nebula is full of pinks and greens and blues and about every color you can think of, and they are swirling and twisting and dancing together in this long stream. It's crazy, right? I mean this star is dying and with its death is some of the most brilliant light in the universe."

"It reminds me," I sat up. "Of the vertical migration. It's magnificent! At night, billions of lantern fish come up from the ocean to feed and it creates this light pulsating from the bottom of the earth. So, we have the light of the stars and the color wheel of the veil nebula coming from the sky and the lantern fish coming from the depths. It's a miracle."

"Hmm." Khalil remarked, giving it a once over. "It's like musical theory."

"I don't know anything about musical theory," I admitted.

"So bored," Kirb added.

"You see lights as miracles. I see musical theory as a miracle."

Khalil rubbed his hands together.

"From Lil Wayne to Samuel Coleridge-Taylor to Beyonce to Wynton Marsalis to William Grant Still. Each person has their own music which reaches across the globe on tiny little phone screens and pulses through ears on sidewalks and in MP3's. The people make the light in the middle, you see? Culture may not write them in the history books, or they may, either way they refuse to be silent. Just like your stars and your fish. Want to hear another song I wrote?"

"I'd love to! Anything but this bored talking." Kirb blurted out before I had a chance to answer.

"I wrote this one about my Auntie Zora." Khalil said before he pulled the trumpet ceremoniously from its case and flipped it over in his hands. He put it in his mouth and tested it with a few pops from his lips. This was a different song, more somber, but equally moving. It did not speak in the same way, but it did take away the last of the energy we had. Kirby's eyes closed halfway through it, and I let his hand go and pulled off my shirt and put it under his head.

Khalil finished the song, put his chalice back into its case, said a prayer and told me goodnight. I waited until I could hear his faint snore before I let what happened come back into my mind.

He had been there, coming in and out all day. Now, we had time to be alone. I wept. I wept hot tears. I wept because he would never know the veil nebula or the vertical migration or the tender notes of Khalil's trumpet.

Chapter Seven

The morning was not kind. Beneath us brewed the awful dreams of mad men and above us rose the wrath of the red admiral. Its dawn was furious. It burned the bottom of my feet and I jolted awake.

The air was greasy, unclean. I could feel my skin as I sat up. It was that late summer heat stick. The only way to get rid of it would be to shower and I wasn't sure if I would ever get to do that again. Kirb and Khalil were sprawled across the boat. Kirb had his neck twisted on one of the sitting boards and Khalil's backside was lifted in the air like a child. Those have to got to be the most uncomfortable sleep positions I ever saw, I thought, and yet they were both sleeping soundly. I stretched my arm, took a breath, and tried to decide whether or not I should wake them or sit there in the silence.

The water was shaken, full of a murkiness I couldn't recognize. The water had been churned in the night and choked weeds and decapitated dandelions floated tranquilly on the water's surface. But there was more.

There were moving black blotches. They twitched and convulsed and spasmed, jerking toward the surface with grief, with a desperate ache to escape. I picked up the oar and stirred the water. It moved. It breathed. It struggled. I peered over the side of the boat. The water was grimier than usual, as if a great gyre had been turning it while we slept, pushing sand and black blotches to its surface. One of them moved its legs and I finally knew what they were.

Crickets. Thousands and thousands of black field crickets. Their eyes were blank, frantic. I knew crickets had compound eyes and could see in all directions, could see the bog they were drowning in and also the sky above them. Their mouths opened and shut, opened and shut, filling with water. Their antennae moved through the muck, searching for an answer, for some reason or stimulus to explain what was happening. Some stopped, drooped down, stilled. But then there were the ones who didn't stop, who couldn't, those that furiously kicked their hind legs to jump. I felt wrong watching them die, watching them struggle, but I couldn't turn away. It reminded me of when a disaster happens on the news, and we all tell one another. "Did you hear how many people died? Did you hear what happened in-" Dear God. They were saying that about New Orleans right now. Did you hear what happened in New Orleans? I wondered how many had died, but not in that same curious way. They were people I knew and even if they weren't, they were part of my home. I felt sick. I wanted to throw up the emptiness and hunger in my stomach. But I couldn't turn away.

I trembled as one of the crickets quit kicking its hind legs. That's how it happens. It all just ended. All at once, we were fire, water, and thunder. A cigarette butt floated next to the dead cricket and stopped.

I paddled, trying to get away from the cemetery of crickets. I used long strokes, switching from one side to another. All I could hear was my paddle against the water and the jingle-jangle of the handle on Khalil's trumpet case. After my arms and hands had got good and tired, I put the oar back in the boat and drifted, folding both hands behind my neck and sitting back.

A cricket jumped in the boat and I smiled. One of the little buggers was going to make it. Maybe we could take him to the Superdome with us, as a fellow survivor of the great water wasteland. Then another jumped in, shaking its legs dry. Then another and another and another.

They poured in like locusts in the dust bowl, a squall of black fury, chirping and flapping and biting and jumping.

"Wake up!" I screamed. Kirby shook his head awake and Khalil stood up.

"What the?" he exclaimed.

More came in. We tried kicking at them, but it wasn't fast enough. Kirby picked up the oar and swung it, but it only caught a few. They climbed up our legs and onto our backs, scurrying up our chest and happily pouncing on our necks and heads.

When I felt the first bite, I shrieked. Kirby's eyes widened with terror while Khalil grabbed his trumpet case and held it to his chest in an act of protection. I got bit again and again but as soon as we brushed one of an arm or leg, they came right back.

"Let's get out of here!" I commanded and I grabbed an oar while Kirby and Khalil sat down in their cricket long johns and pushed the water with their hands. In a frenzy we paddled for about two hundred yards, but it was no use, they kept coming.

Khalil pulled his hands from the water.

"Let's tip the boat!" he yelled. "It's the only way to shake them!"

I pulled up the paddle and took Kirb's arm.

"Buddy, we have to get in the water to get rid of these things."

"Help me, Ernest!" he cried. "Help me! It hurts!"

I held onto him and nodded at Khalil. We both teetered the boat until it capsized, and we all fell into the water. There were a couple of lingering crickets hanging on my head, but most were gone. I made sure Kirb was okay, and Khalil and I tipped the boat back over. There were a few water-logged soldiers we tossed out along with some excess water, but we were back on the row in no time.

"I have never!" I said.

Kirb sulked in the back of the boat.

"I want to go home," he said. "I want some cereal and milk. I want to watch wrestling. I'm tired of this boring boat. I want to see Mama! Where is my Mama? Where is she?"

"We will get there soon enough Chubbs," I said. "I promise. Mama is okay. She's always okay."

He didn't move.

Khalil took off his shirt and wrung it out before putting it across one of the sitting boards.

"Kirby," he called out.

"Yes?"

"Is that all you would eat right now? I mean if you could eat anything? All you would want is cereal and milk?"

"I might also want a grilled cheese," he said.

"Nothing else? No chocolate cake or apple pie?"

"That might sounds good."

"What would you have to drink?" Khalil said.

"A Coke," Kirb said.

Khalil's faced beam.

"Yes, an ice-cold coke sounds amazing right about now. What about you Ernest? What would you eat?"

"Ribs from Geoffrey's, with that same ice-cold coke. And a side of baked beans with some potato salad and a big biscuit with honey and butter."

"That sounds pretty good!"

"Yeah, ribs," Kirb added.

"And I'd sure love a slice of my wife's carrot cake," I said.

"You're married?"

"I am."

"Oh," Khalil thought solemnly. "Did she make it out of the city?"

"I don't know," I said.

I put my hands between my legs.

"She left," Kirb blurted out. "She doesn't like marriage."

"That's Mama talking Chubbs!" I hollered at him. "You don't know what Janus has been through! Everything will be just fine. You'll see."

"Ernest hit her," Kirb said.

My anger vanished, replaced by a rush of shame and embarrassment.

"I did," I said. "And I'll regret it every day of the rest of my life."

The chop of the water quieted as we slowed down.

"A cheeseburger," Khalil said loudly.

"What's that?"

"That's what I'd have, a cheeseburger. But not any cheeseburger would do. I want a giant cheeseburger with grilled onions and mushrooms and Cajun spice and mayonnaise and pickles and tomatoes."

"Oh!" he exclaimed, as if he had forgot something. "And fries so greasy and salty you have to wipe your fingers after you eat them."

I laughed for the first time since the storm, since I had tried to take my own life, and it felt uncomfortable but cathartic.

"That sounds divine" I told him.

"Anything for dessert?"

"My auntie's homemade blueberry pie with a scoo- No! With two scoops of ice cream," he said. "So cold that you have to put the spoon under hot water just to get it out of the ice cream box."

"Ice cream. Ahh!"

"I might love some ice cream Ernest," Kirb said. "Can we have some ice cream? Please Ernest? I'm so hungry. I might just want some ice cream and a coke. Please?"

"I promise we can have some ice cream as soon as we find a place to eat," I said. "Do you think you can help me and Khalil look for a place to eat? We could really use your help on this one."

"Yes, Ernest. I will look," Kirb said.

"You let me know as soon as you see a place, okay?"

"I will!"

Khalil sat down and I picked the oar back up. It felt good to paddle and the heat stick had been washed away in the water.

"My auntie used to tell me that if you killed a cricket, it was bad luck." Khalil said. "How many years of bad luck do you think we got now?"

I chuckled.

"More than we can count," I said. "That's for sure."

"You can push me" he said as he checked the trumpet case. "You can push me but I will fall on soft earth."

"What is that?" I asked.

"What?"

"That thing you keep saying," I said. "I've heard it now a few times."

"Oh! Something my mother used to say to me."

"I love it," I said. "Where's it from?"

"Actually, I haven't found it anywhere else," Khalil said. "Not even the mighty internet pulls anything up. I kind of like it that way. It makes me think maybe it's my family's. The whole thing goes, 'You can push me, but I will fall on soft earth. You can throttle me, but I will breathe through my eyes. You can punish me, but I will weep for your salvation. You can bury me, but I will crawl out, feet first, dancing the *danse macabre*, naked as a skeleton!'"

"That's great man," I said. "I'll have to have you write that down for me when this is all over."

"You got it!" Khalil exclaimed. "But don't you try and say that your family came up with it. That's the Gabriel's. You feel me?"

"Loud and clear," I said.

The morning seemed to go by fast as the leftover water on our backs kept us cool and the friendly banter kept our spirit's light. Kirb and I sung some Backstreet and Khalil told us about his schoolgirl crush, which was a girl named Kassandra that he described as a fun loving girl that wore scented lotions, liked to ride her bicycle, and loved coconut shaved ice topped with condensed milk. His plan had been to surprise her with a coconut shaved ice with condensed milk for lunch this week, but the hurricane had stopped his chance at romance. We all could only hope that things would return to normal, and he would see her again. I thought then of Janus and what I had done to her. I said a secret prayer to God that he would keep her safe, even if it meant I would die. As long as Kirb and Janus were safe. Well, and Khalil, and I guess Mama too. As long as they were all safe, I wouldn't mind dying. I was supposed to die anyway.

We started to recognize things. The tops of buildings rose on the horizon as we paddled toward them in awe. The Superdome wasn't far away now. The light burned brightly. I had never before studied the light, but I watched it now with anticipation as one might watch a movie or scroll through their cellphone screen. It charged and surged until it wasn't yellow anymore but white. White hot heat that climbed into your skull. I felt the anxiety of being trapped more than I had since the hurricane had started. My skin itched. I was hungry.

Interstate ten stood like a hydra monster, half of it drowned and the other half rising to the sky. A van was perched on the edge of it with writing that read: *Please don't loot, it's all we have left. God Bless.*

We paddled passed it slowly, each of us wondering if someone was still inside.

I was about ready to call out to see if I could reach somebody when Khalil dived into the water. I didn't have time to look before Kirb jumped in after him. I froze, unsure of what to do. I had to find out what was going on first. Then I saw them. A young boy of around eight was trying to hold his younger baby sister of I'd say three above water while he held onto one of the interstate's cement pillars. He was bobbing up and down and choking on the water as it passed his mouth and nose.

Khalil was fast, putting the girl on his back while he waited for Kirb.

When Kirb arrived, Khalil showed the boy how to wrap his arms around Kirb's neck and they all swam toward me. I paddled as fast as I could to meet them, excited to see someone else, to have something meaningful to do. I could tell that Kirby was struggling to keep his face above water, but somehow it wasn't long before both the kids were in the boat. I took off my shirt and gave it to them, followed by Khalil and finally Kirby.

"What's your name?" Khalil asked the boy.

"Benny," he said.

"And how about you darling?"

The little girl didn't answer.

"Her name is Anna," Benny told us, as he made sure that his sister was comfortable, swaddled in two of our shirts before wrapping the third around his back.

"What were y'all doing in there anyway?"

"I was trying to make a swim for it," the boy said. "My Mommy died back there in that van a few days ago and I wasn't sure we were going to make it if I didn't try and leave. Then Anna saw I left and jumped in after me. I couldn't make it back to the van, so I was just trying to keep her alive."

"You're a brave boy," I said. "Very brave."

Kirb smiled proudly at Benny.

"You're a big boy!" Kirb said. "And strong!"

Benny nodded.

"We are headed to the Superdome," I said. "We will make sure you and sister get there safe."

We picked up the oars and went back to work.

"Where were you coming from in that van?" Khalil asked.

"St. Bernard Parish, sir."

"Damn! That's a long way! What are you doing all the way up here?"

"Trying to get away," the boy said. "It was real bad down there. You couldn't even see no houses or nothing. The village got destroyed and the sewers came up. It smelled so bad! And my Daddy died. Mommy was trying to get these white people to help us because they had a lot of food, but they wouldn't help anyone that wasn't white."

"Bastards!" Khalil let out, cutting Benny off.

"Are you sure?" I said.

"Yes, sir," the boy said. "They even blocked the roads so none of us could get in."

Khalil cleared his throat. "Ernest, they have been trying to keep us out of there for years."

"I can't believe it," I said, shaking my head.

"I know. But it doesn't surprise *me* at all." Khalil told me angrily, emphasizing the "me" as much as he could.

"What do you mean you know?"

"It's racism," Khalil said. "You wouldn't understand. You can't understand."

I was annoyed. How dare he tell me I couldn't understand? We were friends. We had been through Hell together and he couldn't relate to me? I took him off that roof dammit!

"Well you can't understand what it's like to have a little brother with a disability or to lose your wife in a hurricane!" I nearly yelled, letting the anger swell up inside me.

"You're right," Khalil said calmly. "I can't understand that, but I can listen to you and I can be your friend and can help you in the ways that I know how. That's all any of us can do, but you saying what's painful in your life doesn't take racism away and it doesn't compare. We can't ignore things by saying other bad things that happen to us. That's not how it works. Then racism gets put off and put off and swept under like America has been doing for way too long."

He threw the oar down.

"Think about something for minute," Khalil said. "9-11. Not that long ago, right? What was the response by the government? They came right away. They helped people right away. What was the response of the people in the United States? They pulled together and we grieved the losses together. Mostly white people. Mostly rich people. Now, there are a lot more black people in New Orleans and we are a lot poorer. It's been *DAYS* since we have been out here. We have seen a couple helicopters and some crazy people fighting over food and looting a Best Buy, including the cops, but what we haven't seen is anybody helping each other, besides the people that live here. I'm willing to bet this country isn't going to give a damn about New Orleans the way they did about 9-11. You watch! Nobody outside of New Orleans is going to be shedding tears and waving flags and saying how horrible it was that all the people that died here died. They will probably blame us for it, that's usually how it goes."

I took a breath.

"I'm sorry," I said, not knowing what else to say.

"Yep." He let out. "If only 'sorrys' could change something. But they don't. You all living in your Whiteopia with your frozen yogurt stands and your mini malls, nearly pushing somebody off the road in your car so you aren't late to get your five dollar cup of coffee. And you expect us to give you a smile and hand out cookies or something. I'm tired. We are all tired."

I didn't know what to say. I'd never had a five-dollar cup of coffee and I wasn't a fan of frozen yogurt, but I could see exactly what he meant. Living without the hunger of living. I hadn't felt that before, but

I'd wished for it. I had seen Kirby be judged and I felt it, but I couldn't feel what Kirby was feeling, not how it really was. This was even more distant. I knew I would never be able to understand what he went through, but it didn't mean I couldn't admire Khalil. I admired his passion. I admired his youth. I admired his anger.

Kirb went over to Khalil and plopped his chubby arms around his neck.

"I like you Khalil," he told him and that crooked grin of his brought out a happiness in Khalil's face.

"I like you too my friend," he said back, and right then I wished was Kirby. I wished I had his love because that's more important than understanding, to love someone fully, to love every person fully, even if you can't understand them fully. It reminded me of Dad and the Knights of the Round Table. Arthur made the table round so that everyone had the same say, so that no one was higher than any one person.

Kirby was an honorable man and Khalil was too, or at least he was going to be. For fourteen, he was a better man than I was at nearly 30. He had not hesitated as I had done at the Naval base or gawk in terror as we had all done at the store, but he jumped with Kirby freely into the water and splashed towards the children. I was ashamed and jealous.

Dad believed that Kirby was the best of us. Once, I had asked him what Kirby's place was in our English heritage and his reply was: "Oh! Son!" as if there was something I needed to see that was right in front of me. "He's Percival. One of the most important of all Arthur's knights. He was sent on a quest to find the Holy Grail but found much more than that. Percival came across the Fisher King, a man who was devastated by age and ennui. His whole land was ashes of disbelief, all the trees black and the rivers muck, and the people starving. Percival was a bit scared of the king, so he had to go on a journey, a life journey, a spiritual journey to discover his true purpose. And it wasn't easy! He had to face death. We all have to face it. When he came back to the Fisher King, his true purpose was revealed. All he had to do was ask one question: What ails thee sire? And the whole land was healed, and the King gave Percival the Holy Grail, the one instrument that could heal mankind. All Percival had to do was ask if the King was okay, to empathize with him, to see him as human. That's what we all need son. There were those that thought Percival was a fool, but he was the only one that could find the grail, the only one that dared to ask the Fisher King what was wrong, the only one, ultimately, that could heal him. Kirby is our Percival. He is the only one that can heal this family." Only one? Then what was I? His squire? His brother? His shadow?

"You are an honorable man," I suddenly told Khalil, to get out of my own head. "Just like King Arthur."

"King who?"

"King Arthur!" I said. "You seriously don't know King Arthur? He's the most famous King that ever lived."

"I don't know King Arthur," Khalil said. "What did he do?"

"He started the Knights of the Round Table, men that cherished honor and chivalry. My Dad used to tell us the stories almost every night."

"I loved Dad's stories," Kirby added.

"I heard a lot of stories growing up about honor, but they weren't knights," Khalil said.

"Who were they?"

"My favorite was probably Cetshwayo Kampande, the Zulu King," he said. "He was fierce, but honorable. I liked Marcus Mosiah Garvey a lot too, because he fought for the freedom of Africans more than anyone else. And of course, Malcom X. He said the things that weren't easy to say but that were on everybody's minds. It takes courage to do that. Those are the people I learned honor from. Them and my Auntie Zora. She was so strong. She never backed down from anyone, but she was kind too."

I was quiet. So, Khalil had the honor of Africans and the honor of Americans and the honor of New Orleanians. Khalil truly was an honorable man.

Rescue boats zipped by and we felt that we had finally made it. When we got close to the Superdome it was clear that it had become an island. The parking structure was covered in water, with only the top poking out, which we tied the boat to. Would it ever come back? Was it now the lost city of New Orleans like the lost city of Atlantis? A place where people had been but were no more. Would divers come looking for Jazz instruments and French promenades? What pieces would be lost forever? Maybe our whole history would be buried and hundreds of years later scientists would search the rubble until the sands shifted and New Orleans became an idea, a fiction.

An army helicopter lifted off overheard as we took turns loading up the kids until they had both reached the top. I made sure Kirb and Khalil made it before I climbed up myself. By the time I could stand on solid ground there were so many people around us we couldn't hear each other talking. They were all like us: haggard and hungry and exhausted.

It was pandemonium. There was trash everywhere, piled high with expectation and fear. There was shouting and pleading and crying and howling. I expected there to be a sign that said, "Abandon all hope, ye who enter here."

We were all so tired. We hadn't known how tired until we could rest. We could rest now. What nerves I had were gone. I did not feel shocked or dismayed. I only kept going. That's all I felt I could do. *Just keep going.* But I did not know the purpose of it.

The rest was a blur. The helicopters had already taken Mama from the rooftop and two days later we found her outside one of the gates, wrapped in a thin blanket, pores seeping the rotten stench of whiskey. She did not speak of the storm, nor asks us to recount our story. She thought it was all God's plan and wasn't worth retelling, as it might put into question our own separate trials.

After a few days, we migrated to Uncle Rick's in El Dorado, Arkansas. We stayed there for months until we could come back home. I spent a lot of time watching old movies and eating snacks. Janus had made it out too. I found out from one of her cousins about a week after the storm. It took months to find her when we came back and by then she had moved into the Geisha House and was so deep into the drugs I barely recognized her. I begged her to come home. I even slept outside the door one night, before the Mamasan kicked me out. Sometimes I wake up from a cat nap in the middle of the afternoon and I call out her name, thinking that she is in the other room reading a book or watching TV, and it takes me a few minutes to realize that she is gone, and I had forgotten what it was like to be lonely, that for that brief moment I had forgotten what it was like to be alone, but like cream rising to the top on whipped butter, the alone always comes back, the tremor in my left hand acts up, and I know exactly where she really is.

I wanted an explanation. I wanted somebody to tell me why, why I had to be sad, and why there were people out there who didn't have to be. I'd been happy with Janus, but I hadn't spent enough time enjoying it. I didn't know how happy I was until I wasn't happy anymore. That's why I had to get it back, to make it the way it had been, but even better this time, so good we couldn't do anything *but* be happy and everything else would fall away like the rain pushing out the southern sun. I know! No matter how happy you get, you will always be missing that one thing, that one thing you can't put your finger on, even though you try everything to find it. It's a cosmic juggling act. We can never have all the things we want at once and the only permanence we have is impermanence. We are longing and longing and longing and never stop longing and I guess that's tragedy if I ever knew or will know what tragedy means. But I was determined to beat that tragedy, to throw something in the face of that chasm and let it know human beings didn't have to live like that, even if it was just one family. One family, one man could change the way it all works, if he believed it. What we love can kill us if we love it strong enough. It can also bring us back from death.

The children were taken by FEMA to trailers with the other 125,000 lost children. I remember the last time I saw Khalil. He had found a friend from school and was headed to stay with them in Texas. As Khalil had walked away, he stopped, turned back, and walked again. He looked older, creases of our journey sewed into his eyes and hands. Every time afterward that I spoke his name it was with reverence and there were times I questioned whether or not he even existed. I'm sure if he heard me say that it would make him chuckle, pat me on the head, and remind me of stars, trumpets, and magic.

Looking back on it all, he was right about a lot too. When the Twin Towers went down, we felt as Americans that we were experiencing that tragedy together, but with Katrina, it felt different. It felt that New Orleans experienced it alone. That instead of having our culture with us and with our suffering, we felt that our culture was watching us suffer. We kept waiting for it. We kept waiting for the country to shelter us, to *feel* with us, to comfort us. After all, what does it matter if we are a country, and we can't protect one another? Is it only protecting ourselves that matters? Then we might as well abandon all we know that is American and fend for ourselves. Either that, or learn to come together, but not the idea of togetherness that you see on a Time magazine cover, the real thing. It's like family, you always know someone will be there. That's how I feel about my neighborhood, do you?

I remember I watched a news program a few weeks later where some Midwestern young lady that they labeled "architect" on a blue tab in the bottom of the television screen was being asked about our city and said, "I just don't see the relevance of a city like New Orleans." The relevance of our city? I thought. The relevance of our homes? Of our lives? How could someone make a judgment like that? And she wasn't the only one. There was serious debate about whether or not they should just let our city sink into oblivion. Thank God that didn't happen.

I'll never forget Khalil. When I think of the storm, I believe he was the most important person I knew. Watching him walk away, I remember it being the first time I wanted to keep living, and not for Kirby or Mama or Janus, for something more. I wanted to live to show the world that our city is important, that our lives are important. Some may talk only of the looting or of the Superdome or of the relocations because that's all they saw. But I know what I saw in my neighborhood and that New Orleans is made up of neighborhoods just like mine, just like yours, and that each person has their own version of what happened and all those versions are as important as any one of those versions. Devastation doesn't follow a code that you can just look up in some book and say, this is how it all went down in New Orleans in August; this is what a hurricane means. You can't put some number on the things the water took away, not in how many people died, not in how many animals drowned, not in how many houses were sunk by the Mississippi's Manifesto. You see, you cannot define the storm, for all of us it was different, and for all of us, it was the same. Those are the moments in life where we become more than the single person we think we are, we become a series of memories, strewn together like drops of water in the ocean.

Not one man can pick where he's from, not one woman neither, but the places we are make the stories we become. Only these stories matter because that's what keeps the tragedy alive. It sounds damn illogical to keep something like tragedy alive, but if someone else sees the pain, then it lives. Like trying to see where someone else has been. Isn't that enough? I mean *really* trying, not just going through the motions, but *believing* in their story, *feeling* it. That makes us both alive. That makes us all alive. And the more people that see it, the more will believe it, and maybe then, they can stop it from happening in the future. But you have to speak up. You have to say something. Otherwise, your voice can disappear into the humdrum, the buzz that never stops, it's like the equator of sound. If you listen real close, you can hear it. Or you can use your voice to rise above the equator and become something not better necessarily, but mysterious, and therefore worth trying to understand. Those who are wise and stay silent rob the world of wisdom.

So, for me, the image of Hurricane Katrina will always be the single trumpeter with no socks, feet cracked and broken on top of an old church rooftop playing a story to save all of our souls.

When it was over and the water had gone and the armor was built up again, we went home, and there, bruised and missing most of its branches, was the live oak, still weeping what moss remained, dripping off the last of the water.

I lost a lot. We all lost something. And even after it's been a while, you can see it in those vacant faces, peering into what seems like nothing. Those faces are looking out at the storm, thinking about what is gone, and if you've been there and you know that sight, then you know there is something even more there, that there is that burning question that all of us have to ask: How come I get to live? How come I didn't get washed away? If you think about it long enough, you'll know, that the dying was the easy part, the living is the part that hurts.

That was the moment I knew that I had to free Kirby and Janus.

As soon as we moved back home, Kirb and me picked up working for Mr. Dottol selling vacuums. We were making great money for a while. People needed vacuums. There was a lot to clean up. After we tried to get back to whatever normal is, business slowed, but I got used to it, you know? And I was good at it. As long as it paid the bills and got us all to a better place, then it was worth it. I'd been saving what I could ever since.

Chapter Eight

I checked the shoebox before we left in the morning. The cardboard was wearing thin, and the orange emblem faded. It was a timid coffer with a bold soul. I counted the nine hundred and twenty-five dollars, which was just a few hundred dollars short of what we needed to leave. Then I counted it again to make sure. Rashad Phillips had told me it would be twelve-hundred dollars, for the first month's rent and the deposit. I made sure that Mama wasn't outside our room or peeking through the crack in the door before I put the box in the heating vent over the closet, pushing it back as far as my arms could reach.

It took a while to get Kirb out of bed. He kept telling me how much better of an idea it was to stay home and watch TV and eat cereal than to go out and get tired talking to people while "boring walking." I told him that once he had his own room and his own house, he could stay in bed all day if he wanted and I would go do all the selling and boring walking myself, but that I needed his help today and besides we might go out for a coke. The coke at least got him in the shower and then I tied his shoes, and we moseyed out over the pavement in that morning torpor that feels like you aren't asleep, but you aren't quite awake either.

I studied the sky the way one does when he is content and the clouds almost touched the ground, giving barely enough room for the swamp and the wild grass to breathe. The fall afternoon was painted in brushstrokes with thick layers of memories and those things forgotten, but not lost. It reminded me of this painting I used to stare at when Kirb and me went to Sea Ridge High School. It was a reprint of the painting of The Battle of New Orleans with "Defeat Is Not An Option" painted sloppily underneath in red and black letters (our school colors). It was full of the pageantry of war: the contrived alignment of soldiers in rows like children's toys, ghostlike figures with brass buttons that nearly faded away into the grey, white, and blue.

I imagined the sound of muskets and swords clanging against one another and the smell of death, the fear of it, as young boys fell into the mud, only to be trampled on by the hurried feet of the soldier behind.

One soldier stood on the hillock among the finely ironed blue and red uniforms in ruffled trousers and a buckskin coat that's arms were pulled up to his elbows. His eye was fixed on his rifle sights, and he looked *through* the enemy, not at him, and I envied that courage, that determination. I didn't like envying this man in a picture who so easily could forget fear and time and so I tried to ignore him by getting lost in the clouds. I remembered how as I would look deep into the white folds and grey streaks and the procession of soldiers walking from the water, Josh Stymer would come up behind me and I could feel his red hair and freckles as he asked me "Why you always staring at that darn painting?" I'd pause for a moment and say, "I don't know," which would leave him shaking his head and walking away, but it didn't stop him from asking me again the next time he saw me and repeating the process.

If you haven't lived in a place like Louisiana you might not understand why it makes any good sense to keep asking a question over and over again when you have a pretty good idea what the person is going to answer, but there is something about it that you get used to, and if he would have stopped asking the question I might have missed it. I might have even found him and asked him if everything was alright with his family. Just because something doesn't make sense, doesn't mean that it isn't comforting, that it doesn't give you the world you got. The truth was, I really didn't know why I would stop and stare at the painting, but I kept doing it, and it wasn't something I planned out, but once I saw it, I'd *have* to stop and look at it. It became one of those reoccurring moments that lasted beyond itself, that lingered into other moments and could be picked up again by the scent of perfume, a walk with your brother on a fall morning or the warmth of coffee in your stomach.

We walked into the city and met Seth, embracing him as we had done since we all had come home, hands gripped knuckle-white around his shoulders. Under the sun, the asphalt looked like stars, the shadow of a round streetlamp, a black moon.

"Alright darling," Seth said affectionately to the city. "Me and my boys would like to pass a good time down these here streets of yours and we would like safe travelin' if it's all the same to you. We love you and honor you, and who wouldn't want to, you being as beautiful as you are!"

And he raised his arms high and shook his hands, as if channeling the city's marrow, and before he could put them down a long red van hit the side of a white mustang that was turning left a few hundred feet in front of us. The sound clapped against my elbows and my right hand churned the still air. Kirb jumped to my side as a fire blazed up in front of the mustang and the driver ran out and used his jacket to fan the flames. The driver of the van opened his door and fell face first to the ground.

The tourists froze, as if in a dark wood, their shouts and chatter muffled. The whole street gasped at once like we were seeing the distant blue eyes of a stranger across a crowded café, a stranger we were intrigued by but hadn't yet learned to trust.

In a trance, I let my sight blur a little. The vehicles became white and red blotches smeared across a black canvas, somber and somehow empty. All the noise in my eyes felt empty. I think it's because life was fragile then, that for a second or two it was a delicate flower, petals crushed in the palm of an eager hand and all we had left was the ability to gasp.

The van's front end was smashed up real good. Smoke silently edged its way out of the sides of the hood and the broken pieces of the headlights and bumper were sprayed out over the road. It felt quiet, but it wasn't. It was one of those moments where you look back and think you should have run over there, but you are so shocked, you don't do anything.

People crowded around the accident and cell phones came out of pockets to take pictures and video so they could post the trauma for the price of a "like" or some transient comment about how terrible it looked and was everybody okay. Nothing can happen anymore without a phone. Our mythologies have become websites we haven't visited and pictures we weren't there to take. To say that *you* were there that day! The day of the accident in New Orleans! Then you can tell your grandchildren how *you* had taken a video clip on your phone of the man falling onto the famous Canal Street, helpless and alone.

I've seen more than a couple of times people in a frenzy looking for their cellphone, hair askance, sweat pouring down their neck, all the while muttering, "My phone. My phone," in the same desperate tone that you could imagine they would use if they lost a child or a family heirloom. There isn't a minute in a day where someone is free, when they are standing in a line or in the bathroom or just have a break in a conversation that they don't pick up their cellphone, looking for something that they can't exactly describe.

People believe that the whole of humanity is locked up in those little black rectangles, and as a salesman you have to admire whoever pitched the idea, but it sure seems like a lot of stress just to keep from being alone. I've never owned a cellphone, mostly because of something Seth said,

"The more you own, the more possessions you have, the more that can be taken away from you." And he said it in that way of his, leaning against some railing or taking off his jacket to let the sun hit his skin.

"Seeing those people with their heads down attached to those phones is like watching a dog too big for his owner pulling him down the street," he said. "You stop and think: Is it the man owns the dog, or the dog owns the man? That's how them phones are."

So, I stayed out of it. I stayed clear away from that leash, despite about everybody in New Orleans and maybe even the state of Louisiana, giving me that look of confusion and saying,

"How can you be a salesman and not have a cellphone?"

"It's simple," I'd tell them. "I use this old-fashioned thing called face-to-face conversation."

I could feel the loneliness, how it crept up into your throat and wouldn't let go. I was glad that Kirb was next to me, so I didn't have to stomach it by myself, the metal and the blood and the phones and the sirens.

We stood watching while a police car sped up and a young woman got out and turned the driver of the van over. He was spitting up blood and not doing a very attractive job of it, as it was spilling out the sides of his mouth and all over the woman's hands.

"De-ar God!" Seth exclaimed and an ambulance pulled in front of us.

Two skinny men who moved like toy soldiers hustled out and helped the woman with the driver of the van. There was tenderness in how the policewoman looked at him with her soft eyes, how the toy soldiers held up his head and tried to speak to him, all attempting to call him back, to tell him the story of the life he had still to live.

"What were you doing?!" The driver of the mustang yelled. "Do you even think about anything before you do it?"

"Calm down sir," the policewoman told him, never looking away from the fallen man, never breaking the connection.

"Look what he did to my car!"

"He's not in very good shape. You need to calm down," She repeated.

The driver of the mustang shrugged his shoulders and went back to the car to inspect it.

As the man was lifted into the back of the ambulance, the crowd's fascination was suddenly stifled by the peal of a single laugh. It came from a plump man exiting a bakery and eating what looked like a powdered donut. His utterly disgusting laugh, like a sounding horn, ushered in the familiar street babble and the tourists went on with their walking and the lights of cars rushed by as life kept on.

Seth stepped off the curb and looked at us. "You see?"

He threw his arms up again. "This city protects us! Imagine if we had gone walking across that street and I hadn't given *her* the proper salutation. We could have been right in the middle of all that! Thank you darling! Thank you!"

Then he smiled those big white teeth of his, gave a considerable bow and walked.

We followed, Kirb in tow, who refused to stop looking at the ambulance until the lasts of its sirens disappeared.

"Can you believe that man?" Seth asked. "The one driving the 'stang. He didn't see anything but himself."

He nodded his head and said "Mmm. Hmm. We go searching and searching around for that big villain, that arch enemy, that Satan which is the cause of all our selfishness and greed and evil. We even put a pretty little villain in our movies and books so that we can say that our hero is a hero and our villain is a villain and neither one is anything but good or bad. We think that this evil is in another dimension or trying to destroy us at our job or hiding in prisons or cutting us off in traffic, but the true enemy is right here," and he pointed at his chest. "True evil is within each one of us. You see? We are the only enemy that matters. Inside us is the only real battle that can do anything to change the world. But we go looking around for somebody else to point our brave fingers at so we don't have to meet the enemy inside, so we don't have to see the pains and the desires and the lusts, because if we see all that, then it makes us just as bad as the people we blame for all the bad things happening, and by God, then we might have to actually deal with something and change something, and who in the Hell wants to do something so difficult as that?"

He twirled his cane. "Mmm. Hmm," he said again and then he nodded his head some more, turning those cogs and wheels and getting ready to spit out the rest of it.

"What baffles one's mind though," he continued, "is how much we need the enemy, how it pushes the good parts, how the conflict makes for that internal conversation. Each of us is two people my friends and both parts keep the other in check, if you are listening to them that is. We are the twisted face we run from in the dark. It's us damnit! It's us!"

"I don't know what the Hell you are saying" Kirb blurted out.

Seth got a look on his face like he took a bite of a lemon.

"He's saying we need the bad parts of us as much as the good parts. Or something like that," I interpreted.

"Oh," Kirb answered and looked back again as if to see the ambulance one more time.

"They say" Seth said confidently, "that if your ticker doesn't go bad those damn car accidents will get you. So, most of us got just two choices. Personally, I'll go for the heart. I'd rather have a part of me I love destroy me than some driver that's thinking about his mistress or texting on his damn phone."

"That would be the way for you to go, Seth," I said. "You are a man of the heart. In fact, I can't imagine you going any other way. I'm glad we walk everywhere," I said turning to Kirb. "We won't ever have to worry about something horrible like that. I'm still wrapping my head around it. Right in front of us!"

"Did I might die?" Kirb asked.

"No buddy," I told him. "Everything's going to be alright."

"Will that man might die?"

"He'll be fine, I think."

I kicked a smooth oval rock on the ground.

"Don't you worry so much about dying Chubbs. I'll take care of us! We don't have a car anyway. We are safe. We are safe, do you hear me?"

Seth saw a plastic bag sitting on the ground and he picked it up and threw it in the garbage. He wouldn't go looking for things to pick up, but if he saw a cigarette butt or a bottle or a sandwich bag cluttering up the streets of what he considered to be his darling of a city, more often than not he would pick it up. He was walking a good deal ahead of me and Kirb. I noticed how he plopped his feet on the ground more than he stepped and how it didn't fit him. He looked too good to walk that way. He always looked good. Seth was a muscular man, arms with veins that poked out at the sides and chest round and solid and yet I'd never heard or seen him do any exercise. I envied him for it, as I'm sure many others did. He was aware of his physique, but not in an arrogant way, although it was his wont to inform me and Kirb that it was all about the clothes you put on in the morning. "If you dress well" he would say "and take care of yourself, then people treat you better, they listen to you, and they can tell you are trying. If you don't try, you never get anything done, but you think about not getting things done and those thoughts of not trying are worse than hearing "no" or getting told you are crazy. A lot worse! And somehow, we still keep living in these terrible fantasies of ours. A closed mouth don't get fed, you know?"

I am sure he almost divined me thinking about him and he was about to say something along those lines, when a man jumped out from behind a stairwell and startled us all.

"Hel-lo!" the stranger exclaimed in an overly friendly voice. In the city, you are always weary of other people, there are a lot of disguises and thieves. You have to be quick and keen.

The man was wearing the usual con-man uniform. He was covered in filth and smelled of cabbage that had been left out for a day or two, and he talked with his arms, which wafted the smell toward us. His hair was in a ponytail, and he wore a worn gray t-shirt and blue jeans with frayed edges and holes in the knees.

"Hello," Seth finally returned cordially and continued walking.

The man stepped in front of him again.

"How are you today?"

"Fine pal. Fine. Listen, I don't have anything today for you okay? So, let's save the time and the story. May the goddess of this city keep and protect you."

The story. We had all heard it before. Nearly every city sidewalk or park bench or bus stop or grocery store entrance had someone running out of gas or only needs something to eat or can't find their wallet or's baby is waiting in the car or just plain down on their luck and looking for a warm drink in a paper bag. And if you've lived in the city long enough you've heard about every one of these stories and it don't take but five minutes of following them around the corner to see that gas and food and wallets are all code for junk. Dad used to give them money anyway, every last one of them, and Mama wasn't keen on it at all, in fact she'd give him a good tongue lashing, but he used to say to us, "Boys, it don't matter what they do with that money, what matters is what you feel when you give it. After all, we are Englishmen, Americans, New Orlenians, and above all, men of honor."

I was about half and half on the subject. If I felt like it and I had it, I would give them money, but somedays I wanted to walk down a sidewalk or sit on a park bench or go to a grocery store and be sad about my own problems and not have to worry about somebody else. And there were even other days that I felt this burning desire to ask *them* for something or anybody else for that matter, not money, but something else, something I can't now put my finger on.

"What do you mean?" The man asked, confused. "Are you talking about money? I don't want no money. I only need somebody to show me to the port. Richard is there. You must know Richard! Everyone knows Richard! He is in the port. That's what I heard. Richard is in the port. He lives there."

"Sleep it off," Seth answered curtly, and he motioned to us.

"C'mon Kirb," I said, and we all shuffled away.

"Hey!" the man called out as Seth and I tried to walk fast enough to lose him. "Hey! Hey! I need to talk to you for a minute. Please!"

I saw from the corner of my eye that he was waving his arms to get our attention and so I thrust my eyes forward, determined not to look back. A funny thing about eyes is that it's a lot easier to ignore someone when you aren't looking at them. If you have to look in someone's eyes, you freeze. Why do you think we are so afraid of eyes?

"Hey!" he called. "Hey!" And then the man got close enough to pull on my shirt. "Hey!" I picked up my stride. "Hey! Hey! Hey!" And you could hear the pleading in his voice, it was terrifying and tragic like a shrill scream of a helpless animal and it put in me an urgency to walk even faster.

"Hey!" he called again. "Hey!"

Again and again and we walked faster and he kept coming. "Hey!" He now wailed. "Hey! Hey! Hey! Hey! HEY!"

Kirb stopped.

"Kirb! What are you doing?!"

I imagined him yelling at the man, telling him to quit bothering us like I wanted to tell him, like I wanted to scream at him, "Leave us alone!" But Kirb shooed me away with his hand and let the con-man uniform and stench of death run right into him. Kirby didn't tell him, didn't yell at him, Kirby, with no regard to smell or appearance passionately hugged him. The man was so stunned his arms collapsed under Kirb's fierce grasp.

"It's okay," Kirby said. "It's okay" and his hands widened as his grasp got even tighter and tears ran down the man's face, wrinkles around his eyes beaming.

We left him with directions to the port and whatever was left in Seth's wallet. Seth walked us the last few blocks to the city bus stop before wandering into an alleyway, chattering away about an article he was going to write on the fate of the homeless during the rebuild of the city.

"How much longer?" Kirb asked, almost immediately.

I shrugged my shoulders.

"The bus is supposed to be here at quarter after nine, but I see that clock in the bakery says nine-twenty, so I guess its running late. But don't you worry buddy, it will be here."

"It's kinda bored" Kirb said.

"Well, what do you want me to do?"

"Backstreet?" he asked.

He asked it was as if the word itself expressed some mysterious delight, some passionate plea to be understood. He loved the Backstreet Boys. He had all of their albums on an Mp3 player. He knew all their names and stories. AJ was his favorite. He had two posters of AJ in our room along with about ten t-shirts, a headband, three pairs of armbands, and a stack of VHS tapes from their tours.

Every morning in the backyard Kirb would put his headphones on and sit on a swing and belt out the Backstreet Boys until his cheeks got red and beads of sweat came down his forehead. It didn't matter what time of year it was. Even on the days I took him selling, he would swing in the evenings when we got home. If love has anything to do with devotion, then he must have truly loved them. I think part of it was a tribute to Dad who had put the swing outside for us the first year Kirb went to school. Dad had to fight with the school district to get Kirb integrated. They wanted to put him into Special Ed classes, but Dad wouldn't stand for it. He fought for Kirb to sit in the classes with all the other kids. He wasn't alone. One of our neighbors, a Japanese woman named Ikuko fought for her son Ichiro because she believed if we integrated the kids with special needs into schools it would help people to be more tender, to understand each other more, she even thought it could help with the suicide problem in Japan and talked about implementing it, if she ever went back.

Ichiro had muscular dystrophy and long black hair. He had one of the biggest smiles I have ever seen. Ikuko pushed him around in his chair like a gladiator in a chariot, head held high with the love between them hanging in the air long after they left a room. Ichiro died before Kirb and I graduated. We never saw Ikuko again. There were rumors she went back to Japan. From what I understand, they still don't integrate kids with special needs into classes with the other kids, but my brother and Ichiro never had to take a special needs class as long as they were in school. Kirb could sense the frustration of it all, so Dad bought him the swing set and two or three times a week he would take Kirb out and swing with him.

In Junior High and High School, I had been embarrassed about Kirb's music, because the kids I hung out with listened to Nirvana and Pearl Jam and they saw the Backstreet Boys as some sort of abortive creation made to sell albums to teens with infatuation complexes. We all wore sweaters in July and grew out our hair long and rode on skateboards and called everybody else "sellouts" and "conformists."

Kirb wasn't one to give up on me and he played the music at home until I got to know it myself and even secretly liked it. I was still shy to sing it with him in public, but he was persistent and got such joy from it, I braved humiliation.

"You want to do Backstreet right here?"

"Why not?" he said, his teeth and gums glowing with anticipation.

"Alright," I said, and he took me by the arm and made me stand up on the bus bench.

"My name is Kirby," he said, and he said it as if he was talking to a stadium full of ten thousand cheering fans and he used his hand as a microphone and put the hand-microphone in my face.

"My name is Ernest" I said, and he stared at me, expecting me to start. "Am I origin-al?" I sang in my broken voice.

Then he put the hand-microphone back to his own lips and sang "Ye-ah."

"Am I the only one?"

"Ye-ah"

"Am I sex-ual?"

"Ye-ah."

And as we were singing Chubbs got to thrusting his hips and moving his arms in some dance, he must have seen on one of the videos and he shook me and I danced too and there we were, two grown men, standing at a bus bench singing and dancing our hearts out on a quiet fall morning in the middle of the city. A beat-up red pinto with a couple of construction workers rumbled by and they hooted and hollered and honked and we crowed happily back.

After the song got past the chorus, Chubbs stopped and made a bow and he hit my shoulder, and I made a bow too.

I guess it's like Dad used to say, 'If you don't dance, you'll never learn to love the day.'

We'd been waiting at the bus stop for a good twenty minutes and I combed through the schedule and decided the bus must have come early, so we had another good twenty minutes before one showed up. I was getting hungry.

"Chubbs, you hungry?"

"Mmm. Hmm."

"Go get us some breakfast from that bakery."

"You got money?"

"You know I don't have money Chubbs, c'mon! Go get us some breakfast."

"I got money," he said.

"Let me see your wallet," I said.

It took him a minute to pull it out. I opened it and saw thirteen cents.

"Shit."

"What is it?"

"Thirteen cents," I said. "Chubbs, I only got money to get us on the bus and back. Listen, you go tell that lady in the bakery that you are good and hungry, and I guarantee that she will give you something to eat."

"I don't want to," he said.

"C'mon!"

"Why don't *you* do it?" Kirby asked.

"Chubbs, she won't give me anything. I'm too skinny. You have a baby to feed," I said, as I rubbed his round belly.

"You have to do it! C'mon!?"

He shuffled his feet and then looked up at me with a smile.

"Okay," he said, and I followed him to the door so I could listen in and make sure everything went smoothly.

"Hello!" Kirb said cheerfully.

The woman was fat and happy, and she was slapping her hands together to try get off some flour. Her thick lips smiled warmly, and I immediately felt bad for sending Kirb in there.

He walked right up to the counter and stared at her.

"Is there something I can help you with young man?"

"No," Kirb said politely.

"Did you want to buy something?"

"I do, but I don't have any money."

The woman turned around to a hand washing sink and washed her hands.

"Where are you parents?"

"My mom is at home," he said. "My Dad is dead."

"Oh! Darling," she said. "My Dad's gone too. It's hard losing your father, isn't it?"

"Mmm. Hmm."

"So, you are out in the city all by yourself?"

"Yes," he said sadly.

"That's a scary place for a young man to be, all by his self. Is there anybody I can call? Can I call you mom for you?"

"I'm hungry," Kirb said.

She laughed that uncomfortable laugh that people have when they don't know what to say or do, but it didn't last long.

"Is that all?" she asked. "Well, let me get you a couple of croissants," and she went behind the glass case and picked out two of the finest croissants she had. Then she wrapped them in plastic baker paper and put them in a small white bag.

"Oh! And you will need something to drink. What would you like?"

"Actually," Kirb said. "I love milk."

She handed him a small single-sized container.

"What's your name darlin'?"

"My name is Kirby."

"Well Kirby, my name is Cheryl and anytime you get hungry you can come by, and we can talk."

Kirb picked up the bag and was walking to the window, when I mouthed to him "Thank you. Say, thank you."

"Thank you!" he called out and I ran behind the building and waited for him.

"Good job Chubbs. Now, give me that milk!"

I took one of the croissants and ate it greedily while washing it down with a big swig.

Kirb looked at me searchingly, "Pig!" he said, and I stopped chewing to laugh with him.

"You remember when Dad used to try and make croissants? They were terrible, but we ate them anyway, because we didn't want to make him feel bad. You remember that Chubbs?"

He nodded. "Do you miss him?"

"Of course I miss him."

"Me too," Kirb said. "Would you be sad if *I* died?" he asked, and I turned to scowl at him.

"Knock it off!" I said. " But, seriously, Chubbs, that was amazing how you pulled that off. You are a total bad ass."

I paused and cupped my hands over my mouth. "Watch out New Orleans!" I yelled at the sky. "Kirby is out and he's not playing around!"

Kirb's face lit up and his eyes lifted, and I could tell he was proud.

A lady passed by us pushing a grocery cart full of old clothes stuffed down tight into its bottom with a sleeping bag on top tied with a belt. Five or six black garbage bags were swinging from the side, and she was rubbing on her cheek like her tooth was hurting something fierce. She dragged her left foot as if she wasn't middle-aged, but some old lady about to take her final nap on a park bench somewhere.

She stopped the cart a few hundred feet after us and took a bottle of wine she had hidden in her stacks of clothes and pulled off the cork. She took a good chug and then wiped her purple lips on her sleeve.

It seems that no matter where you go you can't escape the drinking, it penetrates into the front doors and alleyways and wiggles into your stomach like a worm or a bacterium. I even saw Dad drink quite a bit. After a long day, he plugged his mouth with a cold beer, putting it on his chest like a talisman. He did not speak until the beer was gone. He said that he deserved it, that everyone deserved a break. That's where it starts, with deserving. I've seen Mama and a whole bunch of other folks say to themselves that it is something they deserve for working hard all week and having to be lonely and frustrated and why not have a drink or two to get numb? Why not just escape this city with some drinks and some laughs down at the local bar? And when people get to deserving, they don't' see nothing else but that escape, they plan for it, and they wish for it, and then it becomes something different than an escape, it becomes a habit, and some might even say a ritual, since habits are necessary to individuals and rituals are more about culture. I can't speak for any other city in the world, or even in America for that matter, but in New Orleans the ritual of drinking is in nearly every house hold on nearly every block in nearly every part of the city. In our block it's whiskey and beer, in the rich neighborhoods it's wine and cognac, and it seems to me that vodka and gin make up just about everywhere else. Yes, there is a lot of deserving in these neighborhoods and because of it a lot of misfortune and once you get a taste for misfortune than you might as well deserve something even more. Nobody ever talks about it. If you do say something then people get heated up real quick and then they ask you what kind of a son of a bitch you are and where do you get off telling anybody anything about how hard they work and goddamnit you don't know, they deserve it. And I can't answer them, I don't know what it's like, I just know what I see. I know I lost two grandparents and my mother and parts of my father and I don't see it the way everyone else sees it. It's not ethical or religious. I just haven't seen it do anybody any good. I haven't met one person yet that said to me, "Damn! Ernest! I'm so glad I drank that fifth of whiskey last night! Isn't life grand?"

The lady filed the bottle back into her cart and skated away.

The bus squealed up next to us and we got on.

"Hello Kirby," the bus driver said, and I searched the guy's face as we passed but I couldn't recognize anything about him, so I waited until we sat down and then I asked Kirby, "Where do you know that driver from?"

"Sea Ridge High School."

"Oh. I don't remember him."

"He was in ceramics with me. He has a girlfriend. Her name is Jenny. I might want a girlfriend too."

The bus started and the driver motioned for us to come to the front.

"I think your friend wants to talk to us," I said.

We made our way to the driver's seat and stood behind him.

"Kirb! What you been up to?" he asked, excited.

He wasn't paying much attention to the road, and it made me nervous but I let him continue.

"You know, Kirb was the only reason I got through ceramics class."

"Really?" I said.

"My name is Travis, by the way." He offered his hand to me.

"Ernest," I said.

"It's been forever," Kirb said.

"It sure has. I got two kids now."

He pulled his wallet out and handed it to me. "The girl is Cecilia. She is two. The boy is Derik and he's five. Can you believe I'm a father Kirby?"

"Cool man!" Kirb answered enthusiastically. "Where's your girlfriend?"

"Jenny? Oh, we never did work out. She ended up moving to Arkansas as I recall. I met another girl named Sophia. We've been married about six years now."

"I liked Jenny," Kirb said.

"She liked you too. Anyway, who's this tall guy with you?"

"My brother Ernest."

"Nice to meet you," he said.

"You as well."

"What are you all getting into today?"

"We're working," Kirb said.

"Where at?"

Kirb looked at me.

"Garden District," I said.

"Oh! You are doing work up there? Fancy! What kind of work do y'all do?"

"We sell vacuums."

"Oh! Like *Kirby* vacuums!" he said.

I cringed.

"I get it. Kirby selling Kirby's. That's hilarious!"

He laughed loudly and slapped his knee.

"No!" I said, annoyed. "I wouldn't give a handful of nickels for those overpriced hunks of junk. We sell Bullfrog vacuums. They use water and a high-powered filtration system and we can take our vacuums over the floor a Kirby vacuum has already gone over and pull out enough dirt to fill a sandbox."

"Kirbys suck," Chubbs added and I snickered at the irony, but I could tell that the bus driver was taken aback.

"I didn't know," he said. "I'm sorry. Anyway, how much does one of those Bullfrogs cost?"

"With tax, twelve-hundred and eight dollars and seventy-five cents, but we can work out a payment plan if you are interested."

"Twelve-hundred dollars for a vacuum!" he said. "It's a vacuum! You can buy a vacuum for thirty dollars at Walmart. Why would anybody pay that kind of money for a vacuum? I have my kids to take care of and there is no way I could afford twelve-hundred dollars for something that picks up dirt off the floor."

I sighed.

"It's much more than a vacuum," I told him. "It's also an air filtration system that ensures you are breathing clean air all the time. You never know what you are bringing in from outside, especially driving this bus. And your kids are probably running around with germs and toxins everywhere and it ensure that your kids live happy and healthier lifestyles. Money should never be an issue when it comes to personal health and protection. But I understand where you are coming from, and that's one of the reasons we go to the Garden District to sell Bullfrogs because we know those people have the cash to filter their air from toxins and have the cleanest floors money can buy."

"It just seems ridiculous to buy a vacuum for that much," he said.

I smiled dismissively and Kirb gave him a hug. We sat down near the end of the bus because I didn't want to chit chat anymore. Plus, I wasn't going to hard-sell him, he was an old friend of Kirby's and he was a father anyhow, probably just trying to make ends meet, and it would feel cheap to use his friendship to try and get a few bucks. Even if he did buy one, he would probably miss a few payments and that wouldn't look good to Mr. Dottol.

The bus stopped and an old man got on. He must have weighed a hundred pounds soaking wet. His neck was wrinkled and stuck out like a fall turkey, and he had a neatly trimmed grey beard and droopy sad eyes. The whole problems of the city converged on his forehead and yet no one was looking at him, no one else was feeling his sadness.

I gave him a head nod and he nodded back soberly and then he looked out the window and I wished then that I could see the city the way he was seeing it, with all the experience of living a full life, all the memories of the days gone before.

The old man's hands were shaking, and he noticed that I saw them and clasped them together hurriedly. I guess it's impossible for a young man to know the mind of an old man. It always bothers me the way I see people ignoring old people, pushing them out of the way, putting them in homes, and treating them like they are children. If we put them all away, no one will ever know what they know and they have a lot to teach.

Sometimes Mama will come to me and Kirb drunk and desperate and say "Promise me something!" "What Mama?" We ask. "Promise me you will never put me in a nursing home." "Jesus Ma!" "Promise me!" She demands and even though I want to strangle her with both my hands and give her a quick ticket to a place where no nursing home exists, I still promise her. And I know that she's probably going to ask me again a thousand times, but I promise her just the same. Seeing this guy on the bus, hands shaking and dignity falling deep underground in a single stare, I can't blame her. I mean, this guy is probably a father, probably a grandfather. And it made me wonder where his family is and what he's done to deserve such a tremor in his soul. But I guess that is the way it is in the good old US of A, once you get what you can outta somebody you move onto something else and forget where the whole thing started.

We pulled the cord at the Garden District stop just after the last stop Kirb and me had sold at, so we could tackle some new territory, and we jumped out of the back of the bus with a wave, ready to make a sale.

Chapter Nine

Getting off that bus stop was something else! I'll tell you what! It was like walking through a magic portal into a children's book or stepping into the page of a doctored-up picture in a magazine you see sitting on a shelf at a grocery store.

It was as if the storm didn't even happen here. Every house was a palace with arches like giant's fists and windows so big they could fit a whole lifetime into their frames. They all sat back on a large yards filled with flowers and perfectly cut lawns and trimmed bushes and colored rocks and waterfalls. I felt out of place, like I was going to break something just by looking at it. It was Royal! From the shiny leaves of the evergreens to the polished doorknobs and glossy rain gutters. In the front were the cleanest sidewalks you had ever seen. Even the air was cleaner! And if you breathed it in for an afternoon you could almost taste what it was like to be free. Nothing was old or well used, all the objects looked as if they had been created only for Monday and there would be a change come tomorrow when the name on the calendar read "Tuesday" and all the houses would switch colors and shapes and constitutions. There wasn't a hush in the wind where you didn't hear that solemn word spoken, with the deference one might give to an altar.

"Money" it murmured softly but proudly.

"Money" it pointed at you in a commanding wave of its airy finger.

"Money. Money. Money."

The people there were strange. I had listened to them many times. They talked about how nothing interesting ever happened to anybody and geez how nice it would be if something really interesting actually happened to them. Being bored must be a habit of the rich because I feel like I never have enough time to even go to the bathroom because Kirb is usually pounding on the door trying to embarrass me or telling me he needs to go too.

I don't see how anybody could be bored in a city. To me, each neighborhood is like its own story, full of characters and villains, and heroes, and worker bees, and architects; and each dull lamp behind the window is its own separate sunlight, its own full and rife stage play, waiting to be acted out.

I guess we tell ourselves that once we get a house in the Garden District then we can be happy. That once we get that job and once we get that girl and once we get that car and once we can pay the bills and once we can make sure food is in the fridge and once we don't have to worry so much about losing everything we got, well then, the happiness is sure to come, why wouldn't it?

Once you are already in the fantasy land and you have the house and the job and the girl and car and everything else you ever dreamed of and there is nowhere else to go, the sadness takes you over like it is bound to do and then there is nothing left to hope for. It can be hard to comprehend a man or woman who knows this boredom, this luxury. They have their own sadness, I guess. We all do. There's might be even greater than my own.

Me and Kirb to play out our story and before we got to selling: we had to get prettied up. So, I pulled the gel, a comb, and a mirror out of the demonstration backpack and I got to work on Kirb. He hates when I mess with his hair, and I could tell he was irritated.

"Are you done?" he asked.

"Almost. Hold still!"

I gave his hair one more sweep of the comb.

"Perfect. You look so handsome!"

"Okay, Okay," he said and I let him wander over to one of the houses and he sparked up a conversation with a lady who was watering her flowers with a bright purple watering can.

My hair was being difficult, but I finally got it into the professional and chipper wave that I liked so much. I straightened my collar and licked my finger to get some muck off of my face and put the mirror and comb back into the pack.

Kirb was going at it, flapping his gums real good and charming up the lady and I was excited that he was already getting into it, so I walked over with my salesman smile and they both looked at me, annoyed. I was an intruder to their little party, but I kept staring anyway. I secretly liked the fact that I had the power to make people feel uncomfortable and you could use that uncomfort to eventually get someone comfortable and somehow, they trusted you even more.

"This is my brother," Kirb said cuttingly.

There was a part of me that wanted to slap the little bugger, but I was proud of him nonetheless, proud of the way he could walk up to a complete stranger and make them a friend in a matter of moments. I've been studying people my whole adult life, trying understand what makes them tick, what motivates them, but I'd never say I was good at being their friends, that was Kirb's department, that's why I needed him.

"Ernest," I said, and I shook her hand.

She was an extremely beautiful woman. Her skin was taut, threaded together like a basket of wind and sand and she smelled like magnolia, like the ancient world, like the pollens of rustic plains with no structures but juniper and pine. She had long brown hair, curled and kempt. Her eyes were large and oval and were outlined with black mascara that made her look like a gypsy.

She must have known the cave where stood the silent skulls of kings or at least understood such mysteries that common folk like us could not. She was a Garden District treasure, but I resented her. No girl can ever be as beautiful as my wife and any beautiful girl just reminds me of her and then I resent them being beautiful.

"Nice to meet you," she said, and her voice was elegant and polished and I could tell she had had a lot of schooling and I was nervous to talk too much and betray that I hadn't. I could talk human anatomy or scientific theory with her all day, but I didn't feel comfortable with my mastery of the language, not with people that had refined it.

"Kirby was informing me that you boys are headed to work," she said. "He's very reluctant to go."

"It's true," I said, and I cleared my throat. "Would you be interested in seeing a presentation about the cleanliness of your home?"

She smiled.

"I'm busy with the garden, maybe another time."

"Do you know anyone who is home right now that might be interested?"

She put her hands on her hips.

"Um, try two houses down. Francine Rabelais."

"Sounds great, thank you." I said and I grabbed Kirb and started to leave.

"Wait!" She called out. "Wait just one second! Why don't you two come and pick out a flower and you can take it home to your Mama? Mr. Kirby said that you two live with her."

"Well, ma'am," I said. "We have a lot of work to do today."

"Please?" Kirb pleaded.

I sighed.

"I guess we have time for one flower."

"Wonderful!" she said. "Just wonderful!"

She led us around the house and over a broken stone walkway with rosewood lichen growing around the fence. There was a small pond. Before it, tall lake weeds bent and straightened like a procession of people clamoring toward a shrine, a sun shrine, a water shrine, a temple of calm waves.

The garden was surrounded by guardian box elder bushes. Chrysanthemums blinked in yellows and pinks and whites as we tip-toed past the delicate lips of lavender which reached toward us. Sunflowers called out above neatly trimmed rose bushes and tiger lilies watched us with their beady black eyes. The cones of blue hyacinths were statues that pointed at red carnations with white highlights.

"What do you y'all think?"

"It's beautiful," I said. "I've never seen anything like it. Not in our neighborhood."

I blushed.

"Well, don't be shy, pick something out," she said.

I was overwhelmed. The chrysanthemums were too spiny, too aggressive. The tiger lily was too weak. The roses too cliché. I couldn't disturb the carnations; I didn't want to upend something so benevolent. There was something about the hyacinths that didn't sit right with me. I surveyed the flowers one more time and finally saw a lone dandelion underneath some morning glory and I picked it.

The lady scurried over.

"Now, how did that sneak in there? Give it here and I'll get rid of it."

"This is the one I want," I told her.

"Well honey, that isn't a flower at all, that's a weed."

"All the same," I said. "I think I like it best."

She nodded and went to Kirb who was eyeballing a tall purple iris.

"Is that the one you want honey?"

"Mmm. Hmm."

She pulled some clippers from her back pocket and neatly snipped the stem before handing it over to him.

"For me?" he asked, and she touched his face with the palm of her hand, tracing his jaw line and said "Yes, for you. To remind you how amazing you are and how much the world needs you."

Kirb nodded and started smacking his lips and I hit his arm.

"What?"

"Tell her thank you," I said.

"Oh! Thank you."

"It's my pleasure Kirby. Y'all have a good day now."

"Thank you, ma'am," I saud. "Your hospitality is much appreciated, and it is my hope that you find peace in this lovely fall morning."

As we moseyed back over the broken stone walkway, I said to Kirb, "How do you do it? You talk to that woman for five minutes and she acts like she has known you her whole life. I mean, what the Hell did you say to her anyway?"

"Nothing" he said smiling and he had that damn pride seeping out of him right into the ground beneath our feet and all I did was shook my head in mock disbelief.

"I swear Chubbs! You are the biggest ladies man I know."

"Mmm. Hmm," he said.

Right before we made it to the Rabelais house, I threw my dandelion into the gutter and wiped my hands. Kirb didn't let go of his iris.

The house was a two-story red brick with a huge wine-colored door. As I descended the wooden stairs, I noticed a black gargoyle knocker that gave me the creeps something fierce.

"Wow! Chubbs, this place is a true luxury house! We might be able to sell two of them here! You ready?"

"Yes," he answered solemnly, and he looked at his feet.

Chubbs could talk to a complete stranger like it was nothing, but when it came to selling, he got real shy, and sometimes it would get so bad I would have let him stay outside, but him being there motivated me to make things happen, and if I would have left him home every day with Mama she'd let him watch TV until his eyes fell out.

A sprightly looking woman of around thirty-five or thirty-six answered the door in her bathrobe. She was drying her hair with a towel.

"Hello," she said.

"Hello Mrs. Rabelais, ma'am. My brother and I would like to have a minute or two of your time. Sorry to get you out of the shower and all."

"I'm catholic," she said soberly. "I don't want to change the god I believe in."

She started to close the door.

"No ma'am," I said. "It's nothing like that."

She paused to look us up and down and then threw her towel over her shoulder.

"Well, alright then," she said. "Come in."

She opened the door and Kirb and me walked into the one of the most quiet and clean front rooms either of us had known. The floor was a polished mahogany that you could see your reflection in, and the couches had those fluffy little balls like you see on the bottom of theater curtains. It looked like the couches had been sat in maybe twice. The only sound you could hear was the slow tick from the pendulum of the grandfather clock, placed next to what must have been a picture of her with her husband. He was considerably older than her, bald with long grey hair at the neck. He was smiling, she was not.

"Give me just a minute," she said, and she disappeared into the caverns of her house while I pulled out the parts of the Bullfrog and hurriedly put it together. I wanted to get it ready before she came out, so Kirb and I could be standing next to it.

"Chubbs, make sure you smile when she comes out" I said as I positioned him like a twenty-eight-year-old mannequin, putting his arms to his sides, and pushing on the small of his back to get him to stand up straight.

"Fine" Kirb said.

"Listen, I know you don't want to do this," I said "But, I promise it will be over soon. And if you think about it this way, if we get her to buy something, then we are that much closer to getting our place! And once we get our place, I promise you can stay home a little bit more and I'll take these trips by myself, okay?"

He nodded and the woman entered. I stood tall and grinned big, putting my arm around Kirb. Her appearance was much changed. She wore a blue mini skirt with a blue suit vest that showed most of her breasts, which held a bright diamond necklace. Her silver blonde hair was put snugly into a bun, and she was wearing sparkling blue and silver shoes with freshly smeared rouge on her cheeks.

I was at a loss for what to say.

"What are you, Superwoman?" I blurted out ingenuously.

Her face turned giddy, girlish even, and vulnerable in a way that it seemed she hadn't been in a long time, as she wore the expression so candidly.

"Well, what did you boys have to show me?"

I'm not one for going right into the presentation, as I like to allow time for small talk, which makes the presentation flow naturally and allows the customer to relax. When a customer is relaxed you have a lot better odds of getting them to buy something. Building trust and making small talk is a salesman's real and true job. But the way I had looked at this woman, and I guess more than that, the way I had *seen* her, I didn't feel like talking like that because it didn't seem that a woman with so much hope in her deserved to be talked up by a slick salesman from the other side of town. She deserved something better and something that Kirb and I couldn't give or couldn't understand and for lack of anything better to know or to do, I started.

"Do you own a vacuum ma'am?"

"Yes," she said.

"Is it in that closet behind you?"

"How did you-"

"It's what I do ma'am. May I?"

"Go, ahead," she said.

I opened the closet and turned on the vacuum, vacuuming as thoroughly as I could and then I turned it off.

"May I use your kitchen faucet ma'am?"

"It's just past the dining room" she said, and I could tell that she was puzzled by me running into the faucet and I went in and filled up the Bullfrog's collection tub and went back into the living room where I attached the top and started the machine.

I quickly went over the spots I had with the regular vacuum and then I turned it off. I picked up the collection tub and showed it to her.

"You see how dirty that water is?"

"Wow!" she said, and she acted surprised, but I got this feeling like more than anything she was enjoying watching me run around like a fool.

"Now, obviously your vacuum isn't doing the job, and the bottom line is that it lacks the power and the unique technology of the Bullfrog 2000," I said. "The Bullfrog has three times the engine power of a normal vacuum and because it uses water it never gets clogged, and you never have to replace the filter."

I picked up one of her pillows and put it in a plastic bag that I carried around for presentations and I started the Bullfrog and put the pillow inside the plastic bag, making sure I put my hands around the nozzle so that only the suction from the hose could get into the bag.

The pillow shrunk as the air got sucked out of it and I waited until it couldn't take anymore, and I turned the machine off and took the pillow out and handed it to her.

"Feel it!" I commanded and she gently put her hand across it.

"It feels more soft and fluffy doesn't it?"

She nodded.

"That's because the Bullfrog takes out the dirt that you don't see and remember," and here I looked her in the eye, smiling warmly, not enough to show my teeth, but enough to show her I was being genuine "just because you don't see it, doesn't mean it isn't there. And if you think about it, how often does anybody treat their upholstery? Almost never! The Bullfrog will not only clean your floor better than any vacuum, but it will also clean your couches, your blinds, your upholstery, and even those beautiful hardwood floors I saw in your entryway."

I pulled up my belt a little, a habit I have when I get confident in talking.

"And let me ask you this," I continued. "Why is it that doctors never get sick and yet they see sick people all day long?"

She shrugged her shoulders.

"It's very simple: Eucalyptus oil."

I pulled out the vacuum hose and put a couple of drops of Eucalyptus oil in and turned the machine on.

"Can you smell that?" I took a deep breath myself to make sure it was working.

"You see? The Bullfrog is actually an air filter as well. And if you prefer a different smell, we have fifty-two distinct flavors. I'm going to put in a couple drops of our most popular fragrance, summer nights."

I waited a few moments and inhaled again. "That's a very comforting fragrance, isn't it?"

"Yes, that's good," she said, and she crossed her legs and put one hand over the other very softly.

"And not only does it smell amazing, but the Eucalyptus oil is still cleaning and filtering the air."

I paused to see if it had sunk in and got myself ready for the money talk. This was the hardest part about selling: the sales conversation.

"So, what do you think?" I asked.

"Well, it's quite nice I guess," she said.

She guesses? I thought. Oh! Boy! This was going to be a rough sale.

"Well, do you see yourself owning one?"

"Sure," she said, and it didn't seem that she was going to give me much more than that, so I just went for it.

"Should I fill out the paperwork then?"

"Okay," she said and not knowing else to say I sat down and filled out all the paperwork and put twelve-hundred and fifty dollars down on the price line and handed it to her.

"You just need to fill out your basic information."

She looked at the application and calmly filled it out while I looked at Kirb. He was hypnotized by the grandfather clock, and I decided not to bother him.

"So, is it okay if I write you a check?" she said.

I was shocked. She was going to pay in full?!

"Yes, of course," I said. "I can't leave this machine with you, but yours will be shipped within the week if that's okay."

"Sure, that's fine" she said, and she pulled out her pocket book. "Who do I make the check out to?"

"Ernest Larsen ma'am."

"Is that your name?"

"Yes ma'am."

She smiled. "Well, that's a handsome name," she said and she handed me the check. "And you," she paused. "You are a handsome boy."

At this she touched my wrist.

"And what does a handsome boy like you think about all day when he is selling and selling and selling with nothing else to do?"

My breath sped up. My heart thumped loudly in my chest. I couldn't speak.

She unbuttoned her top shirt button revealing lacey white lingerie.

"Do you ever get lonely Mr. Ernest Larsen?"

She scooted real close to me.

"Cuz I get lonely every single day," she said.

My face flushed. How did she know I was lonely? My blood started to boil, but I wasn't getting mad, my blood was boiling somewhere else. I wanted to grab her and take her and find comfort in her lonely arms, to feel loved and needed and touched and to get lost in that voluptuous figure and to be her fantasy and to let her be mine.

As I was getting carried away my breaths became even shorter and shorter until time itself slowed down so much that all I could think of was the movement of the pendulum of the clock, ticking over and over again like my heartbeat. And those fine white breasts! How round they were! How perfect! I could even see the tip of her nipples pushing through the fabric.

I saw Chubbs and his mouth was half open and his look of being absorbed and helpless made me feel as sober as a preacher about to give a sermon on Sunday.

"My little brother is here," I forced out.

I felt exhausted from the journey. That's what a body can do; it can take a perfectly good man and twist him into a damn pretzel.

"I have to go, my little brother needs to get home," I said. "Chubbs! Let's go!"

Kirb walked toward me, his eyes still on the grandfather clock, and I didn't know what the hell he was thinking about, but I yelled out to him, "Get the stuff!" And as he sloppily put it away in the backpack, I handed her the receipt.

"It will be around five business days Mrs. Rabelais." I said and she greedily grabbed the inside of my thigh.

"Come back tomorrow if you like," she said. "Or the next day. Or both. He always works late."

I nodded and swallowed and when we were finally out the door I took a deep breath. I needed to see my wife.

The next two houses slammed their doors in our faces, but we got action on the third.

The house itself seemed out of place. It was about two times smaller than every other house on the block and instead of being right up front on the property, it was about a half an acre back on the lot. There is something that draws me to houses like that; there is an unspoken character to them.

If you look at the outside of a person's house, nine times out of ten you can tell what their personality is. It's not like you can tell whether or not they are Catholic or Muslim or like to read or watch soap operas or anything, but you *can* tell whether they are going to dismiss you or whether they will look you in the eyes or whether they will at least pretend to be kind. I don't know if it's the type of people that choose certain houses of if they try to fit the feeling of the house once they move in, but take a look around your neighborhood, you'll see.

Houses like that one we were at, were a complete wildcard, but usually they were odd enough to at least hear any proposal out, even if it was to reject it.

I made Kirb knock on the door even though he didn't want to. It's good for him to do stuff like that. I like him to know that there's nothing in this world to be afraid of, and besides, if you get afraid of doing little things like knocking on doors, then the list of things you are afraid of might get bigger and bigger until you can't even walk out of the house without asking someone for help.

An older man answered the door in a plaid shirt. His face was perturbed and tired. His mouth drooped and his eyes were watery and apish.

"Good evening, sir."

"What y'all selling?" he demanded.

"Give me five minutes and I'll show you," I said and I could tell my enthusiasm had an effect on him because he face brightened.

"Well, I do appreciate honesty in a young man. Y'all come in," he said.

We entered and he showed us into his living room. It was crowded. There were crocodile teeth and pictures of race cars and a giant statue of Jesus. Food plates and beer cans littered the space around the chairs, and old books were stuffed between every space that wasn't on the floor. It smelled like old leather and chopped wood.

While I was admiring a lamp shade made of snakeskin, the man of the house motioned to his wife, who entered the room. She looked a little too proper to be married to a hillbilly type like himself. She was plump and cheery and wore a yellow and white summer dress and her straight brown hair was short and perfectly combed.

"Hello young man," she said politely.

"Hello ma'am."

"Hel-lo!" Kirb hollered out.

Apparently, the man hadn't seen Kirb when we walked in because once Chubbs spoke, the man's eyes got wide as the Mississippi and he couldn't stop staring. My blood was heating up quick, but we had vacuums to sell, and I figured I'd get his attention on the money he was about to spend.

"How's your morning?" I asked as I sat down on a loveseat next to Kirb.

"Who you voting for, for governor?" the man replied, whistling air through his teeth, like he had a piece of meat stuck in them.

"I'd rather not say," I said.

"Don't tell me you are one of those."

"Excuse me?"

"One of them goddamn tree hugging liberals."

"Sir, my daddy told me never to discuss politics or religion, especially with friends," I said.

"You tell me who you are voting for, or I'll kindly show you the door son."

"Okay," I said. "You want to know who I am voting for?"

"Yes," he said.

"Nobody sir. I feel like politics like I feel about sewage. I'm sure glad it's there or we'd be in big trouble, but I don't want anything to do with it."

I gave him a look, the kind of look that you get used to when you are a salesman, the kind of look that says I know that we are both alive and breathing and that deep down we are more similar than we are different and you want to be happy the same way I want to be happy, but let's get on with it.

He chuckled.

"Well, I can respect that at least," he said. "Damn politicians don't know anything anyhow."

"You said it."

"Yep!" Kirb chimed in and then: that look again. And then, my blood again.

"I'd like to show you both a quick presentation, if I may," I said.

"You may," answered the wife and she plopped down on a brown leather rocking chair.

I set up and went through the routine of getting their vacuum, filling the tub with water, vacuuming with their vacuum, then with the Bullfrog, and then I showed them the water, and everything was going great. The wife was just as amazed as she should have been, but then I looked over at the husband and I'll be damned if that big dummy wasn't still staring at Chubbs. My blood was hot, but business is business, and I was pretty sure I could still close the wife.

I started in, "Now obviously your vacuum isn't doing the trick and that's because it lacks the power of the Bullfrog 2000" and here I heard the husband ask his wife, "What's wrong with that boy?" And he started in with that whistling again, that air pushing through his teeth and my blood was hotter than a Jul-y afternoon, but I tried to keep going. "The Bullfrog has three times the engine power of a normal vacuum and-"

Then I heard it. I heard that dumb son of a bitch say something he was going to regret for a long time.

"Has he got *the downs*? Or what?"

"I don't right know what you mean sir," I said.

"What's wrong with him is what I mean."

Then that whistle again, that happy and ignorant whistle that I wanted to push down his throat with the generation that gave it to him.

"That's not an honorable way to talk sir," I told him.

"I'm just trying to find out if the boy is a mongoloid," he said. "He sure looks like one."

That was it. I threw the dirty water from the collection tub right in his face and before he could muster up a look of surprise, I was on him.

The first punch sent the chair on its back, and I dove onto his midsection and pummeled him with my fists. I could hear the wife's muffled screams, but my rage was insatiable. I hit him and hit him and hit him until all I could see was the dark red of his blood puddled up on his face and something, a stillness in the wet air, stopped me.

Apparently, the wife had been trying to pull me off him and I hadn't even felt it. She was crying and carrying on and pleading with me.

"Please stop," she said. "Please, dear God stop."

My hands were shaking and covered in blood. It was terrifying and yet, the blood excited me some, and I trembled with the ecstasy and shame.

Where's Chubbs? I thought and I frantically panned the room until I saw him sitting on the floor, pink as a cherry blossom in spring, staring at the carpet and smacking his lips. I went to grab his arm and he pulled back.

"C'mon Chubbs, we've got to go" I said.

He just sat there.

"Grab our stuff! We've got to go now!" I screamed and giving me a look of disappointment, he finally got up, grabbing the pack and the vacuum as we rushed out the door.

I didn't see where the wife went, but I'm sure she called the police and an ambulance and all I could hope for was that I hadn't say my name and that she didn't check with the neighbors and that if she did, Mrs. Rabelais didn't tell her anything.

I grabbed Kirb and forced him to dash down the block as fast as we both could until I ran out of breath.

"I'm tired," Kirb said after a while.

I noticed then that Kirb had been carrying the vacuum parts and the pack the whole time we had been running. I almost broke down right there.

"You carried the vacuum?" I said. "I totally forgot about it!"

A car was calmly coming down the street, so I pulled Kirb into the bushes.

"I just-" he started.

"What is it?"

"I just don't want you to go to jail," he whispered.

"I'm not going to jail Chubbs," I said.

He lay back and stared up into the sky and then the guilt came, thick as country biscuits covered in white-pepper gravy. The guilt wasn't for the moment, but for the past. For the many times my hands had been bloodied and how each time I thought it might not happen again, but it kept happening. After each incident I felt like a part of my honor was gone, not because I thought what I had done was wrong, but because I couldn't control my anger.

I didn't blame Kirb for thinking I might go to jail. Kirb had seen me be arrested three times for assault. Thank God he hadn't seen what happened with Janus.

The first time was a few years back when Janus and I had first been dating. We were walking down the street, on our way to the movies, when some school boys catcalled her and I don't care to remember what they said, but a man of honor doesn't put up with such things and so I asked them nicely to show some respect for a lady and this clown had to belt out, "If I saw a lady, I would." I broke his jaw and knocked out three of his front teeth. When I went to court, I stood right in front of the judge and told him exactly what had happened, with no remorse.

"I'm not sorry sir," I had said. "The way he was talking to my girl, he's lucky I didn't send him to the cemetery."

The judge snickered and I could tell from his large gut, baggy brown skin, and deep southern drawl, that he was part of the old New Orleans, the venerable port city that harbored so many men and women of honor, the kind that didn't mind getting their hands dirty, so long as it was an honest day's work, the kind just trying to toil their way through all the muck and mess to find that bit of peace at the end of the horizon. We walk among such men and women, and they carry with them burdens and voodoos and histories that don't take but a snicker or a raised eyebrow to understand. I dare say they are the most interesting characters still left in America. I could have sworn the old judge gave me a wink and the city dropped the charges.

Second time, I slapped a clerk at Kim's Market for saying the "r" word, which if you don't know is the word retarded and I can't think of a more offensive word in the English language. Kirb and me have been fighting that word since he first understood what it meant. I won't say I haven't used it. When I was younger, I used a lot of words I wasn't supposed to, that's one way we learn to speak.

I was going at it with some buddies in grade school when Kirb heard one of them say the "r" word and got real sad and went to smacking his lips. I took him aside and asked him what the matter was, and he answered that he didn't like that word much. I asked him why. "It hurts *my* people," he answered. I've never used it since and every time I hear it, I feel obligated to say something. If I hear it in a movie, I walk out. If a movie star I love says it, I don't watch their movies anymore until I hear a public apology. I have abandoned music groups and books and even friendships, but I've maintained a stronghold on my family's honor. I don't tolerate words that hurt other people, especially ones that insult them based on things they don't have a choice over. I don't like words against women either, which there are more of than I'd like to count. They don't have bad words like that for men and I don't think saying things like "you throw like a girl" or "you push that bench press bar like a woman" are doing anything but throwing gasoline on the fire. I've never regretted telling someone they were pretty or that I enjoyed their laugh or that they had good heart and good character, but there are many words I've said that I regret because they were words created to cause sorrow.

The third time I got arrested, I broke one of our ex-neighbors legs with a piece of a fence post because they told Mama she was a whore for marrying my daddy when she was only seventeen.

I got away the second time, but the third time I did six months in county. The judge told me he could have given me a year in prison for aggravated assault and warned me in that thick southern drawl "Mr. Larsen. You are a crusada and new Ahleans is a dahk city where a crusada can git hisself in a heap ah trouble. I'm givin' you a stint, but you best stay fa fa away from hea son. I'm a step down soon and those young fellas comin' up care mo about the letta of the law and much less about the law isself and the wahld we have to live in."

I thanked him but told him that even prison couldn't keep me from defending the honor of my family and he gave me one of those paternal head nods, as if he approved of me in a way that most men couldn't and I felt a kinship with that old judge and I wished we could have talked through an afternoon over a glass a lemonade.

"You are one in a million son, God bless ya" he said, and they handcuffed me right there in the courtroom. Kirb jumped up off the bench he was sitting on with Mama and ran up to the deputy.

"Get your damn hands off my brother!" he demanded.

Kirb doesn't get mad much. He's forgiving and kind and soft spoken, but if anyone ever touches me or Mama, he gets into a rage that nearly rivals mine.

The deputy was frozen, he knew if he chided my brother in front of everyone, he would look like an asshole, but he couldn't just set me free, so he breathed at Kirby to warn him. It was a wheezy breathing, and the courtroom was so tense you couldn't hear anything else.

"Chubbs, let it go," I said. "In the law's eyes I made a mistake and that means I have to go to jail. Right or wrong, that's the way it is, and if you don't sit down you are going to cause more trouble than you can handle. So, go take care of Mama."

"Get your damn hands off my brother!" he repeated to the deputy and by this time Mama was behind him and she grabbed his shoulder.

"C'mon now dahlin'," she entreated.

"No, Mama! If Ernest is going to jail, then I'm going too!"

"I have to go Kirb," I said. "This man is just doing his job. I need you to take care of Mama while I'm gone. You're the man of the house."

He nodded.

"Do you understand buddy?"

"Yes," he said, as all his anger exhaled into heartbreak.

I did six months, read *Grey's Anatomy* forwards and backwards ten times and came out and took the MCAT. I got a very good score and I have been meaning to put in my med school apps, but I can't leave Chubbs for that long. I can't take him with me either. Even if I could, I wouldn't have any time to spend with him.

The wind blew across the tops of the bushes and their red berries rang like bells of ruin. I looked over at Chubbs and he had that same look of defeat he had had in the courtroom when they put me away. He held the purple iris to his nose and moved it to his chin, stroking his face. He was fanatical the way he held it, the way he eased it to his lips like a sacrament.

"My flower," he said pensively. "My flower."

I hadn't heard any sirens and so I figured we should risk it and get on out of there. We high tailed it to a pay phone and I called Mama.

"Mama?"

"Where you been?" She demanded.

"I told you Mama. Me and Kirb went to sell vacuums."

"You told me you were taking me to lunch."

"No, I didn't," I said, and I sifted through my memories thinking maybe I had forgotten, but I hadn't. *I never told her that!*

Mama did this a lot. She'd tell you things that weren't true and she would say them with such confidence that even though you knew her and even though you knew she was making it up, you still questioned yourself.

"You promised that you would take your Mama to lunch." She scolded. "Now, you tell me boy, is selling a vacuum more important than spending time with your own mother?"

"I can't make it to lunch Mama," I said. "But I will be home for dinner."

I heard her scoff before she put down the receiver.

Chapter Ten

Once we got out into that late afternoon air, sticky and sweet, ripe with forgetfulness and youth, and so full a single breath might stick to your neck and stay there until you woke up the next morning, I convinced Kirby we should go home.

"I might like to go home," he said. "I want some milk and a grilled cheese."

I shook my head.

"A grilled cheese?"

"I want milk and a grilled cheese," he said.

"I can do that, but you got to earn it," I said.

I didn't want to take the bus because I wanted Kirb to get good and tired before we went to sleep.

So, we departed on a long walk, and as we were walking, I felt sad. Some part of me felt guilty for the old man I'd left beaten on the floor, but mostly I felt sad because I couldn't stop thinking about Janus.

The little things. The way she smelled of perfume and a corner bakery. How she always loved baking biscuits and cookies and pies and I'm not ashamed to admit I gained more than a few pounds eating her carrot cake. The way she would tickle my back when I bent forward while watching a movie, the laughter that wasn't so much a laugh as it was a giggle. And there were other things, the things no man needs to talk about to make clear to anybody but his wife. I felt it. I felt her, and I knew the last part of me, of that life, would leave; that if I didn't get the money together for the place out on Lafayette by the end of the week my last rebellious stroke would vanish, and I would end up with Mama forever.

I wanted to get home and count the money in the old shoe box. I think we almost had enough! We should be getting a little over two hundred from the sale, plus the nine hundred and twenty-five would add up to a pinch over a thousand. Now, if I could sell a vacuum or two tomorrow, then I could get enough to move us in and buy something nice for Janus.

We walked through a corner of The Quarter. My eyes leapt from building to building, soaring through the Creole townhouses with their bright oranges and reds, the hanging plants, the flashes of light that came popping out of windowsills, the long curves of arched balconies, the shuffling street vendors in their white coats.

My shoes jumped into the clatter of feet which paraded against the aged stone walkways, and we were in, part of the carnival that never ended and seemed only to reach its peak during February, when we all put on costumes and decorated masks, and celebrated music and dance and desire. But it was there, even in September. You could see it on the surface of the city's skin, where trembled anxious table legs, where the loose rocks were weathered by waiting, where the aching for release from the day-to-day was only purged by the string quartet on the corner with its bop melody.

The people that work in The Quarter wearing their temporary masks for the tourists, those faces that we all must put on every time we walk out the door to go to work, and behind each stare you could see that familiar look saying, "I recognize you. I recognize you live here too and that you know how it is to put on this face." You would nod then and be understood while they skipped and danced and sashayed back to the tune in color of green paper passed eagerly from dazzled eyes and thick wallets.

I noticed an old café, it was yellow, and had four matching yellow street umbrellas, and a single waiter with slicked back hair was scurrying from table to table, like a mouse caught in a box. The whole place seemed to be made of cardboard or gingerbread, and it occurred to me that this whole section of the city was a giant façade. That the parades and the pink headdresses and the green and purple boas and panache and beads and streamers were hiding something the rest of the world couldn't see. The more I thought about it, the more I thought that this extravagant gala would just phase itself out someday, that the golden masks would drop and the pieces of cardboard would fall down and the gingerbread would melt and smear, and everyone would finally see that New Orleans is something more than a street, more than a parade, more than a celebration, that it is a whole city, full of living and breathing people, people who know how a heart can break, but still keep going, not because they know it's the right thing to do, but because it's tradition, because it's our history.

You could feel the two French brothers who fought to build this town from the marshes and how everyone thought they were foolish and how they kept going anyhow. Could feel the Spanish in the cypress and brick. Could feel the Haitians and the free people of color and the Irish, could feel the songs, the plaintive and at the same time joyful voices. They come as a stillness in the late afternoon of fall, when the long and hot and miserable summer finally heaves its last sigh and everything blends together, and it's not peace necessarily, it's something different. It's the will to go on. That's our history. We are stubborn and proud. We are also kind and longsuffering.

But you don't get the feeling of actual history here, not the kind you can rope into a book. In fact, it's not so much historic, as they say, but unhistoric, as in the sense that you don't feel like there is anything *but* history, and yet *you* are there, living and breathing in the right now. It's overwhelming. It is that kind of energy that makes you feel worn out and the kind of curiosity that keeps you moving from one place to the next like a cat on a hot tin roof.

We walked away from The Quarter, and the farther and farther we got away, the more the Creole townhouses turned into Creole cottages, and the more the devastation from the hurricane cried its salty tears in busted-out glass and piles of wood where houses once beckoned Kirb and me back to our neighborhood. People lived there and we understood them. We lived in the same place and spoke with the same climate, the climate where the blue worn-out window slats slap in the wind at night and the ten-dollar box fans push the air around the living rooms in the morning and time moves slow, dripping like water off the rain gutter.

I didn't like walking through those skeletons of the city, no one did, but there was no way around it. It felt profane, like you were stepping into someone's living room without them being home, and each splinter of wood and shard of glass held those frightful memories of destruction, of anguish. This is why the stories of the common people are rarely told, and mostly forgotten. Even our triumphs are only heroic if they are under some exotic circumstance, some marketable anomaly, where everything works out gift wrapped in the end. Our stories are stripped of their passions, our desires chained up in these piles of wood and glass. They are broken, breathless. It's not because they aren't interesting, it's because they are hard to tell and hard to hear about. But we love and suffer and bleed in the same collective shout as everybody else and yet it seems to me you are always hearing about how the world is full of good men and that these good men are some class of people by themselves living in some place you've never heard of, but everybody is talking about. He's such a good man, don't you know? What a good man he is! And we are meant to think some good man is waiting around the corner so we can tell our story to him, and not so he can help us, we can help ourselves, but by God so he can listen. But despite all these good and fine and decent men, a lot of people suffer and even die without anybody hearing a word about it.

"My legs hurt," Kirb said, as we made it just a few blocks from our street.

"It's not that much farther," I said.

"But my legs hurt!"

I sighed.

"Do you want me to carry you on my back?"

"Mmm. Hmm," Kirb said, and I let him jump on my back, while I positioned my arms underneath his legs.

"Alright," I said, "I'll carry you as long as I can, but if I get tired, you are going to have to walk, okay?"

Kirb didn't answer. He put his chin on my shoulder, and I hoofed it, laboring a little as I adjusted to a full grown man on my back and still watching the houses as we passed.

Chet Ellers was sitting out on his front stoop underneath a single two-by-four, that I remembered once being an overhang his father used to sit under. His Dad would spend hours out there on the porch! I don't think I ever walked by without seeing him there. The house itself was nothing special. It had stock white siding, with a stock black gate door and stock black gate railing surrounding the porch. Terry Ellers, the father, had sat on an old metal chair looking out in the streets and waving at anyone that walked by. His wave was so solemn. It was more like a pledge than a wave, palm facing you, fingers pointing to the sky, and he gave with it the most genuine of smiles, and the fact he was missing his front teeth didn't take away from his smile, it somehow added to it. Now, over the years, you may have seen Chet playing in the yard a time or two, or even his mother chasing him around the fence posts, but no matter what, there was Terry, sitting on that porch waving and smiling. When the storm hit, Chet lost his mother and father, and the white siding got torn down, and the black gate fell and there were two trees from either side of the neighbors that crushed the porch covering down into the ground. You might think Chet should have left that house, or maybe he should have built a brand-new house right on top of it. Many folks were faced with the same choice. Some of us though, couldn't say goodbye. You see, this is a place where women and men have grown old believing things. One generation believes something and then they grow old and then another goes on believing something until they grow old, and by the time you are born your beliefs are as much a part of you as your Daddy's brown eyes or the healthy sense of anxiety you get around spiders. Building a new house over your father's house is something some of us can't do. So, Chet, who wasn't much of a carpenter, or much of a student, spent the last few weeks down at the community library getting the information to go back to that house, and get his fingers and thumbs good and sore screwing up rebuilding it. And he did screw it up! More than once! But it never stopped him from walking to that library or punishing those fingers and thumbs the next day. Eventually, he didn't screw up the siding, and then he didn't screw up the door frame, and then he didn't screw up the porch or even the windowsill, and as I positioned Kirb on my back, it seemed that he was doing a pretty damn fine job of not screwing up that overhang his Daddy used to sit under. And there Chet was, sitting under the two-by-four, and wouldn't you know it? He waved. He waved with that same solemn stroke I had seen his father do a thousand times before, but there was something different, and I didn't realize what it was until Kirb and I were almost home. Chet hadn't smiled.

We stopped by Mr. Dottol's and got two hundred bucks for the Rabelais check and a receipt for the rest of our commission once the check cleared.

"Make me a grilled cheese," Kirb said before we even stepped through the door of our house.

"Are you serious?" I said. "Give me a minute for crying out loud! I need to check on something."

He turned on the TV and plopped down on the floor with a bag of sour cream and chive potato chips, taking a handful and happily stuffing them into his mouth.

"I just don't understand why you won't make me a grilled cheese," he said.

I ignored him and I made my way back to the room. I pulled over one of the twin beds and stood on it while I fished the shoe box out of the heating vent. I opened it greedily and took out the money we had made for the day, so that I could put it with the rest and count it all together. When I saw what was in the box, I dropped it. There was only a twenty-dollar bill! The other nine hundred and five dollars were gone! And with it, the breath was gone too. There was the heart, it drummed harder and harder against my breast. There were the eyes, they watered and burned. There was the gut, it churned and exploded. There were the trembling hands, the taut jaw, the sweat pooling at the hairline, but there was no breath. And even though common sense told me that it was worthless, I frantically went through the heating vent, seeing if maybe the money had got blown around, but there was nothing but dust and the certainty that someone had taken it.

I thought of places it could be and furiously pulled out my pants pockets and flew through old laundry. I checked under the beds and sifted through papers in the closet. I even got an old flashlight and took it into the vent to see if maybe I had missed something.

I bowed my head and gaped out the bedroom window.

The sun was taking its last stretch, and the sky itself had broken off into shards shaped like giant icicles, and they were melting and falling down, down into the horizon, down past the water and the houses, and down even further than the gravel, down into the darkness of something that hadn't been accounted for. And I tried desperately to grab onto one of those pieces with my eyes, but I couldn't, they kept slipping away, slipping further and further down into the chasm of the earth, until the sun was gone, and all that remained was that tiny shoe box, helpless on the floor.

Getting away from Mama meant everything; it meant the promise of a new life, of hope. As long as Kirb and me were living with Mama, we would always be beholden to her whims, trapped in night after night where even going to the bathroom could be tragic. She would wait there, in the vulnerable places, in dark corners of the house, pleading for help or screaming in anger.

I thought that becoming a man would change it, that getting a job would give me the freedom to leave, that getting married would somehow liberate me from her, but the only future I could imagine without the weight of Mama around our necks, was a future somewhere else. A future with no guilt, with no past, with no whiskey. But something was pulling us back, some unseen force like the gravitational pull of a small planet kept driving us into her hot breath and cigarette smoke, and she always was waiting, twisted smile on her face, somehow knowing this was our inescapable fate. Mama was a horsefly in the swelter of an August heat wave, buzzing and buzzing and buzzing around, and all you could do was watch while she took bite after bite from your flesh. Tonight, she wasn't going to get that pleasure, because I was going to be waiting for her.

I went to the bathroom and found the mirror. I barely recognized myself. My eyes were bloodshot. I had a scratch on my forehead and blood was smeared over my chin, neck, and hands. A thick smear of red covered the collar of my shirt and extended over my left ribcage.

I had another man's blood all over me! Some poor bastard. It looked like he had come from the woods, deep in the woods as they say, and who could blame him for being that way, when he hadn't known anything else? She was a sweet woman, his wife. Thinking of her hurt more than thinking of what I had done to him.

I had violated their shelter, had forever stained it with my fury. I had walloped some old man, not my equal in strength, but some withering shell. And although I hadn't done it for survival, to feed my family, or to defend them from an enemy, I had done it for the only reason that made it all worth it, which is honor. A man must always defend the honor of his family, and if he doesn't, he ceases to be a man, he becomes a coward, and I'd rather waste away in the oblivion of a state institution, than lose my honor as a man.

I searched my face for some sign of being human, for some line or crack that would explain why I didn't feel anything, but all I could see were the cruel folds on my forehead and the blank stare that must have come from some creature I imagined inside of me. In some way I regretted that I felt nothing.

I washed the blood off of my hands and into the sink and it turned bright as it swirled away into the drain. Blood wasn't what I thought it was. It was fleeting and fickle and could be washed away and forgotten.

"He deserved it," I said.

I washed what blood was left off my face and neck and came out of the bathroom.

I made Kirb a grilled cheese and we watched *The Backstreet Boys All Access* on VHS. I didn't want him to know what was coming. I wanted him to feel safe in the idea that we were still going to leave.

After half an hour or so, Kirb fell asleep on the couch, and I carried him to his bed. I went out into the living room and sat down, turning off all the lights but the lamp next to me.

The room was full. There was the green paint on the walls, the sofa, a loveseat, a coffee table, two lamps, a rug, and a television. They were all there, the things I had known as my past, but there was something different about the textured ceiling. It was lonesome. The hanging curtains were also lonesome. The rogue strands of frayed carpet were lonesome. The ceiling fan blades were lonesome. The hushed rocking bench on the porch was lonesome. The white brick fireplace with the gold trim was the most lonesome of all things. This collection of artifacts was the loneliest place I had known. I tired looking it, so I closed my eyes and listened.

The Goldsmith's black lab barked one last time at the Robinson's terrier. A plane roared overhead followed by a sputtering helicopter. Every few minutes a car drove searchingly through the neighborhood, leaving a dust devil of sound, which echoed in the cavern of our living room. I could hear the middle-aged housewives gossiping as they walked past the house. I couldn't make out their words but understood the muffled cynicism and peals of laughter. Feeling the weight of the heat on my chest, I retired to the kitchen to get a drink. I flipped the tap on, and it whined and hissed until finally producing a small stream of liquid and I put the glass under my nose, as if testing its purity and vintage, the way one might test a wine or a good glass of cognac. The water smelled of bleach and chemicals. I sampled a small amount. It was dry and pasty, and a film formed around my teeth, tongue, and throat. I finished the glass and sat back down. Through the blinds I saw a solitary streetlamp and its yellow stare made the shape of the Navy Cross. I had seen this cross many times. If you look close enough at a light, really peer into it, it's hidden inside. I remembered the cross even in the human bodies that mulled around parks and bus stops and how they stood feet together and arms apart, each person a light, hoping to be seen and all of them same.

A gentle rain fell, and its effects were hypnotizing.

I tried imagining what I would say to Mama, how I would yell at her for taking the money, how I would demand that she give it back, how she would produce it and I would reluctantly forgive her. I tried even more *not* to forgive her, to hold on to that lustful hate, but the rain kept dripping and dripping and dripping and wearing me down, and before I knew it, I was asleep.

In what seemed like a few moments, the door woke me up.

Mama, fumbling with the keys, came in and shrieked.

"Dear lord boy! Why are you sitting in that chair with the lights out? You nearly gave your Mother a heart attack!"

After I oriented myself, I assumed a good hot scowl.

"Why don't you sit down Mama?" I said. "We are going to have a talk."

She put her purse on the end table and ducked into the kitchen and I could hear her putting ice in a glass before she reappeared and carefully sat on the sofa, folding her skirt underneath her thin legs before she sat down.

"What is it?" she said, as she sipped her drink with her wooden stare, eyes numb and rolling back in her head.

She was still there, unshaken. Still the formidable Mama I had known as a boy, the one that could bully and threaten in one breath and be sweet as caramel drizzle on vanilla bean ice cream the next.

"I kept some money in a shoe box in the heating vent in my room," I said. "There was a lot of money in there, money I was saving, and today I went to put some more money in the box and all that was left was a single twenty-dollar bill."

She smiled. It was a wolfish smile. She took another long sip.

"I know," she said proudly. "I had to use it."

My blood fumed underneath my chin. It fired up my neck and into my mouth. I was trying to stand up to her, as I had wanted to for so long. Childhood holds that grip on us, it refuses to let go of the image of your parent as something more than human, some entity affixed to you by destiny that would give you guidance and support even in the toughest of times, so you could become great. And even if she wasn't that, even if she would never be that there was a part of me still believing she had it in her, that all mothers or fathers *must* have it in them. As the idea faded into the cigarette she flicked into the ashtray, discarded like the money I had saved, I knew that in order to change you need to destroy the heroes and demons of your childhood and let the grip loosen, so you can be free.

"I had to use it," I repeated in disbelief. "I had to use it? That's all you have to say for yourself? Do you know how hard I worked for that money? How long I've been saving it?"

"Well, it's not like you told me about it," she interrupted. "The only reason I even knew it was there was I was going to tell you that I had brought you home something for dinner a few days back and I saw you sneaking around in my heating vents. Imagine my surprise. If I would have known that you were *saving* it, I wouldn't have taken it. But we were behind on the electric bill and the gas bill, and I figured that you would want to contribute to the house, since you are a grown man and you' re staying here for nothing."

"Nothing!" I said. "I buy all the food for the house! I do *all* the cleaning! I take care of the yard and I take care of Kirby! I was saving that money for something special, something… Well, something you wouldn't understand."

"What?" she said. "What were you saving it for that could be more important than your mother or your brother?"

"I was saving it so Kirb and me could move the hell out of here!" I blurted.

"I see!" she said. "I see now! You were going to leave here without even telling me! You were going to take my boy from me! Well, over my dead body! You will never take my boy from me! Pssh! Leave me here all alone after all I've done for you! I'm your mother boy! I went through pains you'll never know to bring you into this world. I've cradled you since the day you were born and picked you up after what you did to yourself and to this family! You have no loyalty! And you talk so much of honor! What honor can you have if you would leave your mother this way! All by myself and take my boy too? You are a pig!"

She nodded her head, agreeing with the logic. "Yes, you are a good for nothing PIG!"

She said it to hurt me, and it did. I didn't want it to and that made me mad. I wanted to see something human in her, something like remorse, but she looked at me in that calculating way of hers and I imagine if she could have licked the heartache off of her fingers, she would have. Yes, she was still there, all of her, every moment of her seeping out of her twitching lips and taut forehead. The way she taught me to sing when I cleaned the house, how she whispered adages to me above the pale nightlight plugged into the wall, even how she scolded me for not eating enough or crawled in my bed after Dad had died. Crawled in my bed with me, as a teenage boy, dressed only in her underwear and how she cuddled up next to me and how I never knew whether I would wake up in puke or urine or blood or bone dry and molested by her hot breath on my neck. I had pitied her and had been afraid of her, had loved her but wanted to forget her.

"Pig?! I'm a pig?" I said. "How about you Mama? You drink so much the whiskey company would have to go out of business if you stopped! You don't know how to be a mother. You never were one even when Dad was alive. You haven't taken care of me or Kirby our whole lives besides having a house for us to live in, which Dad bought. The only thing you have ever done is let other people pay for your life while you sit back and watch it happen. You don't ask how our day is or what we are feeling or any damn thing that matters to us. All you care about is that glass and the ice and the liquor you put in it."

"Is that so?" she said.

"It's the truth!" I said. "And the truth hurts, doesn't it mama?"

"There you go again!" she said. "You and the truth! Mr. Honor! Well, I know what your Daddy said to you. I know why you think that."

And she was silent for a minute. She even set her glass down on the table and took a few slow breaths.

"You see, my son," she stared, very sincerely. "You think everybody should be perfect, should hold honor so high and never hold up anything else, but people aren't perfect, people do things, bad things even, and that doesn't mean that they themselves are bad. And you probably think the world is different than your Mama, that the world is more like you, but what you don't realize is that most people don't tell you the truth about nothing, they just tell you about their life the way they want you to see it, the way they wish it was. So, all these conversations in the neighborhood are just gums flapping and when you tell them to someone else they have even less of the truth in them then when you heard them, so they just turn into fiction and there ain't no more truth than that."

I couldn't think of anything to say. The lonesome artifacts stared at me, and it was obvious that Mama fit right into them, fit right into the space right next to the impress where Dad used to sit on the sofa.

I shook my head.

"I needed that money," I said. "You don't understand."

"You don't understand boy. When you are young, the best is ahead of you. When you are old, the best is behind you. Losing my father took a part of me away, just like losing your daddy took a part of me and I've tried to do everything I can to get those parts back, but I can't. So, all that's left is this smothered heart."

She put her hand on her breast.

"Nothing makes a woman older than death," she told me, using that same hand to fish out another cigarette.

"You men can be as old as you want to be," she said. "And it don't cost you nothing. But, when a woman is old, it cost her everything. She don't feel wanted anymore. And not being wanted is painful. *So* painful. You try and try to see God's plan for what it is, because after all, the lord knows best. But no matter how much you understand or don't understand, you're still left with the pain of it all. Knowing and not knowing is both pain, the worst kind of pain you can imagine, and the older you get the more pain you've had, until your body gives out, because that pain beats on you like the wind and rain on a courtyard rock. So, yes, I drink. I drink because it takes the edge off the pain, and I don't have to live with it every damn minute of every damned miserable day."

Mama gave me that hungry look, the one aching for something, for something mysterious and dark, and I almost felt bad for her. But that was her way, to shock you with something tender after she did something horrible, so that you let go and she could get away with it. She'd been doing it as long as I'd been alive and probably some before. It makes you wonder where a person learns a wicked trick like that, if it's the parents or the city or the way they've been loved, but no matter how much you turn it over in your mind, you never really find out, do you? Even if you did, it wouldn't stop it from happening.

"Just because you've had pain Mama," I said. "It doesn't make it right for you to do some of the things you do."

"Maybe you're right son," she said softly. "Maybe you're right."

I nodded while she put her head back on the sofa and looked up at the ceiling.

"But being right isn't everything either. You see, you can say all these moral things, all these beautiful and perfect things, the best way one should live, you can say them until you are blue in the face, and you might even get somebody to agree with you, but most of us will just go back to living the way we did anyhow. I wish-" and she stopped here to pick her drink back up.

"I wish that choices were different, that they were more simple and direct, like left and right. You could say then 'I'm going left' and you would end up on the left side, or you might say, 'Today I'm going right, and you would end up on the right side.' But the way it stands making one single choice is about the most complex thing there is, because you can't tell what the outcome of that choice is going to be, and you might as well have no light in the middle of the swamps at two in the morning in December. We can't change the way we is son. I'm just the way I am and you are just the way you are. We are stuck."

She drank the last of the glass and probed the ice cubes with her finger.

"Time for a refill," she said.

She would always be the damsel and my father the gallant knight who had saved her, broad-chested and smelling of aftershave, powerful yet gentle, kind and above all honorable.

Mama was telling me something about herself, something I didn't care to listen to that night, but in her own way she was telling me she was sorry. She wouldn't remember in the morning, she'd deny it. Yes, Mama would deny the conversation. She'd deny that she had been drinking. She'd deny taking the money. She'd even deny the puke she left under the rug outside the bathroom when I asked her to clean it.

As I left her there in the dark, she protested for a kiss, which I did not give her. I knew there was no sense in trying to get the money back. All I could do now was think of another way.

I lay awake imagining coming home from a long day of sales to Janus and Kirb at the beautiful house on Lafayette. They were so happy to see me! And I, I was so happy to be home. Even the sun seemed warmer in that house! I stepped through its threshold to get nearly tackled by Kirb. Then Janus kissed me, and it was a sincere kiss, one that felt like she hadn't kissed me in a long time. "What do you want to do today hunny?" she asked. "Anything you want," I said.

"Anything at all."

Kirb's snoring made me open my eyes. It was cold. I could see the heating vent and it was still open. I was going to get a necklace for Janus no matter what. At least there was that.

Then, it came to me. We could get the money from Janus! Yes! She must have had some money put away. She was always good at putting money away. She would know that this was best for her, best for me, best for Kirb. Once I gave her something nice, everything would be alright. I could explain it to her. I would give the deposit to Rashad Philips, and we could finally be free from this house.

Chapter Eleven

I knew exactly where I had to go to get the necklace for Janus. There was no other place I could go. I wasn't superstitious like Mama. I wouldn't chase my sons down at seven in the morning on their way to school, panting and frantic in my bathrobe with curlers in my hair because they didn't give me a kiss goodbye, or look at the numbers on a dollar bill before I left it as a tip because I didn't want to give my luck away to our waiter, or have an anxiety attack for a week because my family accidentally walked under a ladder on our way home from church. But I did believe in the mysteries of life. Mysteries are their own little gods and goddesses and what we can't understand about them is what we wish for in ourselves. I believed in places and their power, even if that power was the collection of fantasies I built up in my own mind. The source of the power doesn't matter because it connects us to that place, and then all those places you've loved and mythologized in your life become a part of you.

The jewelry store was like an old cabinet of memories, there was not one dull shelf. And coming up to it with Kirby on the morning after Mama had spent most of our money, I wasn't any less enchanted than I had been the first time I had seen it, which as I recalled had been when I was around seven or eight.

It was just Dad and me. Kirb had bitten off a piece of his tongue tripping on a garden hose and was sidelined with Mama eating popsicles and watching cartoons. So, Dad had taken me out for the day. He needed his own break because he had gotten into it with Mama a few nights before and was looking to make it right.

"Sometimes," he had said in that deep and soothing voice of his. "Sometimes, you've got to *pay* for your mistakes."

He winked and smiled, in that way that made you feel like he was telling you a secret, and I wouldn't understand why he smiled until many years later, but I smiled then anyway, because he was my father.

"You must die my boy!" he had called out passionately. "You must die! Each part of you that grew when you were young must die. Your dreams must die! The honeysuckles outside the church must die! All of creation must die, heaving its last sighs into the cold air, reaching finally upward in a long mournful choke. You must die to love! For love is the recognition of someone else's pain as they recognize yours, both dead enough to know that the only real resurrection worth mentioning is dying to love. Because so many of us die, a little bit here and there, but everyday more. We die in our routines, going to and from work. We die each time we kiss, and each kiss dies, throwing off its husk like an exploding sun. We die in complaints about weather and politics. We die in the same meal cooked the same way every Wednesday. We die as we stop to say hello, as we stop to nod, as we stop even to make eye contact with another person. We all die. You must! But, above all, you must die enough to love."

I remember getting the chills hearing him speak, from the beauty of it. It's like that with good words; you can feel them before you really understand them. It took a long time for me to understand his, his *real* meaning, but the words he spoke haunt me, as good words tend to do when we forget the rest of our lives for a moment and listen to the silent hum. You might call that hum existence or the universe or connectivity or the creator, but to me it's something more familiar, like my father's whistle on those steps, or the buzz of a bumblebee on a June stroll through the sticks.

"You must die to love," he had said.

So, we went to Francoise Pelagie's, which at the time was the swankiest jewelry store in all of New Orleans. I remember the name itself was this grand riddle that seemed as if it had come down from heaven like divine brilliance and I had somehow missed the lesson in Catechism. The steps were wide at the bottom and became more and more narrow as you got towards the top, which did a good job of giving your eyes the impression your feet were leading you somewhere higher than what nature could provide.

Dad took my hand and led me up, and as we got about halfway, I could see the building's gray façade, its murky windows, and large heavy white doors, which stood like an age-old gate carved with sculptures of ancient warriors in round helmets, commanding chariots and wielding spears and long swords.

It was a place where there was no death, no sorrow, no crying, no pain. It came over me like thunder, like a rumbling voice through the wind, like a wave of water crashing over the top of my head, and just when I thought I couldn't be more overwhelmed, *she* walked by.

Her hair was blonde and pulled perfectly back into a small ponytail. She wore round rimmed sunglasses above a thin nose and pouty but resolved lips. On her neck was a black band, which matched her large black shiny belt, wrapped tightly around her lime green skirt. She moved like a snake in a basket being lulled by a flute, hypnotically swaying to and fro, to and fro, to and fro. As she reached the giant doors, a man appeared out of thin air, rising from some enchanted smoke, just to open the door for her. She breezed in and vanished and I remember thinking that she was the most interesting and perfect woman I had ever seen, and that to go into a place she had wanted to go into would somehow help me understand what perfection was.

Dad gave me a good slap on the back and when we made it to the top of the stairs I read the sign in my head: FP: Jewelry. The big blue lettering looked like a fresh paintbrush stroke and underneath was inscribed in gold the year 1899.

Before I could think any more about it, Dad ushered me through the doors and we were overwhelmed by glittering light, by the wall painted as a sky full of stars which poked through the shadows of the deep dark walls like torches of the night. The glass counters teemed with gems and sparkling bracelets and pins, and over the largest wall of the store, in white sparkling letters it said, "Francois Pelagie's: The only place where the stars fall from the sky right onto your hand."

As we ambled to the back of the store, a clerk glided across the floor, smiled, an ensign of the highest of temples.

"How y'all doing? Welcome! Isn't it a beautiful day?" he said, and the way he said "y'all" was the most damn charming thing you had ever heard, even though we said it plainly at home to each other every day.

Dad stopped at the brooch counter and the clerk, a middle-aged man with wavy black hair perched himself in front of us. His expensive cologne climbed warmly in my nose and when he pointed his smile at my father, I could see a gold tooth on one of his canine teeth.

"Something I can get out for you?"

"Yes," Dad said after thinking for a moment. "That one there," and he pointed at a large brooch that popped like a white firework surrounded by gold circles.

"The Victorian Rose?" The clerk said. "Sir, it has no equal in brooches."

The clerk pulled it out from under the counter and gave it to Dad, slipped it to him over the counter, a private whisper between palms.

Dad met the brooch with greedy eyes, and as he peered inside, looking into it, far into its delicate gold and diamond frame, the left side of his face beamed.

"How much is it?" Dad asked.

"Three thousand." The clerk said, lightly tapping his finger on the counter. "But I'd be happy to give it to you for twenty-five hundred, seeing as it is such a beautiful day and you've brought such a handsome boy with you."

I blushed.

Dad, without even second guessing said, "I'll take it" and the clerk scampered away with Dad's credit card. Dad bent down and handed me the brooch.

"What do you think?" he asked.

I turned it over in my hands a couple times and tried to look at it how Dad had looked at it, with that same thoughtfulness, that same purpose. The more I did, the more beautiful it became. I knew then why they called it the rose. Behind each individual diamond were gold folds shaped like petals, with a large golden rose in the center.

"It is amazing," I said and the giddy smile that followed from Dad told me he was happy and so I was happy too.

Before we left, I combed the store carefully for the lady in the lime green skirt, but she was nowhere to be found.

While we were walking down the steps a man ahead of us was digging through a bag he had gotten from the store and dropped his money clip. Dad drooped down and picked it up. He shuffled through the money, and I saw more than a few hundred dollar bills and come to think of it, I'd say there was nearly a thousand dollars, almost half the price of the brooch itself. Dad wasn't a rich man, even though he had an occupation that was supposed to make him rich. I wouldn't have blamed him if he would have just put the money in his pocket and kept walking. He worked hard my Dad, and he loved hard. I was about to suggest that maybe he should keep it, after all it was a lot of money and the man who had dropped it sure looked like he wasn't going to miss it. I believed Dad sensed me and whatever passing thought he may have had of keeping the money was gone. He ran it over to the man, who curtly said "thank you" before throwing it carelessly into the bag.

When Dad made it back to me, I couldn't help but ask "He didn't even care, did he?"

To which my Dad replied that I had better sit down and I asked him if he meant right there on the steps of Francoise Pelagie's, and he said yes, so I did.

Dad pulled up his belt.

"Honor isn't easy, son," he said. The best things in life aren't easy, but they are worth it."

He bent over and caught my eyes.

"You remember Lancelot?"

I nodded.

"When he went into Corbenic, a dragon attacked the city. Everybody left in fear, even King Pelles. But Lancelot stayed to fight. It took everything in him! The dragon was one of the most ferocious dragons that had ever lived. It had teeth as big as a car and one single breath of fire could take out fifty men. Lancelot stood eye-to-eye with it. To face it, he had to face death and fear and every insecurity he had ever known. He went through the horror of all that, not to save himself or to gain glory, but to help the people keep their homes. He killed the dragon and saved the city.”

Dad put his thick leathery hand on my shoulder. I understood. I told him so.

You should have seen Mama’s face when Dad gave her that brooch, she was truly happy then, and I’ve often wondered since how much she thinks of that day. I see her sometimes, when she doesn’t know I’m looking, and she pulls the brooch out of her crowded jewelry box. She picks it up delicately, as if she thinks she might break it, and she stares at it, not in the way that Dad or I had stared it, but with a wretchedness, almost a loathing. Once, I even saw her put it in hair and look in the mirror. I expected her to smile, but she just examined herself carefully, and then, not even a moment long enough to take three breaths in, she put the brooch away.

I have remembered Dad’s words on the steps in front of Francoise Pelagie’s on many separate occasions in my life. They have remained inside my head, waiting for when I needed them, when I needed the strength to go on, and even when I didn’t have the strength, they were there to comfort me.

“How much farther?” Kirb said after the first couple of steps, letting his shoulders fall forward and his chin drop.

“We still have to go all the way up these steps,” I said, and as he was complaining to me about how far we had already walked to get there and how tired and hungry he was I tried to remember more about our father, his expressions, his face, but all of it came out faint. I sighed, looking down at the ground, wishing I could hold on. But you can’t stop it. You can’t stop how the memory of a man fades, day after day, how you lose part of that man until there isn’t anything left but a ghost, and that ghost can’t talk, not in the way the man that made him could. Eventually, you even forget how the ghost sounded, until it isn’t a ghost anymore at all, it’s just the words you remember them saying.

I took Kirb’s hand, and he reluctantly climbed up a little farther with me until we reached the step that Dad had stopped to talk to me. A young couple walked past us, playfully arguing about what to have for lunch and the young man stole a kiss from his companion, and she grinned and gave him a good pat on his backside.

I thought to myself, what a cruel idea that life continues on so happily after we are gone. There should have been some crevice in that step, there should have been some crater, like a meteor leaves in the

Earth's crust, but there wasn't. The step was serene, it almost seemed happy, and I wanted to crush it with my boot heel for being so damn happy when my father was gone, for not remembering what had happened.

"How much farther?" Kirb repeated.

I led him up the remaining stairs, to the white doors, and I paused for just a moment before I opened them, to let out the morning's last breath.

The inside was exactly the opposite of what I had remembered. The paint had faded on the wall of stars and instead of a room full of clerks and customers, there was only the couple that had passed us on the steps talking to a young and overly eager clerk, and then one other solitary clerk, who stared aimlessly out the murky windows. Even the lettering that once said how the stars would fall right onto your hands was faded.

We walked back toward the clerk but stopped next to the couple. They were looking at engagement rings and as I peeked over their shoulders to see what ring they wanted to wear for the rest of their lives, I noticed that their hands were touching and the young man was tenderly stroking the tip of her fingers, and then, time shifted. Or maybe I shifted into another time. But seeing those two picking out a ring, so joyful and full of hope and recognizing that feeling, that unmistakable feeling of being complete, because you realize someone else is just as incomplete as you are, I couldn't help but think of that summer.

It was summer and you knew it was summer because there was no escaping the heat. We were right in the middle of it. Some days it would get so hot that your mind would get turned around sweat droplets on your forehead and that blazing and beating sun, so you'd sit underneath your porch trying to escape it all, but then that hot wet air that blows off the coast would get angry and so it would punish you, in the way it knew how, which was to burn right into your cheeks.

About then you'd realized that it was so hot you just couldn't stand another minute of it, so you'd know that you had to take a swim. And somebody might ask, "Why don't we go to the swimming pool," and then you would reply with your own question, which is "why would anybody in their right mind go to the swimming pool when we got a whole ocean just miles away and no fee to get it?" So, there you were, out of the sun, into the car for a few hours and finally in front of the cool waves of Henderson Beach State Park. There we were, me and Janus, and she was wearing that black bathing suit, the one piece that I said was so old fashioned, but that I'd be sorry if I saw her throw away.

We lay on the beach awhile, towels sitting between tufts of beach grass, listening to the gulls, pointing out the occasional sailboat, and sometimes just staring up at the sun and letting the heat sink into our skin.

"Did I ever tell you on was on the swim team in High School?" she said, as she looked up from the sand.

"No, you didn't."

"Yep. I was on the swim team for three years," she said. "My specialty was the back stroke. I only ever got beat on my back stroke two times and I got a bad start the first time. My finger slipped off the ledge and it just threw off everything else."

I tried to imagine her in her one-piece suit and swim cap, chopping through the water with those tiny violent splashes of arms and legs and I could see the swim coach from the other team saying to himself, "Damn that Janus! We just can never get her on the backstroke."

"I wasn't very good at anything else," she said, almost speaking to herself. "But nobody could beat my back stroke!"

She grinned and did her best to find my eyes through the sun.

"I think it was because I love swimming on my back."

She turned over on her hip.

"Did you ever just lay there in the water?" she said. "You know, on your back?"

I told her I had.

"Did you notice how everything just melts away? That you feel like you're floating above all your worries, that there isn't no pain or suffering and their ain't no trouble, no trouble at all in the world or any other place? Like it just makes sense."

I looked over at her, head propped up on her hand, elbow in the sand, and right then, it came to me, like a drop of black ink on a clean white paper: I knew I was in love with her. It frightened me at first, that loss of control, that idea that somewhere inside her head, underneath the beautiful skin, and near blue-black eyes, and the mouth full of teeth, there was either the condemnation or vindication of my heart, and by proxy my soul, since souls and hearts are connected in the way the earth is connected to the ground or the blue is connected to the sky.

"Well have you or not? Don't keep me waiting all day!" she said playfully as she flicked a little sand at me with her free hand.

"Not until right now," I answered, sober.

She dropped the playful air for just a moment, and I could see an inner warmth come across her features, and knowing she accepted it, that she was open to the way I felt, I didn't feel scared anymore. I had faced it, had gave it a good licking, and my fear was exactly where it should be, in her hands.

"Can I ask you a question?" she said, and the way she asked, it seemed as if it was something she had been thinking over a while.

"You bet," I answered.

I sat up.

"What do you want to do with your life?" she said. "I mean, do you know what you want to be?"

I had heard this question before, more times than my mind had the tolerance to hear it. I had heard it from school counselors and Mama and Seth and even Mrs. Walker, and I always found it such an irritating question. I mean, aren't I doing something with my life right now? And what the hell should I be doing that I'm not doing? But, coming from Janus, the woman I loved, it didn't sound so much like battery acid, but more like the soft coo of a dove. And I imagined that it was a fair enough question, feeling you loved someone and wanted to be with them forever, as love should be.

"Well, there's nothing more I'd like to do," I said, "then to be a doctor. A family physician, like my father."

Here, I chuckled a bit.

"You know he was the only doctor that didn't make money? He took all the sad saps that didn't have any insurance. He shrugged off their payments and told them to buy groceries for their families. Word gets out real quick and a lot of people loved my father, but sometimes it seemed like the bread barely made it to the table. I know our neighbors helped out some and I'm sure if Dad would have asked, people would have given him near anything, but Dad had a lot of pride. He was an honorable man, my father."

I gazed above Janus, as if to see him standing there with his strong hands, deep voice, and that smell of shaving cream and leather he bandied about in the air as he walked.

"I got the grades to get in somewhere" I continued, "and I did real good on this test they have you take to get into medical school, it's just-" and here I paused and took a good sigh, "it's just, I worry about Kirby. If I go off to school, I don't know what will happen to him and Mama would raise Hell before she let me take him away that long. But I still want to go. I still think I can, if I can figure out a way to take Kirb with me."

She let it sink in. She stirred it around in that brain of hers and gave it a proper silence, the kind of silence that something like what you want to do with the rest of your life should warrant.

"Sure", she said with confidence. "You could do that."

She was sure. She was sure, sure right down to the blue of her eyes, and I think I could have told her I wanted to be a puppeteer and she would have stirred that around in her brain, just the same way she had, playing out the rest of our lives in a series of breaths, and been just as sure I could do it and she could support me in it. And in that way, love is like faith, it's a belief in something that's not rational. As long as you keep believing, love can carry you through almost anything, but once you let that go, you're defenseless. That's how people fall out of love, they quit believing.

"Race you to the water!" she said and stood up and ran.

I took off after her and caught her in the tide, picking her up by the waist and tossing her.

"I love you," I said.

She stopped and looked at me, as much and as close as anybody can look at a person and said, "I love you too."

I felt that finally admitting those words sealed the sacred pact that meant we belonged to each other, that love was giving forever a certain part of you to another person, and in many ways, I wasn't wrong. But you find out if you've been around long enough, that right and wrong are too far apart to be the same and too close together to be different.

We went out deeper into the water and her eyes got more blue and dark the deeper we got. She swam away while I wasn't looking and next thing I knew, I heard a few splashes and she was out. Out so far, I could only see her slick red hair, bobbing up and down like a happy seal. She smiled and waved and then pointed out to the endless expanse of the sea, as if to ask me if she should swim away even farther and try to catch the sun. I shook my head and motioned her to come back, and she did, and I tickled her until she gave me a good long kiss.

Afterwards, we dried off and went for a walk in the fields and the light wandered off into the horizon, scurrying like a stink bug across the highway. I held her hand and we didn't have to say anything because it was enough. It was enough to be together and to have drained the day out of the summer for a laugh or two. It was enough to touch each other in the darkness, knowing that the other person was there. You see love isn't as complicated as we make it. Love is single-minded, it forsakes all things.

I was about to tell Janus how perfect the day had been when a single light flew up out of the field, followed by another and then ten more and then a thousand more until the whole field was chock-full of tiny bulbs of dull yellow light.

"Fireflies," Janus whispered.

I did not dare to speak. I just watched. It was a chorus written for the eyes, but you couldn't pick up the timbre or the rhythm, you could only watch in awe as each tiny figure zipped through the dark sky, leaving behind some white-hot shape, some temporary proof that they had been there, that this night could solely be this night and not anything else. It was something that happened only because it happened. Just the same way you need water to live or food to eat. You can explain why the body needs those things, but not how the body came about to need them. They are just because they are. That's fate and I was fated to be with her forever and I knew it.

We sat down underneath the hovering lights, and I slowly pulled off the strap of her swimming suit. She didn't move and as I went to pull the second strap off, her shoulder stirred just a bit to help me. When I pulled the swimming suit down, she lifted up her hips to let the last of it come off. She had goose bumps on her chest and arms, and I touched her, hands shaking, and she moved closer to me, and kept moving closer to me, until she whispered in my ear, "Yes, darling. Yes."

That night we became one. That night gave way to a summer of nights where the details changed, but the end result was the same.

Then, fall beating on the leaves and the back of your throat with that sea taste sweet and salty in your mouth, your left-hand tremors and you realize she's gone.

In that way Francoise Pelagie's was a place outside of time. It was a place I experienced the past, the present, and the future.

Drearily, Kirb and me made it to the clerk who was using the reflection on top of the display case to fix his tie and didn't even notice we had walked up.

I shivered. It felt like a cold and damp fruit cellar. I could nearly smell a rogue jar of apricots that had been left open and was rotting away amongst the old wood and dirt.

The clerk, startled, said "Oh! Hello!"

"Hello," I said, and as his head came up from the counter, I noticed his gray wavy hair and it was familiar. I couldn't put my finger on it until I saw his contrived smile highlighted by a single gold tooth, as shiny and as potent ever, which poked loudly out his mouth.

"You've worked here a long time, haven't you?" I said.

"Been here twenty years last month," he said, and he adjusted his tie again and I espied a crop of liver spots on his chin and neck.

"What can I help you boys with?"

"Hello sir," Kirb said and perused the display case. "We might find some jewelry for my brother Ernest's wife."

"Okay," the clerk said, in this official air, which I guessed was a voice he thought he had to use with people. "What kind of stone are you looking for?" he said. "What quality?"

"Can I see your necklaces please?" I asked.

"Of course," he said. "Let me pull out our finest for you."

He reached down below the counter and pulled out a tray of necklaces. They were bright and sparkly, and each seemed even more extravagant than the next. I felt small underneath their gaze. I dared my hand to touch one and it was like touching grace itself. They say precious stones are just rocks, but being near one, touching it, it's the earth's perfect window, a window into something beyond us, something ordered and perfect, something like eternity.

"Do you have any emeralds?" I asked. "Emeralds are my wife's birth stone."

"Very good sir. A gentleman with some taste. I'll return shortly."

As he walked away, I turned to Kirby. "What do you think Chubbs? Do you like any of them?"

"They're okay," he said. "How long do we have to stay here? It's bored."

"Not much longer buddy," I said. "Just hang on."

The clerk returned and put the necklace in front of us and there was a huge emerald on it the size of a fifty-cent piece and the rest of the necklace was made up of small diamonds. I held it in my hand and lifted it up to the mirror. It put a silence on everything it was in the presence of. I imagined putting it around Janus's neck and how her face would light up as I clipped in the clasp behind her pale white shoulders, just above that wistful grove of freckles on her spine, and I would watch her parade the necklace around the room like my very own royal lady.

"How much?" I asked excitedly.

"Let's see, sticker is seven five, but I can give it to you for seven."

"Seven hundred?"

"Seven thousand," he said.

I looked down at the ground. I would have given anything to take it to her right then. I would have spent any amount of money if I had it.

"Can you make payments?"

"Of course, sir," he said. "We have a layaway program. The first payment needs to be at least twenty percent, so it would be fourteen hundred. Will that be credit or cash sir?"

My heart sunk. I had only the two hundred from Mr. Dottol, but I was going to have to save at least a few dollars for groceries. With Mama being upset, she was bound to go on a long drinking binge and in case we didn't get the house I might also have to pay for a hotel stay or two.

I cleared my throat.

"Are there any necklaces that you have for say one hundred and fifty dollars?"

The clerk mused, perplexed. That face of his was digging deep in his mind to try to think of something, but after a minute or so, he exhaled and shook his head.

"I'm sorry sir. We don't have anything even close to that price range in here."

"That's alright," I said. "Thank you for your help."

I was hurrying to the door when I heard Kirb say, "It's okay, I'll pay," and I turned around to watch him pull out all his money and put it on the display case. It was probably five or six dollars in bills and twenty or thirty cents in change.

The clerk was stunned.

"Thank you, buddy," I said as I walked over and picked up the money. "Don't worry. We are going to find another necklace."

"I don't mind," Kirb insisted, "I can pay."

"No, Chubbs. I really don't want this one."

"Okay," he said, and I gave him the money to put back in his wallet, and as we left Francoise Pelagie's I knew, as sure as I knew anything, that this was the last time I would walk out its white doors, down its long steps, and onto the street.

All happiness and sorrow have their roots in desire, I thought. Loving something is not easy, not when you have a mind that mucks it up all the time with your expectations of it. When you love a person, the expectations get even higher, and we have even more chances to muck it up. That's why love doesn't last too long for most people. The challenge of love isn't looking past somebody's flaws, it's overcoming yours, that's the only way you can see who they really are and love them for it.

I saw past Janus's flaws. I saw her in a way no one else did. If I couldn't get her that necklace, I would get her the best one I could. She would love it! I know she would love it! Because it came from me, from my heart.

I was trying so hard to be excited, but I felt out of control. I felt the feeling I'd felt that day, the only day I seemed to remember and was trying so hard to forget, and then, it was all creeping up on me again, entering in through my nostrils and covering my brain like a warm veil of smoke, and it was like the moment when you wake up in a panic and you don't know why, but you are afraid.

Chapter Twelve

By the time we got outside the sun was covered in a veil of clouds and the light came down in spurts as the sun shuffled in and out, in and out. It was afternoon and people were walking with the purpose that comes at the end of a day but in the middle of the week. Instead of looking at each other, they looked *through* each other, through even the city itself, and if you watched a person long enough you might even see the tiny balloon of thought where they imagined their comfy desk chair or lazy porch swing. The balloon was tugging them to it, carrying them from the city to their houses.

The breathing itself was shallow and snappy and the voices were curt. Stepping out onto the street to walk, felt like stepping out into the fast lane on a freeway with nothing but your belt buckle and a glass of water.

There was an excited mob outside White Magnolia, one of the cities many locally flavored bookstores and I saw Lance Frederickson, a friend from High School, waiting in a line that wrapped around the building, so I decided to stop for a chat.

"Lance!" I called out.

He turned with that puzzled look, like when your eyes adjust to your room after waking up in the morning, the same one you get when you hear your name in crowd, and you don't at first realize who the person is or where you know them from.

"Cheese!" he said, finally recognizing me. "Cheese, is that you?"

Kirb and I jogged over.

"Yeah, it's me buddy," I said. "How you been?"

Lance was someone that understood what it was like to be tall and too skinny. He had virtually the same dimensions I had except for a mop of curly blonde hair and full red lips. We played basketball together and he was the one player I actually got along with on the team. Lance and I would sit on the bench and crack jokes. I was usually the one who got caught and so coach never thought I was serious enough about the game. As a punishment he made everyone call me cheese ball and after a while it just became cheese. I never minded it much and hearing it again felt like putting on an old winter coat, it was warm and cozy.

"I'm doing alright," Lance said. "I just applied to med school for the second time, so you better cross your fingers. If I would have had your score on the MCAT I would have gotten in already."

At this, he pulled the arm of a red-headed young man who was standing next to him.

"Hey! Joey! This is my friend Cheese. He got a 42 on the MCAT! Can you believe it?"

Joey lifted his eyebrows. "Wow! That's amazing!"

"Yeah, I'm telling you," Lance said. "Cheese would score a hundred on ever test in Anatomy. I'd always ask him: how much did you study? 'An hour or two,' he'd say. I was like you have got to be kidding me?! I mean I was getting mid-eighties and I studied six to eight hours a week."

"Yeah," I said. "But then there was English class. I couldn't buy an A."

"You didn't have to!" Lance exclaimed. "Coach taught English and even though you were a cheese ball, he still got you passed the class with a C minus, and you didn't do a damn thing!"

Lance assumed a semi-serious tone. "Tell me you *finally* applied."

I shuffled my feet. Hearing him brag about me made me proud, but ashamed. I hadn't done a damn thing with my life. How do you tell your old competition that you are still in the same place you were ten years ago? I was that guy, the guy that hadn't done anything. I was a vacuum salesman for crying out loud.

"Not yet," I said. "Right now, I'm just trying to take care of my wife and Kirb. I'll get there though. Even if it takes a hundred years, I'll get there."

"Oh! Yeah! Joey! This is Kirby," Lance said, as if the revelation of Kirb standing there had just come to him.

"Nice to meet you," Joey said and Kirb answered with a dismissive "Hi."

Joey's face flushed, the way a red head does when they feel the spotlight on them, and it reminded me of Janus. It reminded me of all the little moments when she blushed, when the veins in her face had responded to her adenylyl cyclase and dilated, creating that perfect pink face.

Ah! Science, I thought to myself. Seeing Lance and thinking about the rush of reading those books and learning about botany, zoology, and chemistry. I felt that long and cruel absence of not studying those things.

I had spent most of my childhood reading Ranger Rick magazines and when Dad died, the only way I knew how to connect to him was by reading all of his medical books, over and over again until they became as much a part of me as they had been a part of him. Science was the one way I knew how to view the world that was personal. I didn't have to share it with anyone else.

"Kirby it is so good to see you," Lance said. "You still listening to The Backstreet Boys?"

"Mmm. Hmm." Kirb said proudly. "I love them."

"Kirby knows every lyric to every song of The Backstreet Boys," Lance said. "We used to jam out in the halls, you remember Kirb?"

"Of course," Kirb said, and he smiled that wide smile of his, with his tiny teeth and his big gums and made you smile just looking at him.

"So, what are you guys doing anyway? What is all this?" I interjected.

"Oh!" Lance said. "We are standing in line to get our books signed by Arthur K. Wild."

"Arthur Wild? Who's that?"

"You don't know Arthur K. Wild?!" Lance said. "I'm surprised. I'd safely say he is the greatest writer in the twenty-first century."

"Really?" I said. "What's so good about him?"

"He's all about that Renaissance thinking," Lance said. "Not limiting yourself to just one thing like they are always trying to get you to do. Remember how in High School they wanted you to know what you were going to do for the next fifty years of your life by the time you are a junior? It's like, c'mon now! Wild believes life is too full for that, that you should have many passions, many loves, and if you do find one thing that you love, you should learn about all other aspects of life so that it will make you more genius with the one thing you love the most."

"Sounds interesting," I lied.

All I could think about was science, about the neurons firing in my brain faster than the speed of a bullet, and how each flash gave me a memory and how that reminded me of stars forming from massive molecular clumps that break off into gaseous cores, each forming an individual star. Or how the simple process of speaking involves so many things, like your lungs to power the voice box, and how the voice box vibrates sometimes a thousand times per second, and that the voice box alone creates a simple buzz and that for speech to work correctly you need the nose, mouth, and throat to work in harmony, all to push out a simple "hello." And then there was Darwin. How the first time I read Darwin I would find the answer to everything that had been and would be again. It was specifically the moment when I read about hearts ease flowers. The connection he made between how many cats in a given area related to how many hearts ease flowers was in that same area. That the cats ate the mice, and the mice ate the humblebees that pollinated the flowers. How I finally felt then like I understood something meaningful about my existence. I only needed to look for these subtle connections to put my life into a code I would understand.

"It is more than just interesting Cheese!" Lance said. "I am telling you; this guy is a madman with words. You *need* to pick up *Elegy*, it's his masterpiece. It will change the way you think. They say that the philosophical novel is dead, but *this is* the philosophical novel. It's so seamless. So thought provoking, you know?"

He stopped.

"Hey, what are you guys doing this far out in the city anyway?"

"Just down here getting some jewelry for Janus," I said.

"Oh," he seemed suddenly pensive. "I heard what happened," he said. "And I really just wanted to say how sorry I am. Nobody should have to-"

I cut him off. "Thank you," I said. "We really need to get going, but it was great seeing you, Lance."

I could tell that I hurt his feelings some, but I didn't want to go over it all again. I didn't want the awkward, 'I'm sorry' and the more awkward 'it's okay' because it's really not okay. I understood that he felt he needed to talk, that sometimes we all need to talk, and sometimes we just need to hear things that everybody says in those situations, but I had heard enough of it already. Kirb and me walked away without saying much more, other than goodbye.

I should not have stopped. I should have known that remembering the other me was a mistake. There comes a time in life when your talents become painful. It was too painful to think about passion, about the things I couldn't do, that no matter how much I wanted I couldn't grasp. Happy moments are more fleeting. Pain is like a deep trench and once you hurt, you go spiraling down into that trench until you reach the bottom, where all of it is waiting. Seeing Lance had sparked the journey to that terrible place.

"Can you imagine Chubbs?" I asked to pull myself out. "Standing in line to see an author of fiction? I mean real life, I get that, but some made up story? Who does that? It's just crazy. Especially the guy he was talking about. He sounded like a real quack."

Kirb laughed. "Quack," he repeated. "Yeah, how bored."

We walked a few blocks until we ran into a pawn shop. The red and yellow sign was twitching, writhing and spitting out light, like some wretched creature struggling for its last breath.

I stopped. Looking through the windows I could see aisles of old lawn trimmers, floors with bent bicycles, shelves lined with rusty rifles and the walls full of thirty or so failed garage band's guitars. It occurred to me that I might be able to get Janus's necklace here at a discount, so Kirb and me pushed through the barred doors.

The placed was bright, so bright you almost had to shield your eyes and it gave you the feeling that they wanted to see everything you were, that they needed no secrets but the ones you were going to buy or sell over the counter.

The owner was a brawny man with thick glasses. He was balding but had a full-grown beard. He wore a shirt that was too small for his large belly, which was poking out above his beltline, and he was eating a sloppy Joe, which was spilling over his lips.

"Howdy," he muttered, mouth half-full.

The place smelled of raw onions and seeing the sweat on the owner's forehead, I didn't have to guess where the smell came from.

"It smells like runions in here," Kirb said loudly, so loud I'm sure the owner heard it, and I wanted to laugh, but I felt like it was in bad taste.

"Shh! That's a man's body odor," I whispered.

Kirb laughed out loud. "Body odor," he repeated.

Up at the counter, I asked to see the necklaces. The owner put his sandwich down on a piece of white paper and then wiped his hands on his pants. He turned around and produced three metal boxes full of necklaces. They were in no particular order; they were just thrown together in a pile of precious metal and shiny stones which reeked of disappointment. There were diamond necklaces, but they were missing the Francois Pelagie luster and I wasn't sure whether it was the weight of what these necklaces had meant to someone else or just the fact that they were used, that they were old, but I pitied myself for looking at them, and even more because I was about to buy one.

"Do you have any emeralds?" I asked.

"Nope. I got amethyst. I got garnets. I got some knock off sapphires, but I ain't got no emeralds."

I looked through what he had as he popped a finger in his mouth and sucked some of the sloppy Joe off of it and I picked up a decent diamond necklace with a single pendant. "How much is this one?" I asked.

"Six-fifty."

I sifted through a few gold chains, then some sterling silver crosses, and some white gold lockets, but they all seemed so bland. Finally, at the bottom of the last box I found a bright white pearl necklace.

"Wow! I like that one!" I said. "How much?"

"Two hundred."

"Two hundred" I said to myself, mulling it over.

"How about one-fifty?" I asked.

"Fair enough," he said.

"Do you have a box I can put it in?"

"Yep," said the owner popping another finger in his mouth.

"I'll take it," I said.

He brought his finger back out and snatched the necklace out of my hands. He wrapped it up with the care of a butcher wrapping meat and slung it over the counter. I paid him, pushed it deep into my pocket, and then Kirb and me hurried outside, me wanting to remember nothing of the place, Kirb ready for a late lunch and a coke.

Chapter Thirteen

Geoffrey's is the finest place for jazz and blues music in New Orleans. The ribs are spectacular, and the music makes one feel at home in a city he loves. Among the bevy of the so called best blues and jazz bars in the city, you can find flashy signs, dancing ladies, chalkboards telling you that jazz will be played there all night, drink specials, and proclamations from chipper sidewalk showmen, but the best places for music are the ones that you can feel before you even walk in the door, they have something, something you can't put on a flashy sign, give to a pretty lady, or write on a chalkboard. It grabs you, the grit of the bass on the sidewalk surfaces on hairs of your ankles as you try to peek through clouded windows. Your feet aren't your feet anymore, they've been taken over by the aria of guitar and the warm thud of the kick drum. The music commands your feet to move, and they have to. That was Geoffrey's, a place as spiritual as it was American, with that comfortable brooding and unique flavor that somehow was the key to all that was and will be again.

Geoffrey was a creole that was more ancient than he was old because he carried so much wisdom with him. He had an answer for everything, and they were good answers too. I remember asking him once why a fella that was playing a jazz guitar set was wearing a silk scarf around his neck, laughing a bit because it made him seem so darn funny.

"Well first off," Geoffrey had said in a very serious way, "a gentleman wears a muffler, not a scarf. And second, it just fits who he is, doesn't it? In the way things ought to be, you just look at that man and think: he wouldn't be who he really is if he wasn't wearing that muffler, would he?"

And Geoffrey was right, he always seemed to be right, down to the shined black shoes, the red plaid shirts, and the thin grey sideburns that curled around his chin to make a beard. Yes, even his frame was right. He was short and stalky, and he had the most perfect little gut, it came out over his belt just enough to let the air know that no one regular stomach could hold such a man as him.

He was married to Dr. Plum, who was always nearby. She was a short woman, but her presence was large. When she was in the room, you could feel it. She was always kind but reserved. She held something back from everyone, I imagine. I never saw her kiss Geoffrey, but I caught them eyeballing each other a few times and it was so sweet it was almost saccharine. Her, with her thick glasses and wide smile and him, with his big head and gap in his teeth.

She had hair only about an inch thick that covered her whole head, which was gray at the edges, but a dignified gray, a subtle gray. She always dressed in a suit with long gold earrings that dangled close to her neck. She never wore makeup besides pink lipstick and her smooth brown skin gleamed like a jewel when she smiled. She'd kept her last name and added Geoffrey's to it. His name was Geoffrey Lanyay, so her name became Judith Lanyay-Plum. Everybody called her Dr. Plum. Even friends she'd had for years, even Mama. Geoffrey called her baby and sugar pie and hot stuff, but I didn't once hear him call her Judith. The only reason I even know that her name is Judith is I looked her up once on the internet in High School to see the school she worked at. She was provost of Southern University, a historically black college, and she took pride in her job, calling the students and faculty she worked with family. "You got to give back Ernest," she told me. "Helping other people is the only way to live. It makes all of the horrible parts of life, palatable. I remember the darkest moment in my life. It was right after my mother passed. I didn't even feel like getting up in the morning, my heart hurt so bad. A friend from church told me that when you are feeling depressed, the best cure is to go do something for someone else. I spent the weekend after my mother died putting together a food drive at the church and I felt closer to God than I ever had my whole life. Maybe she was guiding me there. I didn't look back after that. It's always been about something higher than me, about loving God through others."

Dr. Plum let Geoffrey be right too, although I could sense sometimes that she was biting her tongue to do so.

Yes, Geoffrey was right nine and a half days out of ten, except when Seth came in. Those two argued about everything.

Geoffrey was a God-fearing man, and he didn't take kindly to Seth talking to his bartop and chatting up pictures of dead blues musicians. He even once had a quick word with the bathroom door. Geoffrey believed talking to things like that was idolatry and idolatry was breaking the good lord's most precious commandments. On the other hand, Seth didn't take kindly to being told that God wasn't in every damn thing there was and that if we didn't talk to him, we were committing unforgivable blasphemy. Each of them made such a good point in every argument they had that you couldn't help but listen and wonder why they even bothered arguing at all. Now don't get me wrong, they weren't spiteful about it, they never raised their voices or stood up and walked away.

Geoffrey bought the bar before Kirb and me were born. We knew Geoffrey because he and Dad were friends growing up. Dad used to play baseball with Geoffrey in the neighborhood. Dad said that Geoffrey had a mean fastball and Geoffrey said that Dad was too quick on the bases for his own good. Neither of them played past high school and so Dad went into medicine and Geoffrey met a young girl named Judith Plum from Mississippi that supported his dreams of perfecting his family's barbeque recipes and obsessing about music.

"I never could get the playing right," he'd say, "but I got the ear."

Dad would take us to Geoffrey's every other weekend for ribs starting by the time we could walk. Back then, Geoffrey was running the place by himself with just one other person behind the bar and Dr. Plum was busy getting her degrees. He was always running around the place, cleaning up counters and wiping his hands on his apron, pooling sweat on his forehead, and his mind was habitually somewhere else, searching for some place where he could finally sit down and have a good breath.

Then Dad would say, "Geoffrey, why don't you do us all a favor and sit down?"

And Geoffrey would break that running around to smile at Dad and say, "Resting is for pregnant women and dead people," and we'd all laugh.

Geoffrey stayed running around until a couple of years after Dad died and then things picked up, Dr. Plum got her job at the University, and they hired some people to work the place for him. Geoffrey slowed down then, as if for the first time discovering he could breathe, and he kept breathing until it finally seemed that he caught that one elusive breath he had always been looking for. It even changed the way he spoke. Now, he talks like a true southern man, with that slow and thought-out rhythm, like a dragonfly hovering over a pond, buzzing and humming and nearly putting you to sleep if you listen to it long enough. Every once in a while you might catch him spouting off to somebody in French and then coming back to that southern drawl again, but he does it with the greatest of ease, and nobody's the wiser.

Geoffrey doesn't really work anymore, but he comes down with Dr. Plum to listen to the horn players. Geoffrey loves the horns, especially the sax, trumpets, and trombones. Growing up, Geoffrey had us listening to tapes of Satchmo and Miles Davis that he would make us take home, like "homework for the soul" he'd say. And then he'd ask us, with that half grin in the middle of his face, "Did you hear that trumpet? He plays on that thing like light playing to a butterfly." We'd nod our heads and then he tell us their stories, how they struggled with racism and poverty and even drugs, but that they kept playing music anyhow, and how they were tuned into that frequency so few people had ever been tuned into. He had us believing that those musicians built the buildings of this city brick by brick, with music notes and the triumphs and sorrows of the Harlem Renaissance. And he wasn't wrong.

Geoffrey even got to Dad, and after Geoffrey bought the bar Dad's old rock albums were getting replaced by blues and jazz albums and we were going to hear more and more music and eat more and more ribs.

Dad's favorite musician was Al Jarreau, and he took us to see every show Al Jarreau ever played in New Orleans until Dad died. One night Al Jarreau came to Geoffrey's, and you wouldn't believe it if I told you, but it was the exact day of Kirby's tenth birthday. Geoffrey had talked Al Jarreau into singing Happy Birthday to Kirby after the show and he was so impressed with Chubbs that we went backstage. Backstage was really just Geoffrey's living room upstairs; except he would take out the TV and put some fancy Persian rugs over the backs of the sofas and throw a small checkered tablecloth over the coffee table.

I remember, that as Dad and Geoffrey talked on about jazz and blues and New Orleans, Al Jarreau listened, not in the way people usually listen, where they hear only the sound of the words you are saying, but in the way he could have repeated every word you said, and maybe even the tone in which you had said it. It occurred to me that this is how he made music, and why he is so good, because he listens. And he smelled good too! He smelled like some wonderful and exotic cologne that only a traveling musician would have, probably snatched off a shelf in some far away land, where they made scents the way he makes music.

I was only eleven, but I'll never forget how happy Mama and Dad were. Mama was so different back then, she laughed like the day had a million years of peace ahead of it. She was courteous and proper and kind and the best dressed and best-connected southern lady on the Gulf coast. Dr. Plum loved chatting with Mama then, as they went from politics to society to education. And even though Papa didn't have the money to keep up with her society affairs, he doted on her, and he bought her dresses and hats and shoes every time he could, and I'm sure plenty of times when he couldn't. To make her feel special, Dad even did all the cooking. Every Thursday was homemade fried chicken and biscuits, and every Saturday was beef stew or chili, and every Sunday was either roast and mashed potatoes or pork chops and applesauce. Mama would have us set out the silverware, like she had learned from her society types, with two forks, a knife, and a spoon, and she told us not to throw down the silver, but to put it on the napkin delicately, intimately, because it was an intimate thing to eat food, and true gentlepersons were never in a hurry. Then she would tell us boys how lucky we were to have such a wonderful father and we would be instructed to go tell Dad thanks, which wasn't hard, because we usually got a healthy pat on the back and a warm grin.

It was sad to see that version of Mama go, to see her slip away into our memories, but none of us could help it. She aged twenty years at the cemetery when they were putting Dad in the ground. I imagine it was just like when Moses went to talk to God, every time he came back, he was decades older and I guess it's because God is death himself, whatever he giveth he can taketh away. Mama didn't let that death leave her either, she wasn't one for throwing anything away, and so she wore it on her face the same way somebody might wear lip gloss or a new eye shadow.

I think if Mama has to go to the cemetery one more time, she'll just wither away, and all that will be left is a pile of dust and those sunglasses she picked up on a street sale when I was five. Whatever God had left Mama with after Dad, she gave to the devil with her drinking and pain pills. This once southern lady, this once connected princess of the third coast, whose head she could hold higher than a lamppost, now goes to see the doc at least twice a month to get her "prescription" refills. She has to take us with her, carrying on about her back or her headaches and the doc takes a damn hour just to tell her that she's fine. Then she gets to arguing and dabbing her eyes with a handkerchief and the doc relents because he went to school with Dad, and he can taste the desperation hanging in the air like a peach pie sitting on a windowsill.

Then there's the sigh, that cavernous sigh that reaches deep down from the bottom of the doc's throat where he releases whatever pride he has. He sighs that sigh and then tells Mama that maybe he's not in a position to say she doesn't have a headache or her back doesn't hurt and maybe this time he can write her a prescription, just this time, and then the doc goes back to his life and thank Christ, so can we. Then, before you can say Holy Rollers, Mama's at the bottom of the prescription and she gets started up again and God forbid you didn't go back to the doc with her. Maybe you tell her you can't or that Kirb is tired or just plain that you don't want to because you know she is going for pills and why in the hell does she need you there anyway. Well then, she gets talking in that damn hot and deep voice and asks you what kind of goddamn son you are leaving her in her darkest hour, and how your Dad would be so ashamed he would probably be rolling over in his grave. If you still said "no" then it was how you didn't go to medical school, and how you let your brother down. If it got far enough she'd bring up the dark times, the times when the pain had been so great you couldn't touch your teeth together without feeling your life turn upside down and your stomach and your soul with it, spinning and turning deeper and deeper into the shadows, and she would mention all this, that night and even more, and at that point you would be so boiled up you wouldn't go to the goddamn doc's with her, but it would ruin the whole day, it might ruin the whole week, because Mama would come home mad as the dawn and she would take those pills and pour herself a drink.

Then she would take them for spite, right in front of you and your little brother, slurping on that whiskey and staring at you with those red-hot eyes, and Kirb and me, trapped in that horrible silence, would be fighting off the flames of hell.

But back when we were eleven and ten, watching Mama sit next Dad, chatting cordially with Dr. Plum, who wasn't quite Dr. Plum yet, with that unequaled posture, so poised and light, we never saw the terrible and uncanny Mama, we didn't even know yet, that she existed.

Kirb and me went into Geoffrey's and sat at the bar. Having been there so many times when we were underage, we weren't able to sit up at that bar top and so now we weren't going to sit anywhere else.

Biggs came over and smiled those ivory whites at us, and without acting surprised or happy said, "Well that wind was strong today coming from the sea, but I didn't think for a minute it would blow in you two boys."

Then he put down the glass he was carrying and fixed his belt.

"Biggs, every time you are bartending the bar looks about ten times smaller than it really is." I answered, trying to match his even temperedness, but letting out a little of the excitement I had to see him.

"Hi Biggs," Kirb said.

"Well Hello Kirby," he said in that damn deep southern voice of his that sounded like he could be telling people which maple syrup to buy on TV or putting people to sleep on those relaxation CDs.

"I hope you are keeping this tall skinny brother of yours on the right path," Biggs said. "Because he don't look like much at a glance, but I know he's got *the* trouble in him."

"Mmm. Hmm." Kirb agreed.

I snickered.

"Two Cokes?" Biggs asked.

"Sounds good," I said.

"Actually Biggs," Kirb said. "I think I'll have a be-er!"

"Kirby!" I yelled as I hit him.

"The two cokes will be just fine, thank you very much. Who you got playing tonight anyway Biggs?"

"Julius Styles," he said.

"Styles? Never heard of him," I said.

"He's an old timer," Biggs said. "One of those fellas that's been on tour for fifty years. He's a decent guitar player and he has a hell of a voice. He's usually alone, but right now he's touring with a pianist, and this wicked sax player. He can *pl-ay* the sax. You'll see."

"Sax?" I said. "Oh! Boy! I guess the boss is coming down then?"

"He might," Biggs said. "I'm not sure. Y'all getting two full racks and two orders of cheese fries?"

"Extra sauce please," Kirb said.

"Extra sauce it is Kirby," he said. "Now y'all give me thirty on the food and Mr. Julius Styles should be out anytime to provide the entertainment."

"You're the best Biggs," I said.

We got our cokes and Biggs lumbered down to the end of the bar and chatted up a couple of Puerto Rican fellas I'd remembered seeing in the place a few times before. One of them saw me and tipped his fedora and I lifted my hand and waved.

"Julius Styles," I said to Kirb. "And a guitar player. You know how I love blues guitar."

"I prefer nineties music," Kirb said.

"I know you do, but c'mon Kirb, it's Geoffrey's! And we are getting ribs."

He let that sink in for a minute, before he said in that sometimes dreary voice of his "This place just always reminds me of Dad."

"Me too buddy," I said.

"I miss him," Kirb said. "He just always buy us ribs."

Kirb took a big long swig of his coke.

"Would you be very sad if I died Ernest?" he said.

"You know I would be Chubbs, c'mon."

And before he could ask me again, the lights dimmed.

"Hey, it's about to start," I whispered.

Julius and the band came out and the song started with a long piano solo. I recognized some of the notes as an old Al Green song, but there was something different about this version, it had a lot more loneliness in it. The guitar came screaming in and dropped down into those deep and colorful sounds. Then, like a murmur in a crowd, the sax grew into that low crawl of brass that only a saxophone can reach. The loneliness spread out and filled the room and it was a comfortable loneliness, a familiar one, like remembering the way my Grandma's house used to smell, or the way it felt so reckless and free when Kirb and me would race our bikes through the neighborhood, and it touched me in the place you think no one can ever understand, that place you thought was only yours, but hoped somebody would reach out and touch, to tell you that they get lonely too, and it's okay.

"Come on now!" Dr. Plum called out. "Come on!"

I peeked over my shoulder, and she waved and I waved back.

I thought then that *that* was the blues, *that* was New Orleans, where America finds its true self, the self hidden behind the facades of skyscrapers in New York, palm trees in Los Angeles, and the wave of houses that are the salt and sand of the Midwest. New Orleans is the magic city where everything comes together, where one can remember their past, where one can muse on their future, where one can recognize his loneliness as an old friend, all in a series of scattered notes, played in a small bar to a crowd of ten.

I imagined these places, all this, and even more, until eventually the music stopped. When the cloud of my vision was lifted, I saw Kirb's face lathered in barbeque sauce. He was chomping away at a bone. My ribs were in front of me and as I put my napkin in the collar of my shirt, I noticed there were five or six more people in the place, including some obnoxious young men that were playing pool and drinking whiskey.

Julius came up next to us and ordered a drink. He didn't sit down. His hands were shaking something fierce. I knew that shake well and I'd say it's really more a tremor than a shake. It's like the body is trying to pick up a vibration, like a divining rod doodlebugging for oil, except for this oil was the kind they fermented. Most people might see those tremors and think something sinister about Julius, they might assume something about his character, but I tried not to. Dad used to say that you can't make a good sailor by sailing on calm waters. Judging a man, he had said, was inviting your soul and your life into trouble, because judging someone was as bad as hating someone, and hate, Dad would say, is a sure way to get lost. After knowing the way people judged my brother, I'd be a damn hypocrite if I judged anybody else. I was sure that underneath his dry skin, that blue suit and trimmed black moustache, underneath those fingers that danced so lightly on the frets of the guitar and yet shook so violently, Julius had a sorrow, a deep mystery of pain that no one could understand. I guess we all have those sorrows and mysteries, and the tragedy is that we think they are our own and nobody else knows sadness. We all carry our burdens, our heartaches, and what we do with them, that is the measure of our greatness. Hearing Julius Styles play the piano and sing the blues was a greatness I was lucky to see after a long day of running around town.

Julius drank a full glass of scotch in one gulp, and you could see it move down his throat and into his hands, both of which immediately straightened out.

"That was a great set," I said to him. "I've never heard Al Green played with so much loneliness in it."

"Well thank you son," he said politely, and he held his glass up to Biggs, who poured him another scotch and he dispatched it just as quick as the first. Julius turned toward us, and he noticed Kirb, who was grinning from ear to ear.

"Good music," Kirb said.

"You like the blues son?" Julius said.

"It's okay," Kirb said. "I prefer nineties music."

Julius got a puzzled look on his face and the row of pecan-colored lines on his forehead crumpled up, as if contemplating some untamed riddle.

"Ninetees music?" he asked.

"Backstreet Boys," Kirb said. "Ninety-Eight Degrees, 'N Sync."

"I'm not following you son."

"They are names of pop bands from the nineteen-nineties," I said.

"My favorite Backstreet boy is A.J.," Kirb said. "Who's your favorite?"

"I can't rightly say," Julius said.

"A.J?" Chubbs asked.

Julius chuckled and took another drink.

"Well, if I had to have a favorite," he said, "I guess it would be him."

Biggs poured him one more and he seemed to sip it more slowly.

"I love the blues," I said.

"There ain't nothing more American than the blues," Julius said with the confidence of a couple glasses of Scotch behind him. "No one can touch it. No other country knows it like we do. I've heard some that can copy it real good, but none can master it. No sah, There ain't nothing like 'em. They give you everything you want and then they take it all away."

Here he paused.

"But the blues, son, the blues give a man a reason for waking up in the morning, putting your hat on, and looking out the window."

"Well, I'm sure glad that you came," I said. "Do you have a CD I can buy?"

"I don't. I don't record my music."

He finally sat down on the bar stool.

"You know," he said. "I remember seeing BB play when he was first starting out. Some smoky bar in Manhattan. I thought I'd heard the truth of heaven itself. I never was the same after that night. So, I worked real hard doing chores for my father for two or three months, and then I got me enough money to buy his record. I had kept BB's sound in my head. I kept it with me good and close, so when I put that record on my Daddy's record player and heard what came out, boy, I've never been so let down. It sounded nothing like what I had heard in that bar. There was something manufactured about it, and I decided then, that I wasn't never going to record when I played music. You see, you can't put blues in a bottle. They are like a fine wine or a glass of cognac, to get at their true nature, you got to let them breathe." And he said "breathe" real slow, like it was an action, not a word.

"The blues ain't always the same," he said. "Like the ocean, they can change direction at any time. One night you might play one song one way, and the next night you are going to play that same song different. It all depends on what you're feeling, you know? How the music speaks to you. That's what life is all about son, it's about listening for that music, and letting it speak to you. Every great blues musician never plays the same song twice. Now, don't get me wrong, I ain't saying that I'm great, but I keep trying to be. We can never achieve perfection, but we should never stop trying for it. Shoot, if I put out a CD, I'd have to put a new one out every week."

"Actually," I said, "I think that would be amazing. Nobody has ever done something like that before. You could put out a whole CD of just one song played thirteen or fourteen different ways. You could even have somebody maintain a blog for you and put performances up for the week. It would be a really good way to get your name out there."

Julius laughed and slapped his knee as if that was the funniest thing he had ever heard and then he put his hands back on the table and took a big gulp of scotch.

"Son," he told me, "anybody who gets into the blues doesn't do it for the money and he certainly doesn't do it to get known. Getting known is a sure way to stop that playful lady from coming and visiting your fingers every night on the guitar. And I need her. We all need her. Music needs a muse, just the same as any other thing in life. I play blues because my soul can't live without it. If you are doing something for any other reason, then you are wasting your time. I play the blues to show people how I feel, and if I'm lucky, for a moment or two, they feel it too, and there is no sum of money or amount of what they call fame that could buy that from me."

"Yep, Styles is a purist. I'll tell you what though, he could sure use another piano player." It was Geoffrey, he had walked up behind us and put his arm on my shoulder.

"That piano player is a young buck, that's for sure." Styles said. "But he's got the goods in him. He just needs a few years to find the music, or really, to let the music find him."

"I thought he sounded great," I said.

"Well, Ernest, you know you ain't got the ear," Geoffrey said confidently. "It's not for a lack of loving the blues. You love it so much that your ear has just been plain turned off to anything but the love. You get old enough, the blues become a vintage car, like an old Shelby Mustang or a Camaro. You only appreciate the best ones."

"And you got the ear Geoffrey" Dr. Plum said. "Nobody can deny that."

"It's only because I have a smoking hot wife with the brain the size of the Gulf of Mexico," Geoffrey said with a wink. "I have to keep up somehow."

She whimsically brushed her hand across his elbow before moving toward the stairs.

"I'll see yall later," she said. "I'm sure I have about twenty emails from faculty to answer."

Julius nodded and finished his drink.

"Well," he said, "I'm gonna go sit somewhere quiet and get ready for round two. It was sure nice talking to you boys."

"Thank you," I said.

"Bye!" Kirb called out.

Right then, I noticed Seth sitting in a corner reading, and his ears must have been burning, because he looked right at us, put on his hat, and came over.

"My Larsen boys!" he said. "I never tire of running into you!"

"Seth!" We both called out.

"What's good?" Geoffrey said.

Seth shook his hand.

"Good to see you."

"What did you think of that set?" Geoffrey said.

"He has a good sound. There's a lot of love in it."

"You got a hickey on your head?"

"Excuse me?" Seth said, puzzled.

"There weren't no love in that song," Geoffrey said. "The only man that ever played loved, real love, in a song was Dizzy Gillespie. Nobody else can pull it off. Most music is too simple for real love. Lost love? You bet! Love that ran away and came back? Absolutely. But the kind of love you are thinking? You are out of your mind."

"Charley Parker," Seth said slowly.

"Please!" Geoffrey said, throwing up his hands. "Dizzy was the only one could ever pull it off."

"Charley Parker," Seth repeated. "What does Dizzy know about love? He knows about loving music, yes, he does, but what does he know about showing music *through* love? Not as much as Charley Parker, you can be damn sure of that. You see, my friend, love is a surrender, that's what it's all about. Everybody keeps trying to make love a fight. 'Love is a battle' and 'relationships are hard work' they say, but what love really is, is a surrender of the ego. Once each person lets that down, willingly, then you can truly see the other person for what they are. The story isn't about two people anymore: it's just about one person, that's real love. Listen to the 'The Gypsy' and you can hear the ego flying right out of that saxophone and being surrendered willingly to the gypsy. Love is the mysterious dancer. You have to be looking for her. You have to surrender to her. You get it?"

"Hmm," Geoffrey mused. "You've got a point about love and you are right that Jazz is the preferred music style to show love, but I don't buy it from Parker. Gypsy is a seduction. It isn't about love at all. It's about lust. Lust can be real easy to confuse with love, there's lots of young men and women that does it, but it isn't the real thing. My sweet lady and I got the real thing, so I know. I can see your confusion though, but what you need to do is listen to 'All the Things You Are' and how it turns the slow notes into those jumping wails about one minute in. That's love, the celebration."

""All the things you are?" Seth said. "That was what Charley Parker called YATAG or you are the angel glow. He did a version of it too. Although, I do like the Gillespie version."

They seemed to reach a standstill and the chatter of the room got louder.

"Reminds me of Khalil," I said. "I told you both about him, didn't I?"

Seth and Geoffrey nodded somberly, and Kirby smiled.

"I miss Khalil," Kirby said. "I might want to see Khalil. Ernest, can we see him?"

"I haven't talked to him or seen him since-"

"Katrina," Seth said.

The word was strong. The chatter kept coming and we all checked in to the picture show of our own cold memories.

"Katrina," Geoffrey let out somberly.

All four of us had all been there. It was different for the ones who had stayed. We had seen it. We had lived it.

"You remember how grateful we all felt after it?" I asked. "Like every person we ever loved we got to see again for the first time? You remember that?"

"Of course."

"I'll never forget it."

"I just might want to see Khalil again Ernest," Kirby said. "When can we see him?"

"Well," I swallowed. "Why can't we just hold onto that feeling? Why does it fade away? Why can't we be grateful and happy like that all the time?"

We went back to the picture show, to the cold times. The images played in flashes. How the earth came alive, the transient leaves caressing the moist grass under my feet and the chilled air across my forehead colliding with my nose. The paste of the Tylenol stuck to the sides of my mouth. The skeletal tree arm overhead and the squawk of flying gulls, the cries of fleeing engines barreling by while the frantic footsteps walk up my earlobes. The spray. The eye. All the things we knew, gone. The voices forever garbled in the silence of water.

"God's a busy individual," Geoffrey said, finally proffering an answer.

"And he can't be running around putting a storm to your head everyday of your life to make your appreciate it. Look at Peter, he met the lord hisself and he still denied him when he got scared because he was caught up in that mind of his, the way we all get caught up. If I wasn't a God fearing Christian, I might ask God what he was thinking giving us things to get caught up in that take us away from His grace. But I know salvation is about faith. I have faith He knows what He is doing. It's hard being alive sometimes. But we got to do what we got to do, there ain't nothing more to it than that."

"Bullshit" said Seth confidently. "Pure bullshit."

Geoffrey stared at him with that what-in-the-hell-did-you-just-say look.

"That's a convenient story we tell ourselves, so we don't have to be responsible," Seth said. "We can be grateful if we choose to be, but we have to make that choice. What we have lost in our culture is mythology. All our myths get taken up by movies and series and cell phones. What we need are real heroes and heroines. Because you know what a hero does? What they *really* are meant to do? They strip away all the bullshit, so you are able to realize the beauty of the moment. A hero destroys the illusions in your mind so you can see that the perfection of life is right now, has always been *this* moment. That's a hero. That's what we need so we can hold on to what Ernest is talking about. It's the pause we take to think over the moments that we've had, that's philosophy. The living of it is poetry."

"Well, poetry and philosophy would be nothing without God," Geoffrey said.

"Maybe God is poetry and philosophy," Seth said.

They left it at that. Seth tipped his hat and called it a night and Geoffrey went over to talk to Julius.

"I don't know if I really want to sit around here for the second set, what do you think Chubbs?"

"Let's go," he said.

"Alright, finish your coke and we will," I said.

I ate my ribs, which were cold, but still had that nice smoky barbeque sauce that only Geoffrey could make. Kirb drank his glass down greedily and coke spilled over the sides of his mouth and down his chin.

I watched the three young men playing pool. I could hear them arguing and they sounded like they were in college. You know how those college types can be, they speak about people as if they weren't people, as if people were something apart from people, that the human heart itself represented some dire and final statistic, and that all we could do was sit back and analyze them in blues bars drinking too much cheap whiskey.

Sure, I get the scientific method and impartiality and all that, but a man's a man and a woman's a woman, and you just don't reduce people that way for your own amusement. That's one of the things that I respected the most about Dad, he didn't treat people like test subjects, he measured someone's worth by their actions. I swore to myself that I would never talk with such low honor when I went to medical school.

"People spent centuries believing in ghosts and voodoo and that leeches cured blood disease," one of them said, a tanned fellow in a yellow flowered shirt, with a thick build. He took a shot at a red pool ball, and it hit against the side of the green felt and bounced around the table.

"Now, we've realized how to actually cure disease and look how much better we are," he continued. "The world before contemporary science and medicine was a dark world my friend."

Then a short one, dressed modestly in a white collared shirt and some blue slacks, who wasn't playing pool at all, but was just sitting at a nearby table said, "Well, there's no denying that science has improved our longevity, all I'm saying is where has all that *truth* led us? People are even more restless now than when they did believe in that stuff. If anything, science has exacerbated the anxiety of the human condition. I bet there are more cases of anxiety, panic disorders, and acid reflux than any other time in history. It's an epidemic."

"That's only because we can diagnose those disorders," the tanned one argued as he took another shot at the red pool ball. "Who's to say that they weren't just as prevalent in the past?"

"Maybe," the short one said, clearing his throat. "But science really hasn't found a way to combat that stuff."

"Sure, they have!" the tan one said. "It's called medication."

"If you really believe that medication helps," the short one said. "I'm not arguing that sometimes it does, but what about the times it doesn't? Maybe this type of epidemic isn't solved scientifically. Maybe there is something beyond knowledge, something we can't quantify. I mean isn't that all we do anymore? Quantify! Quantify! Quantify! Everything has to have a numeric value or some sort of practical use and here we are calculating it like a damn walking computer. Technology isn't enhancing us anymore, we are enhancing technology, at least until it doesn't need us anymore. We just have to explain every little thing, and if you can't explain it, it's a rush to the computer to see who can. There's no struggle, no fight. I mean, don't you want to believe in some magic, some secret that we have in us that science can't explain?"

"What, like God?" the one playing pool scoffed. "Who cares about mystery, as you call it, when it's predicated on a lie?"

The third one, who wore a tight black t-shirt and was stirring his whiskey with his finger chimed in, "he's got you on that one."

"Got me how?" The short one asked. "I wasn't talking about God.

I'm talking about being content with what is. Saying that the stars are the stars and that they are beautiful because they are, not because I have some optic glass coldly pointed at them, but because I see them with my eye. That when somebody tells me a story about how the tree in their front yard grew up out of a rogue rainstorm that blew in seeds for it twenty years ago, I don't need to rush to my laptop to find out if that's possible, I accept the story for what it is: the experience. Truth isn't always the best thing for people, it can be very damaging. I don't know where people came up with this obsession with truth. We strut around demanding it, acting as if it is the one and only higher order, when truth in and of itself can be a very relative thing. Most of us concede our own truths," he said, and he sat back down and took a deep satisfied breath.

"So, what you're saying is that you'd rather be ignorant of truth?" the tan one said. "You'd rather be some retard with a brand-new shiny toy, sitting in a corner, slobber hanging out of your mouth, happy as a pig in shit? Is that what you are saying?"

That word again. That word seemed to echo every time I heard it, seemed to follow us everywhere we went.

Kirb dropped his coke, and the cup spilled the last of his soda on the ground. He looked at me, desperate and sad, pleading. He had heard it. I looked back at him as if to tell him I was sorry, but it was not enough, and he smacked his lips in his own tragic and defiant way.

I charged over and stood in front of that tanned young man. I gave him a good and courageous stare. I peered into his eyes, like a lion protecting his stretch of the plains. I waited.

"Can I help you with something?" he asked, and he said it full of that jest that being with a couple of your friends in a bar gives you, but that he wouldn't have said, had we met in the afternoon, just me and him.

"I think you should apologize to me and my brother," I said. I tried not to sound forceful, just frank.

"Oh, really?" he said, sarcasm rising like a tea pot on a hot stove. "And why's that?"

I grabbed his face and turned it to where Kirb was sitting.

"That word," I said, "is an ignorant and stupid word made to demean people with disabilities. Apologize!" I demanded.

He brushed my hand away and shook his head. "You have got to be kidding me," he exclaimed. "It's getting to where you can't even open your goddamn mouth without offending somebody. Listen, pal, I didn't mean it that way, okay?"

"In what other way did you mean it?"

"I just meant," he started. "I just meant stupid, like-"

"Like somebody who has a disability." I finished for him. "That's what it means. It doesn't mean anything else!" I snapped.

"It used to be a medical term for crying out loud!" he said.

"Used to be and are, are a million miles away from each other."

"C'mon Rick, just apologize," the short one said.

Their third friend had positioned himself behind me and he armed himself with a scowl.

"You know what?" The tanned man said. "No! No, I'm not going to apologize. This is ridiculous! You don't get to censor what I say. It's a free county. Free speech? Remember? If I want to say retard or retarded or whatever I want to say, I'll say it. I'm not apologizing, so you can go sit back down."

I was getting hotter than I thought I could control, but I looked back at Kirb and I remembered what Mama had said. I remembered that Kirb was watching, and the bar was watching, and even Julius Styles was watching now, so I was going to try and be civil.

"Listen, I understand y'all are having fun," I said. "But I need you to try and understand something else. My brother doesn't have the ability to just sit back and say that guy's ignorant, that you didn't mean to hurt him. Saying that word really cuts him deep, you know? It's the one thing in his life that makes him feel like he's less than everybody else. You can understand that, can't you? Now, please, do me a favor and apologize to my brother, it would mean a lot to me."

"Can you believe this guy?" he said, motioning to one in the black t-shirt. "He actually wants me to apologize for saying something's retarded."

"Rick," the short one said.

But it was too late. He kept saying it, and each time I heard it, I tried not to look at him. I looked at the pool sticks in their holders and the black circle was like a volcano, boiling hot and spitting and spewing magma all over the carpet. I looked back at his face, full of triumph and pomp, and as he smiled, he pushed out those puffy cheeks and he instantly resembled a red-faced mandrill baboon.

Staring at him I imagined all the times in his life he had probably said it, joking with his friends in bars, playing in the playground, trying to sound "adult" to his father. I imagined everyone I had ever heard say it. I imagined the comedians, the movies, television anchors, and how I heard it uttered on the street and how each and every time, I cringed. I even remembered how the president of the United States had made a crack about the Special Olympics, and how even though he had apologized, how it hurt me, how it hurt Kirby to know that it kept being used, that it could be used with no repercussions. Then, before I knew it, I swung one of the pool sticks across the middle of his chest, sending him to the ground, where I pounced on him. As I was punishing his face, his friend in the black t-shirt tackled me and got me real good on the right side of my cheek. Kirb rushed over and pushed him off me. The man in the black t-shirt turned toward Chubbs and he raised his hand, as if to strike him. As soon as I saw the look of anger in the man's eyes toward Kirby, I was on him, kicking his ribs and face and neck until Biggs pulled me off and carried me outside, my arms and legs flailing in the air.

"Get the hell out of here!" Biggs yelled as he put me down. "I can't believe that you would pull this shit in Geoffrey's bar you disrespectful son of a bitch! You can't just punch somebody out every time you disagree with them. You know, that temper is gonna to be the death of you one day!"

Kirb got in Biggs's face.

"Don't talk to my brother that way," he demanded.

Biggs threw his hands up. "To hell with both of you," he said, and he went back into the bar, slamming the door behind him.

Kirb walked over to me, offered his hand, and picked me up off the ground.

"Sorry buddy," I said. "I didn't mean for you to see that."

I sighed.

"I just couldn't let him get away with it. I tried. I tried to get him to apologize. I just know how much it hurts you."

Kirb looked down at the street. "I don't like it when they treat *my* people that way."

"I know," I said as I dusted myself off.

Kirb stood there with his hands in his pockets. He was giving it all a once over. He was deciding what it all meant. He smacked his lips to get back to the rhythm of his thoughts and I could hear Julius Styles start his second set. It was "Lousiana Blues" by Muddy Waters. I kept hearing "Be, be, behind the sun. Be, be, behind the sun." And I watched my brother try to make sense of the cruelty, of the misplaced hate, of the audacity of our egos, and of the collected moments of a word meant to destroy him.

He cleared his throat and asked, "Would you never make fun of me Ernest?"

"Never." I said. "Never."

"Be, be, behind the sun. Be, be, behind the sun."

Chapter Fourteen

The light of day had vanished, and the second face of New Orleans was on, all done up with its reds and whites and pinks. The neon lights and signs pulsated and pulled you into their dancing vortices, like a tornado in Oklahoma pulling in a curious bovine.

The longer you stared at it, the longer you yourself pulsated, until your mind numbed into a vibration and that vibration didn't do much else except walk towards it all, towards the beauty of the night, which in its own way is just as beautiful as the day.

We walked past an alley, and I could see two young boys about eleven or twelve putting some old newspaper and what looked like wooden chair legs into a rusted barrel. Those boys were about as grimy as I'd ever seen two boys and I made Kirb stop a second to watch them.

"You didn't put enough newspaper in there. How we supposed to have a proper fire?" One of them said, reaching down for some more newspaper.

"Goddamn!" said the other. "You don't know a thing, do you? What the truth is, is that you put too much newspaper in and then we don't have none for the next night. You just like the fires big, and I understand that, its warmer, but you don't think about nothing but how cold you gonna to be tonight. You don't think about tomorrow."

"Well," the first one said as he put some more newspaper on and lit the thing up. "We can always find more newspaper tomorrow. You act like we have all the newspaper on earth right here in this alleyway. This is New Orleans, there's enough newspaper here for a hundred nights."

"That may be true," said the other, "But there's been plenty of nights we burned up all the paper and couldn't find jack the next day and so you get cold and end up crying to me all night. 'I'm cold and I can't sleep' you say and then I have to sleep right next to you and you are just rubbing up against me all night and kicking and calling names out in the dark. And how the hell am I supposed to sleep with you rubbing up against me? So, I end up just watching the alley all night and trying to calm you down."

The first one blushed enough I could see it in the dark.

"I'm sorry about that," he said. "I was just cold is all. I told you I was sorry."

"Yeah, I heard you was sorry the first ten times," the other said. "But it just keeps happening. Anyway, ain't nothing good going to come out of me telling you about tomorrow because you are just going to keep putting that newspaper in night after night and it ain't going to change nothing."

The fire stoked up and it brought both of the boys a little farther away from the barrel and seeing their faces in the now dark alley, lit up by that red and orange glow, they didn't seem like boys, but like aged men, tired and listless, and I couldn't imagine where they had come from or what had brought them there, and I felt helpless. I mean I hear a lot of talk about being civilized. We think we are civilized and that being civilized is everything that a good man or good woman can be. But the more the world keeps going, the less and less the idea of being civilized becomes what I think we all wanted it to be. I mean how could these two boys be in this predicament, trying to warm themselves by this barrel fire, and less than ten miles away there are people driving cars that are worth more than Mama's house? I don't see a damn thing civilized about that. I guess that's the way it is with some things, they change, but we keep acting like they are the same and we keep pretending things like being civilized really exist, and I don't know whether it's the hope for something more or just stupid luck. Truth is, if being civilized meant helping those boys, I wasn't about to do that even if I wanted to.

The darker it got, the more the boys seemed like specters, the more Kirb and me seemed like specters, and all of us were performing some lawless rite of the night, milling around the fire, each breath a short chant, each movement around the barrel an incantation. As I pulled Kirb close to me, as we watched them, I imagined the flailing arms and elbows, the screams and demons and unruly souls. These were the streets where so many have fallen, not unlike a city that undertook a famous battle. This was the place of unearthly beings, where the veil between good and evil was permanently blurred. And if one didn't believe in God in this place, you believed in the Devil, or at least in the evil that he had made. This city, where even in an alleyway you were underwater, like a buried submarine, that if you put your ear up to the pavement it was an ancient seashell. You could hear the faint whispers of the fallen, could feel the breath in the chill on your neck and the bumps on your arms. This personage of the city persists, as if guarded by some sacred and everlasting rite to exist, refusing to be washed away, protecting its secrets and still forging a new wave of mysteries to give to the world, so that its breath can never be silenced. But what can you do in such a city when it is your home? You accept it for what it is, and you love it the way you love any other person, for its darkness and its light. You learn to love the fire. It hypnotizes you. The flames sway back and forth and back forth like a dancer's eyes, teasing you and getting just close enough to you and then pulling away. The flames are life, are the memories of times we've longed for but can never reach again. A part of us will always linger in the flame, in the heat and mess of living, but we can't touch it, it must stay there, flickering away under alleyway walls.

I left the haunted boys to their fire and floated down the street, back to the pulsating neon lights, back to the moon and the streetlamps and the night air hovering above your forehead like fog. As I watched the lights, the vibration took over again, and before I knew it, there I was, right in front of it.

Chapter Fifteen

You won't find it in the city or county phonebook, and I wouldn't tell you the address if you put a gun to my head. It's in the worst part of town, in a place most people have to get lost to find, but some of us just end up there, and there's nothing we can do about it. There were the burnt-out candlesticks lined up against the pavement like a shrine, the shreds of paper and plastic, the red and black graffiti, the cigarette butts, the sweaty men lurking in shadows waiting for an evening of fantasy, and the inescapable aroma of the sewer drain lingering outside the window.

There were no letters to mark this storied building, only a picture, a neon Geisha girl. Her hair looked like a giant seashell, coiled in flawless rows of black that were wound around two yellow hanging flowers. The classic white face was nearly foiled by the side of her eyes which had a red shadow that reached so far back it drilled into the grey bricks. Her red lips were bent into a sultry smile, and it seemed foreign to her ordered face and made her so seductive that the chopsticks in her hair were nearly popping out into the sky. The sign, like the contents of the building it colored, was an illusion. Anybody that had ever walked inside would tell you that the neon frame was the only Geisha girl you would ever see, because the building was full of everything but Geisha girls. And this is how it is with signs, with pictures, they show us what we want to see. No matter how many times we walk through those doors and are let down, we still look at those signs, and somewhere, inside us, there is always something that will believe today will be different. That was my feeling, walking up to the place the neighborhood simply called "The Geisha House."

For me it was more than a name or a house or even a neon sign. For me it was a place entirely made up of the dreadful past, a horrific hourglass turned over the moment you touched the rickety door handle and walked in.

In between us and the door handle was Lou Fitch. He was pacing outside like a vulture hovering over a corpse that had been picked over three or four times. That was Lou, he was always looking for a scrap.

"Cheese!" he said. "Kirby!" He ran up to us.

"How you doing Lou?" I asked with the sincerity that most of us don't usually use when we say something like 'How you doing' because we are just trying to say some extended version of hello, trying to move along the conversation to some other meaningful question or just to say some passing greeting on our way to something more important. But this time I really wanted to know how he was doing because I was concerned.

Lou had been the starting quarterback at Searidge when Kirb and I went to school and over the years had turned into one of the more famous drug addicts. The Geisha House was one of the five or six places you could find him, lurking around for some whiff of a way to make money. It was a great place for him to find the type of people he was looking for because most of the girls were on drugs themselves, so drug dealers stopped there often, fueling up the girls for their long nights of pleasuring, the way you might imagine a food delivery truck stopping by a busy restaurant.

Lou couldn't have looked more different. He had been handsome in high school. Back then he had long brown hair that he wore slicked and a fine alabaster complexion that made him the spitting image of a fancy porcelain doll. He had walked with supreme confidence, head high and teeth wide, and I remember he smelled of expensive soaps and lotions. Standing in front of me and Kirb, he was worn. He was sallow and thin, hair greasy and hidden under a filthy beanie cap with stitches that were coming undone. His face was covered in open sores, and he wore fingerless gloves. The smile that so many of the sophomore girls would have given their first born to see was yellowed and had thick black edges. The confident manner in which he used to carry himself had turned into a shifting anxiety, where he never seemed comfortable in any single moment, where he trembled violently and paced and paced and paced until you thought that the soles on his shoes were just going to fall right off and he was going to have to stop, or at least go get a new pair. But somehow in the untimely and yet ever-present universe, those soles kept holding, and so he kept pacing, walking away from whatever it was he was walking away from. Seeing him, I felt stumped. I remembered many a time I heard whispers of him, asking what had happened to that good Fitch boy who had the whole world in front of him and nothing to get in his way but himself?

"You know man," he sniffled. "I'm doing okay. How are you two? Looking sharp today! Looking sharp!"

"Thank you," I said, "We are good."

Kirb was a bit baffled by Lou. He watched him, waiting to hear more to find out if he wanted to talk to him or not.

"Hey man," Lou said looking down at the ground and shuffling his feet. "Hey, do you have a couple of dollars so I can get something to eat? I haven't eaten in two days."

Without hesitation I reached in my pocket and handed him a five-dollar bill. I know we didn't have much, that we were there to get money, but I had to do it. It was the honorable thing.

"A five? Wow! Thanks man!" Lou said, stuffing it sloppily into his shirt pocket. "It's so good to see you guys. I mean, how long has it been? Who knows man, but I remember a lot of good times we had in high school. Geometry class was a trip for sure man. You remember Mr. Graves? Crazy man, crazy."

"Yeah," I said. "I do remember. I remember every girl in there was half damn in love with you. Graves rightly adored you too."

He smiled and in that smile there was a bit of the boy that played football. It called out desperately to those of us who had known him as a lighthouse beacon on a dreary and foggy day.

"Well Graves was J.V. coach" he said. "So, you know. But do you got the time? I mean, do you have a watch or whatever?"

"It's somewhere around eight, I think," I said.

"Okay, what day is it, like Tuesday?"

"It's Thursday Lou," I said.

"Oh! Yeah! That's what I meant. Thursday. Thursday."

"Hey, do you know if Janus is up there?"

"Janus?" he asked, obviously confused.

I clenched my teeth. Janus, like all the girls at The Geisha House, had changed her name into what she thought would be some glamorous and fascinating flag, some new identity that she could play out night after night without having to remember who she was. All the things she had said, all her touches, all her gentleness were phantoms slipping away into the abyss of my memory, the only place where those parts of her still existed, where I kept them safe.

"Mercedes," I said with anguish. "Is Mercedes here?"

"Oh! Yeah!" he said. "Mercedes is here. I saw her earlier. Upstairs man."

"Thank you," I said. "I appreciate it. Listen Lou, we are going to get up there and speak with my wife. You take care of yourself."

I put my hand on his wrist.

"When was the last time you saw your mother?"

His face twitched and he shook his head as if there was water in his ear.

"I got to go," he said abruptly before disappearing into the catacombs of the New Orleans night.

As Kirb and I walked through the black gate, passed the large neon Geisha girl, I thought about all the Lou Fitches and Januses of the world.

About how there is a whole generation of young men and young women like Lou and Janus who somebody loves and wishes would come home. How it all starts with their hurt legs and back spasms and depressions and how they get to taking pills to make the hurt go away and soon enough it's just cheaper to buy something off the street and shoot it into your arm.

That's the science of it all, the statistics and the psychology and the addictions. But somehow science doesn't explain it. It doesn't explain how human beings are the only species of living things, that not accounting for survival, continues to do things they know will hurt them. I guess truth be told we love the suffering just as much we love the not suffering. I can't rightly say why anyone would want to suffer, but I haven't met a man or woman yet that hasn't found a fondness for suffering in one way or another. I know I got used it. I got used to the screaming and the fighting. I felt something. With all the pain that we had been through, Janus and me, it seemed that neither of us had felt anything, except grief, and so feeling, even if it was just being angry, was at the least, something.

"What's wrong with him?" Kirb asked.

"He's on drugs buddy," I said.

"Hmm! I might want some drugs!" Kirb said.

"Chubbs, seriously, not right now."

"Okay," he said, and he put his head down, resigning to the fact he wouldn't get an answer why any more than I would get an answer why Lou had given everything up to be a street rat.

So, we stood in front of that ghastly and threadbare door, pieces of wood sticking out of it, and I touched the doorknob. As I stepped in, I knew that there was no turning back, that I was going to have to face every terrible thing I had ever known.

The "Mama" who noticed our presence but didn't look up from the paper she was reading, hit her buzzer bell, and yelled "Rine up!" in broken English.

They called her The Mama or Mamasan, but I wouldn't say that to her if my life depended on it. She was the owner and operator of the Geisha house, a fat Japanese woman with golden colored skin and one of the cruelest stares I have ever seen on a person, because it was cold, it didn't see the difference in anything. She stared at you the way she might look at a broken windowsill or a tired old alley cat. And what made the stare so chilling was that I knew it. It was a stare Janus had perfected. She became the stare. She became real smart at giving pain, so smart she didn't even know it, it was just a part of her. And somehow in that smart way of hers, she made it seem like kindness, like she was doing a big favor for you.

It started small and easy, a comment about what she thought you should say to your brother or how she thought you could make better sales if you listened closer to people and she might slip in that you are too old to be living with your mother or that you didn't really fill out the way you should have after your twenties. It was in this way that the Mamasan stare became the drapes of my deprived dreams.

No matter what time of night or day we came, the Mamasan was sitting in the same place with the same glasses and the same paper.

As she pushed her glasses to her forehead, she saw me and said, "Oh, It's *you*."

She hated it when I came in and I hated her.

"I'm here to see my wife," I said.

The Mamasan flipped her paper over. The pitter patter of feet rumbled over us like rolling thunder and before you could say Jack Sprat five or six girls ran up and formed a line to face me and Kirb. Each one of them was dressed in lingerie and they must have all had the same makeup artist because each wore a heap of blue and green eye shadow with long imitation eyelashes. They stood proud and slowly arched their backs, stretching out their frames like slender gazelles, aware of every posture and pose, of every muscle and bone, ironing out every little thing in their body, a steam press getting the creases out of an expensive suit. The last thing to straighten was their teeth and as they smiled at us, so coy and seductive, gazing with that pure desire, the desire that somehow could devour anything, I thought then, that maybe they weren't gazelles after all, maybe they were cheetahs and there was no way to escape, there couldn't be.

"Sexy!" Kirb said and he rubbed his body, smothering his chest with his hands and sticking out his tongue.

The girls tried to keep straight faces, but they couldn't help but snicker. I even thought I saw out of the corner of my eye, the Mamasan crack a smile for just the smallest instant.

It was difficult if not impossible to look at those girls and think about a damn thing but what they were offering, but after searching desperately for Janus and not finding her in the lineup, I found her somewhere else. I found her in those lost and empty eyes, those tired faces, those frail souls held up by a backbone and not much else. I'm sure, like everyone, they had once dreamed. That among them were failed ballerinas or engineers or lawyers. That they once had their weddings and children all planned out at thirteen, that they had skipped rope in a neighborhood much like mine, had ran through the sprinklers with boys much like me. Sure, on the surface you might see those seductive eyes just waiting to draw you in, but somewhere behind those eyes is somebody's little girl and somebody's sister and even somebody's wife.

"Out of here girls!" the Mama barked. "False alarm."

And with that, the pitter patter escaped until it was back over our heads, and in a spell, it was silent.

"You know where she is," the Mama said.

Kirb and me climbed the stairs, past the cinnamon smell and pink numbered doors, past the Egyptian linens hanging from the doorways, and into the narrow and remote hallway, the place where I had learned shame, where I could not hide from what had happened, where I felt eyes from peepholes glaring at me, sneering.

Halfway to the room there was a skinny man with stringy long hair wearing the dirtiest suit I have ever seen, which was two sizes too big for him. He sat in a miniature chair outside one of the rooms and as we passed him, he smiled, and we could see he was missing his front teeth and I felt a pity for that man, a disgust, and an anxiety all at the same time.

I went to that most cursed of rooms, room 124, and knocked, but there was no answer. I knocked again and after not getting an answer a second time I opened the door. Janus lay on her twin bed in her uncouth attire, red nighty halfway off her shoulder, her left breast out, nipple smashed into the flowery bed spread and lipstick smeared across her cheek and neck. The soft and intricate spirals of her red nighty pained me, as if something so delicate could be so violent.

She was groaning and had that wretchedness on her face I had seen so many times before, and it was causing her eyebrows to clinch and her forehead to wrinkle up.

"Baby," I called out softly. "Baby, it's me your husband," and I sat down on the bed.

"Chubbs, close the door," I commanded, and he did.

I took Janus by the hand.

"It's me Ernest. How's my girl?" I said and she tossed and turned as if she was fighting the darkest and most vile demons that anyone had ever known.

Then, suddenly, she seemed to break out.

"Ernest? Ernest is that you?" she said.

I thought maybe that she had opened her eyes, but I couldn't tell because she had so much makeup on them and there wasn't enough light in the damn awful room she lived in.

"Yeah, it's me baby," I said.

"Where's Adam? Bring me our boy Ernest. Bring our boy to his Mama."

"He's gone," I said, and I said it with the last breath of dignity I felt I had left.

"No, he's not!" she screamed. "You bring me our boy goddamnit! You bring me my boy right *now* so his mother can hold him!"

"Alright now. Alright now. I'll see what I can do," I said. "Just calm down. Just calm down now," and I pushed my fingers through her hair, and like a wild mustang she bucked me and bucked me until eventually a calm came over her, and I could see lingering beyond her mask of anguish, the same spry young girl from the swamps. Fighting with all she had, was the mother, Adam's mother. I thought of the first time I saw her hold him, that laughter, that innocence, that joy.

Then it all came down. I couldn't stop it anymore. I couldn't pretend that it didn't happen. I couldn't hold the levees. I couldn't stop the water from rushing in and breaking me. It was there. It was all there. Every moment and every dark thing I had ever known was back in my mind. It was like a big spool of twine. You kept thinking that even though you had used up some of it, it was just going to keep coming and coming, and then before you knew it, all you had left was the spool and nothing to show for it. Yes, the fog that we had been living under was lifted and there I was again at the beginning of it all, sitting at a desk in the clinic.

Chapter Sixteen

The New Orleans Radiology clinic was a quiet place at night, a place where you were forced to confront yourself, to confront all the fears and anxieties you tried so damn hard all day trying to run away from. We've got real good at running away, us human beings, and the more time goes by, the more we invent devices to keep us busy, because if you are nice and busy, you have no time to think. It seems in this highly advanced society of ours that we still haven't gotten over that ancient fear of being alone. We exhaust every energy we have to keep us from facing that all too familiar and yet still remote person that stares back at us in the mirror every morning we get up, wondering, in the same way most of us wonder: how'd I get here and what am I going to do about it?

Sitting alone behind that desk in the deserted office, with nothing but big windows that were black with night, I was forced to confront a lot of things. I was forced to find out if there was anything in me worth knowing, if all the events I had experienced, that were still swirling around in that place called the past, had done anything meaningful for me or anybody else, and if those events were going to mean something to the right now and the yet to come.

Just when I'd get good and lost in the fancies of the future, playing out finishing medical school and saving strangers' lives, I'd get interrupted by the old beige desk phone.

Brrring! Brrring! Brrriing! That's how it rang. That's how it bounced around the abandoned office complex after eight o'clock, against the black and white tiles, against those infernal white walls, off the green pipe looming over the coffee maker, off the giant ceiling fans, off the cone-shaped lobby lamps, until it just rattled around in my head. It didn't stop ringing. It couldn't stop ringing. It had to ring, and I had to answer it. I had to answer it because we needed the money. Janus and I spent all the savings we had on our wedding, and we were just about to welcome a brand new baby boy.

"New Orleans Imaging, this is Ernest," I would say, hearing the words come out of my mouth, but not understanding them as mine, because they had been given to me by someone else.

Doctor Nisha Ghosh gave me those words, with strict instructions on how to deliver them: to be professional and courteous, to sound interested but not too familiar, and to use the same tone every time I answered the phone.

Dr. Ghosh had known my father when she was in med school. He had mentored her into the community of New Orleans, where she held a respectable imaging clinic that handled most of the x-rays in and around the city for radiologists and hospitals. I answered the phones at night and helped Mama with Kirb during the day. Dr. Ghosh paid me a decent wage and was understanding if I had to run home for a minute to be with Janus, as long as I came right back. I was grateful for the work, but I felt I was spending too much time away from Kirb and my wife, and I was waiting anxiously to hear about the baby, and so I took that baggage with me and added it to the beige phone, so that the ring became more than a ring, it picked and prodded, eroding me into a frenetic mess.

I remember telling Janus about it.

"It's driving me nuts!" I had said. "I don't hear the ring of the phone anymore. I only hear one note. That one damn note over and over again. It rings and rings and rings until I just want to scream!"

She flicked her curled red hair playfully and put her hand on the side of my neck.

"You have to find your melody," she had said.

"My melody?"

"Oh, Ernest," she had said in that sincere way of hers, that way where she was so sure of it all, and the fact I wasn't sure was endearing to her somehow.

"Just imagine that one note as a small part of a big, beautiful melody, something that gives you peace, something that reminds you of me and Kirb and the bump."

She smiled and rubbed her belly.

"We will always be here," she said, "and anytime you start feeling like the world is coming right down on top of you, you can find us in that melody."

Then she moved her hand from my neck to the left side of my chest.

"I will always live in the melody of your heart," she had said.

I was powerless, too weak to do anything but what she asked. The next night at work, I listened to the ring of that beige phone until it became that one note, and then I imagined some mixture of blues guitar and piano around it, and the note spiraled in and out of the rest of the music and then waltzed on the desk and then onto my arm and all the way up my shoulder, lively like a sax, a Coltrane sax. In my right hand I held a pencil, and it was as if I was the very first conductor of the blues symphony in G minor, so I swung the pencil back and forth to the tune of the melody of Janus, Kirb, and the bump.

As I was enjoying my newfound melody, I realized I was forgetting something very important: I needed to answer the phone. I chuckled a bit at this thought and then happily picked it up.

"New Orleans Imaging, this is Ernest," I said, for the first time feeling as if I used my own voice.

"She's in labor son."

It was Mama.

I had been so caught up in getting rid of that ring I had nearly forgotten. Two or three weeks prior I held out hope that every ring would be *the* ring, but I found out with hope came disappointment. It was one of those things where you think about something so much, where you keep milling it over and over again in your mind, as if you could make the thing happen just by willing it, and then, when your mind takes a moment to forget, to think about something as trivial as how much the ring of the phone irritates you, it happens.

"I'm coming," I had said, and with that oneness of purpose, I picked up my coat.

I ran straight to the bus stop, shoes clapping against the sidewalk, sweat pooling on the sides of my face, and before me, I didn't see the blur of buildings, I didn't hear the clatter of cars with their engines pumping and grinding; all I could envision was him.

I tried to picture his face. Would he have my curved nose? His mother's pouty lips? What would his tiny fingers look like? Would they have any trace of Dad's time-worn and soft wisdom? What would his feet and miniature toes look like all wiggling and red? I was so excited that I couldn't help but call out, "I'm having a baby!"

Looking around for a response, I noticed that my sound didn't echo, that there was no raucous stir and so I nodded my head. It knew. New Orleans, in its silent way, seemed to accept it, knew that it too had another son on the way, a son it could call its own.

When I got to the hospital, it was full of people, and they all were walking in different directions, some going toward life, some going toward death, and it didn't take a salesman to understand that all you had to do was look at their faces to tell which way they were going.

I went to the gift shop and after passing over the usual white teddy bears and balloons, I found a charming plush pelican. Its large grey throat and unassuming black eyes only added to the gold crown on his forehead. He was so stout and simple, so funny with his wide webbed feet. It was a perfect first gift.

The hall was full of that oppressive noise that can bear down on a man if he listens to it for too long, but I couldn't make out a word, all I could understand was the beat of my heart, pounding and pounding and pushing me forward toward those happy and anticipating faces, all headed up in the elevator to the beginning.

When the doors of the elevator opened, I noticed that even though it was on the sixth floor, the maternity ward felt like a dungeon, in the way that all hospital floors feel like dungeons with their poor lighting and thick walls painted sterile white that doesn't say anything about life coming into existence, or even about it going out, it just says "antiseptic". If it wasn't for the big "6" painted in the hallway in blue and pink, you might have thought you were on the cardiac floor or transplant unit.

I found out from an energetic older woman at the desk that Janus was in room 306. I walked as fast as I could down the hall. Kirb was standing outside the room smacking his lips and staring at God knows. When he saw me, whatever trance he was in, lifted.

"Ernest!" he said loudly, and I gave him a big hug, a hug so big I picked him up off the ground.

"You might be a dad," he said.

"Well, you are going to be an uncle!" I exclaimed.

"Really?" he said, perking up a little.

"Yeah, buddy. And you better be a good one too. You're the only Uncle he's got."

I took his hand.

"Shall we?"

We opened the door and went and in. If the maternity ward was a dungeon, the rooms were like terribly lit attics with the shades pulled down. There were two dull lights on the wall above Janus, who lay there, eyes closed, so fragile with her sweaty cheeks and her light blue hospital gown that I nearly forgot the earth was round.

"Where's my boy?" I asked through the fog of darkness, not really to a specific person, but just speaking out loud.

"They are cleaning him," Mama said, and she stepped out from the shadows.

For a moment, I was at a loss for words. She looked great. She had that young and hopeful look like before Papa died.

"Can I see him, Mama?" I said.

And there was that voice! That voice I had almost forgotten, the voice I used to use to ask Mama to take the crusts off of my peanut butter sandwiches and if I could take my bike down to the neighbors to play.

"The doc said about five minutes," she said.

I turned to Janus and sat down in a chair beside her bed.

"How's she doing?"

"She's tired, so tired," Mama said, and she stood behind me and put her hand on my shoulder.

"You spend all your breath pushing out a baby boy," Mama said. "It tests every limit on God's green earth, but there is no pain more worth it. I remember when I was lying in a bed like that, waiting for the doctor to bring you in."

She leaned up and looked at the ceiling.

"You were the most beautiful boy New Orleans had ever seen. I haven't seen a baby like you since. You had curly hair and everywhere you went, people thought you were a girl, because you had those soft features and big eyelashes. You were so handsome that I had three complete strangers on three complete separate occasions ask me if you were the Gerber baby."

"What about me?" Kirb said. "Was I handsome?"

"Yes, my darling," Mama said. "Just like your brother."

"I was handsome Ernest, like you."

Mama rubbed my shoulders a bit and it felt good. It felt like, for the first time, I had a mother, someone who wanted to ease my suffering a bit, someone who cared about me, if just for a moment, more than they cared about themselves.

"You still are the handsomest boy I know," she whispered in my ear.

"Thanks Mama," I said.

I saw Janus stir a bit, so I took her hand in mine.

"Baby?"

She opened her eyes, and she strained a bit as she did it, they looked so tired and heavy.

When she saw it was me talking, she used whatever energy she had left in her to smile. Her hair was matted down to the top of her head and drops of sweat were on the tip of her nose.

"Ernest," she said in the most tender and joyful of ways. "Ernest, you wouldn't believe it, but we made the most beautiful baby you have ever seen."

I looked over my shoulder at Mama and she winked.

"He looks just like you Ernest."

She paused.

"He's so tiny!"

"I can't wait to meet him," I said. "Are you doing okay baby?"

"I'd do it a thousand more times if we could have a thousand more like him," Janus said.

She stared into the room as she said it and let me tickle her hand. I rubbed my thumb over her knuckles and then she asked, with genuine wonderment, "Can you believe it? I mean, can you believe you are a daddy, Ernest?"

I couldn't believe it. I couldn't believe that something so wonderful could happen to somebody so ordinary. I was just a man, just someone struggling to find happiness like everybody else, working and laughing and sometimes bleeding, and who said I deserved anything, let alone a beautiful wife and a baby to boot, but there I was, with both. That's what pure happiness is, it's a state of shock, one where you can't believe your luck.

Then he came in, held in the arms of a male nurse, a big Nigerian fella, tall and slim, grinning ear to ear.

"Mr. Larsen?" he asked in his charming accent, charming because it was lively and happy and light.

"That's me sir," I said.

"Okay 'daddy'," he said and then that big and tall Nigerian fella walked over and handed me my boy. I felt strange holding him at first. He was so much lighter than I had imagined, and his little red face was so relaxed and complete. I took the blanket off of his feet and checked to make sure he had all his toes and then I counted all his fingers before I pulled the small blue hat off of his head and lightly fluffed his jet-black hair.

"I found it baby."

"Found what?" Janus said.

"I found my melody," I said. "I thought for sure I'd found it earlier tonight, but now I know I found the real thing, right here."

"We'll always be here Ernest," Janus said. "Me and your baby boy."

I felt strange when she said that, like I was watching someone else's life unfold. I didn't know how I was going to do it. I didn't know how I could feed and clothe him, how I could keep him safe from the madness of the world. I didn't know how I was going to be there, how I could be there every moment that he needed me to be, and I almost panicked because of it. But what I did know was that whatever it took, I would do it, that holding him was the most perfect moment I had ever experienced and that somehow it made every moment of my life, every mistake, every tear, every victory, every battle, worth it.

"Have you thought of a name yet?" the nurse asked.

"Adam Jacob Larsen." I said confidently.

"Adam?" the Nigerian mused. "You can't go wrong with that. That is the first name the world ever knew. God came up with that name, and he's not known for being wrong."

He smiled that big and wide smile of his, in a way that I hadn't seen many folks smile in New Orleans or any other place in America and then clasped his hands together, said something in his native tongue that I only understood as some kind of mystic blessing and then added, "Now, I got to go see some other patients, but you buzz me if you need me, okay?"

"Thank you," I said.

Then I turned to the boy. I kissed his soft rosy cheek.

"Hello Adam," I said. "Do you know who I am? I'm your daddy. Yes sir! I am your daddy and I've been waiting a spell to meet you."

I paused, overwhelmed.

"I love you boy. I love you so much," I said, and I gave him a kiss on his other cheek.

He seemed unaffected by my words. He yawned and turned over in my arms. I straightened out his hat and I felt connected to him in a way I had never felt connected to anyone before. It wasn't brotherly love like with Kirb, and it wasn't romantic like Janus, it was more protective, more deep. We shared something, that little guy and I, something that ached in the bottom of my spine and twitched in the knuckles of my fingers, some force that's impossible to put into words. You might argue it was biological, some need built in me to protect my offspring, but I felt it so strongly. It was more than that, I swear it was.

I helped Chubbs hold Adam for a few minutes and Chubbs's hands didn't look too comfortable, but his face did, and he quietly smacked those lips of his as he rocked Adam back and forth.

Janus was asleep. She had done her work and now it was my turn. Chubbs gave Adam to me and left with Mama to go home.

For a while I just sat staring at Adam. Even his breath was a mystery to me, not the process behind it, but just that he was capable of it, that I held in my arms, a boy of mine and Janus's creation, and that he breathed. His nostrils moved as he took in air!

The nurse came back and took him, and I slipped away into the dream that is morning, smiling proudly in the hospital chair, as I nodded in and out of sleep.

When Janus woke up, we played with him and cooed at him and made silly voices with him as every man says he's never going to do and then ends up doing anyhow. Then we took it all in until morning quickly became afternoon again and I went home and got ready for work.

Janus had plans to try and bring him home by the time I got off in the morning or shortly thereafter and I couldn't wait to get him back to the house where we could get him in some proper clothes, and I could start showing him everything I'd ever loved.

Before I left, I talked briefly to the doctor, and he assured me that we had a nice healthy boy and Janus was recovering just as she should be.

I went to work drunk on Adam's touch, his eyes, his chest contracting and filling up with breath, taking the world in and letting it back out. It was all so effortless.

When I got to work, I picked up my pencil right where I had left it and began again the music of Kirb, Adam, and Janus. There was no boredom now, no irrational phone ringing, only them. I answered the phone cheerily and often and even tidied up the desk.

About halfway through my shift I noticed someone trying to get into the door. Alarmed, I walked over and peeked out at the figure, who was savagely jiggling the door handle, but all I could see was a fury of brown hair and red fabric tossing back and forth like an outlaw gale blowing a mess of leaves across a neighborhood street.

I tried another angle and I saw that it was Mama. What was she doing out there? She'd never been to my work in her entire life. Maybe Janus had gotten out early or something, I had thought.

I opened the door and Mama stumbled in. She looked at the floor, holding her purse so tight the tips of her fingers were white. She didn't speak. She peered out over my shoulders like she was trying to find somebody in a crowd, and I was standing in her way.

"Mama?" I said.

She just kept looking over my shoulder! And as I tried to search her face for some kind of clue into what she had to tell me, I noticed that she didn't look at all like she had the night before. Mama was as pale as an ivory dragon figurine on a fall street-walk sale. Her eyes were puffed up and those hands of hers were trembling against her purse, making a snapping sound, and I wondered if she might drop it.

"What is it, Mama?" I said. "Dear God! What is it?"

"Ah, honey," she said.

Then I heard it. Without her saying another word, I knew something was terribly wrong. She had spoken in a way I had never heard her speak before, with pity. In fact, I had never heard anybody speak with more pity in my entire life than when Mama said those two words.

"It's Adam," she said, and before she could say anything else, I dropped down on my knees, right there in the middle of the office lobby and wept.

"Nooooooo!" I wailed in agony. "Dear God, no."

I can't explain what happened next because there aren't words that can rightly tell you what I felt. The closest I can come is to say that it was like waking up in the morning and going to look at the ocean and suddenly finding out that it's not there anymore. That somehow the universe swallowed every drop of water and every fish and every crustacean and algae and coral. All you have left is the gaping hole where the ocean used to be and nothing you can tell the universe or yourself will ever get it back for you.

It took a while for me to stop crying because it wasn't a voluntary cry, it just came out, until it didn't come out anymore, and then Mama put me in her car and drove me to the hospital.

She spent the drive squawking away about life and death and the divine purpose and how in the cosmos of time this all made sense, how it was tragic but necessary and I was meant to learn something that only God could teach me, but I didn't listen any of it. I *heard* it, but I didn't listen. There was nothing she could say. There was so much pain inside me I didn't even feel like I was a human being anymore, I just felt like some imposter that was watching a human being. I watched myself sitting there in the car with my mother. I watched myself look out the window. I watched myself trace the veins in my hand with my index finger.

When we got to the hospital and found Janus, I watched myself watching her as she sat in a hospital chair, rocking back and forth in that cold and dark room. I said nothing and neither did Mama. I didn't even think to ask where Kirb was, although later I found out Mama had taken him to Seth's. I just stood there, waiting for something to happen, hearing the low whir in the room that I couldn't decipher. It was a magnetic noise, a soft hum. I stepped a little closer to her and then I knew what it was, Janus was singing.

Here comes the Sandman, stealing so soft, stealing along on the tips of his toes, and he scatters the sand, with his own little hands, to the eyes of the sleepy children.

She stopped and reached inside a blanket she was holding, and I guessed that she must have folded up the blanket and was pretending to sing to him, imagining that he was there. Then, she sang some more.

Go to sleep my baby, close your pretty eyes, that lady moon is sleeping throughout the darkened skies, the little stars are peeping, to see if you are sleeping. Go to sleep my ba-ah-ah-by. Close your little eyes.

I watched Janus rock that bundle in silence. I felt that to interrupt her would be to interrupt the natural order of life.

Mama put her hand on my shoulder.

"They are going to want him soon," she said.

"What do you mean?" I said.

"She can't stay with him much longer son, it ain't healthy."

"Wait, she's got him? I thought-"

Mama pointed towards Janus, and I saw Adam's pale finger outside the blanket, and I knew then that what was left of my boy was getting put to sleep one last time by his mother, rocked from this world to the next.

"Let her be," I said, and I led Mama into the hall.

"Do you want to hold him one last time?" she asked.

"I can't right now Mama." I said, feeling nothing but confused, numb, angry.

"I understand," she said softly.

"I want to know what happened."

"Maybe we should go sit down somewhere and have a drink."

"No!" I said. "You tell me here!"

"Okay. Okay," she said. "Your wife was talking to me about monarch butterflies and how her and her granddad would watch for them in the fall and catch them off of the bridge by Lake Pontchartrain and then they would stick a pin in 'em and put them on boards, sometimes while they were still alive. Can you imagine that? So, she'd been having all these terrible nightmares about butterflies chasing her around New Orleans screaming 'Help me! Help me!' and she was getting to the point where she didn't even like talking to her own grandfather because it reminded her of those goddamn butterflies so much, and so she came up with a plan and she was about to tell me what it was when I swear on heaven above that she stopped dead in the middle of telling me and we both looked up at the clock.

"Ernest, I will never forget how we both looked at that clock and it said nine-eighteen and I felt it. I felt the darkness of something coming toward us and I looked at Janus and she felt it too and we just sat staring at each other, both of us afraid to say anything, lest it came true, and then the doctor came in. I've never seen a man standing up that looked so sick, and he spoke with a boy's voice that said 'Oh my God. My God. Oh my God' and then Janus said 'What? What is it?' and he just kept looking sicker and sicker and I thought he was going to melt away onto the floor, but he spoke in this trembling voice, son, this awful and trembling boy's voice and he said, 'There was a student nurse and she was feeding the baby, and he choked.' 'Is he okay?' Janus asked him and he just said it again, 'He choked. He choked.' And then he put his hands against the wall and slid down to the floor and he sobbed and sobbed. Son, I ain't seen a thing like it before.

"Then a nurse came in and she told Janus and me that Adam was dead, and Janus cried a terrible cry and she could scarcely breathe right, she was retching, and wailing, and carrying on, and I was worried if she was going to just drop dead right there. When she calmed down, she asked to see him and that's when I came and got you."

"Choked?" I thought to myself. It didn't make sense. I had just held him. I had just felt his heartbeat in my fingertips. Dead? How was it possible? I thought of God and heaven and how I guess it makes sense to say to some people that God needed another angel and that he took him to test me and my family like Mama had said, but the way I saw it standing on that polished white floor, with Mama next to me like a marble statue, and the stench of chemicals seeping into every damn thing, there wasn't any sense in death. Death is hard to deal with when you are prepared for it, but this was something else, a transient evil that had been floating around the earth and decided to drop on us at just that moment.

It took nearly three hours to get Adam away from Janus and I was the one who had to do it. The cold corpse lay heavy on my hands. I didn't want to look down at his face, but I had to see him. I had to see that he was my son and that the life had indeed left him. His face was peaceful, but bloated and wrinkled and I could tell his eyes were starting to sink and I remembered seeing Papa and how his eyes were sunk in and it made sense to me that God would take a man's eyes first because your spirit or whatever you become needs to see just like anything else and if one energy becomes another energy like all those smart folks at the college say, then why not an eye for an eye.

I carried my boy. I held his face to mine, and I put our foreheads together and I closed my eyes. It was the last moment I spent with him before the funeral.

When I found Janus, she was sitting in the hallway, looking as uncomfortable in her own clothes as I'd ever seen her. I went to hug her, but she wasn't having it.

"I can't," she said. "I just can't."

I shrugged it off.

"You ready to go home?" I said.

"He was still warm," she started to sob. "He just looked like he was sleeping."

Chapter Seventeen

As the fog of the moment came comfortably back, I heard the chatter from the room next door and drank in the smell of cigarette smoke that rose from the ashtray.

I could hear Janus struggling to breathe, like a piece of plastic was stuck between her throat and lungs. It was an awful sound, wounded and fragile, and yet so powerful that it sliced through the air like a carving knife through a cured ham.

I opened my eyes and carefully rolled her onto her side. The noise didn't stop, but it slowed down enough to where you could actually hear breath travel to her chest.

I remembered when Janus and me stopped talking. How we learned to talked only in the way that people talk to reaffirm to each other they are both still alive. We said 'hello' and 'how are you' and 'what you been doing today,' but we never said anything more. It was a full silence, a powerful silence. It is these things we know without saying that break us. We pretend they didn't happen, that they couldn't have happened, and this leaves us with no explanation of why we are broken. But the gears keep turning despite our silence. The gears keep moving, clicking away into each other, like the tick of a grand and awful pocket watch. And as much as us being silent was a protest against the gears, a defiant shout into the meaning of all that had happened, or lack thereof, it didn't stop the watch from ticking or those gears from pushing and pushing and pushing along.

Janus had put up Adam's baby picture on the mantle in Mama's house, and it stood there, looming over us like a shrine. When the room was full, we all tried not to look at it, but when we were alone with that picture, we coddled it, talked to it, we even kissed it. It became the focal point of the room without anybody ever acknowledging that it was. There were times when just seeing it, I shuddered. I still couldn't believe that he was gone. So, because I had to live with the pain anyway, I played the moment over and over again in my mind. Mama coming to work, me going to the hospital, Janus rocking him to sleep.

I started making up alternate versions. In some, I went to the hospital early and asked to see him. The student nurse went for a walk and had a cigarette and Adam came home with us. In others she choked another baby, and I tried not to feel better about it, but I couldn't help that I did. Sometimes, I didn't even leave the hospital, I stayed and watched over him all night. In one, I told Mama to just take him and run, to run without looking back, to run and run until she got home. She was on strict instructions to lock all the doors and not let anybody in but me. I would get him to safety. I would hold him so tight. I would protect him. But, no matter what I dreamed, no matter how many times I played it out in my head, he always ended up in that tiny coffin, dressed in that tiny black suit, wearing those tiny black shoes.

Janus fell into a deep depression. I tried everything to get her to snap out of it. I bought her flowers and took her out to movies, and I took her back to the beach a few times to try and recapture our magic night. I even suggested that maybe she should go back to school to help get her mind off things, but nothing shook that austere face, lips clenched so tight no air could get in, with the steel jaw that held her grimace in place like a large white pillar in an ancient Greek temple.

As Janus got worse, we all tried harder to make her feel better, and the harder we tried, the worse she got. Kirb would go to rub her back and she would tell him that she didn't like to be touched anymore. Mama would be cleaning up our room and Janus would throw a fit and scream at Mama and ask her why in the hell she was always trying to change everybody because nothing in this damn world could be changed anyway, so we might as well just keep what we got.

I kept my distance. I was trying to be a husband in the only way I knew how, but it seemed more often than not I was asking her what was wrong and trying in vain to fix it. It got to the point that all we did revolved around Janus. We tiptoed around the house, painfully aware of every twitch in our faces and every creak in the floorboards. We brought her Iced Tea and then she sent it back because there was three ice cubes too many. We made some more and brought it back again. We were all hiding from it in our own way. We were offering up what we could to her, devoting our time to her, because she was the mother, she knew more than any of us could know. But, what we didn't want to understand was, is that all her fussing wasn't about her at all, the ice cubes and touches and clothes on the floor didn't have a damn thing to do with her, everything inside her, all the longing and despair and frustration, all of it was trapped inside that blurry picture sitting on the mantle, haunting us all with its silver frame and dark brown matting.

Janus and I slept as far apart as two people could sleep and still be on the same bed. We had a ritual. In the middle the night, she would take her clothes off and get on top of me. All I could see in the darkness was her wane face, aching and desperate. All the brightness had gone out of it, and she didn't look much like a woman anymore, she looked like a small boy or maybe even a young man, a lonely young man. Then, when she realized that my body wasn't going to let us make love, she would roll off of me and hit the bed in frustration. It wasn't every night, but I'd say she would give it a good try at least four or five times a week, with the results being the same. The more she tried, the less I was able to perform my spousal duties. And then, when she'd knock back a couple of glasses of whiskey with Mama, she'd get stirred up real good and slap her shoes against the floor and accuse me of being with somebody else.

"Who are those sluts at work?" she'd ask, and I'd answer that for the most part I worked alone and that there wasn't anybody alive for me but her.

"Then, who's Jen? Who's Misty? Who's Stepanie?!" she'd holler out, and it would take hours for her to calm down and I would have to swear up and down that I'd never heard any of those names and sometimes I'd get mad and scream at her and we'd give each other a nice back and forth until Kirb went and hid in the bedroom and we would have to go find him, sitting in a corner somewhere, smacking his lips and trembling.

Janus broke the past with a cough, as far away in time from those nights as she could be, and Kirb started from the window, sensing in the way he did, that something wasn't quite right with either of us. He could pick up a feeling the way most people could pick up that slight ticking in the bathroom you hear sometimes while you sleep. That ticking that swells and swells in your eardrum until it burrows into you, so that in the dreary state between sleep and waking, you are forced to search your lazy mind for an answer, and you go swimming around in there for a while, while the ticking keeps gnawing at you. It takes what seems like hours until you realize the most obvious solution: the ticking is water dropping from the faucet. So, the way that you get up and turn off the faucet is the same way Kirb knew to come over and sit down on the bed. He was smacking his lips real good and it seemed to get louder and louder and sometimes after a long day of walking around, like we had been, his smacking could be enough to drive you up a wall, but at that moment, it gave me peace.

"Kirby's here to see you," I told Janus.

She shivered and I could see his name had brought her out of the darkness for a moment and the shiver climbed up her torso and popped open her eyes. They were black and glossy and terrified, but as Kirb came into focus, something changed. They were somehow more delicate.

"Hey Chubbs," she said weakly. "I love you."

"I love you too," he said.

Her eyes shut and she picked up another shiver and went right back out, tossing and turning and sweating, descending back down into the darkness.

Kirb reached out and took her hand. He saw the scars on her arms, the track marks on the soft side of her elbow and winced. He pulled her arm onto his lap and traced the scars with his fingers, as if he was healing her, as if he was forgiving her, telling her that all was understood, that the pain was seen and heard and that she was still loved.

"Did she try to hurt herself?" Kirb said.

What he really meant is did she try to kill herself and all I could say was, "She *is* hurting herself buddy."

"Does she might die?" he said.

I didn't know how to answer him, didn't want to think about if I should answer him, but I knew he would ask again.

"I hope not," I said.

"How about you?" he said. "Would you might hurt yourself again?"

"No."

"Would you might die?"

"I have to die someday Chubbs," I said. "We all do. But I promise I'll never hurt myself again."

Kirb nodded. Sitting there holding the pale and clammy hand of my wife and listening to my brother smack his lips while he traced Janus's scars, I thought of the many wives and husbands and children that were locked away in cathouses and old folk's homes and office cubicles. How as much as we try, we can't get them out. We can't tell them where the door is or how to get there because it wouldn't make a damn lick of sense. They could be driving down the highway or boiling catfish in a restaurant or operating on a broken leg, life still wouldn't make sense to them, because they are lost. They have that feeling. You know it. I know you know it. It's the feeling that something is missing. You can't put a finger on it, so you just keep going to your job, keep eating the same dinners, keep sitting in the same chair and having the same conversations, because you figure eventually you have to find a way out. I know what that feeling is, because I feel it too. I have felt it for years. Every time it gets cold, or the moon is covered up by the clouds and it is so dark you can't see your hand in front of your face. For me, it is the hurricane. It always goes back to Hurricane Katrina. That's where I stored all my pain and misery. In that day. In that week.

The storm was finally at its peak, its anger flooding over me, and I knew I had to go back. It was the only way to move forward. It was the only way to heal.

I let my eyes close again, let my mind run through the dark forest, scramble desperately over the endless water, staring wildly into the raging night until it landed underneath the knobby branches reaching out into stars.

Chapter Eighteen

Kirb sat there with Janus, tracing the track marks on her arms, hearing with his hands all of her scars, and feeling, as we were all feeling, those moments of the storm. They hid in the quiet spaces of the night, when the sounds of the city crawled away into the corners and cabinets and caverns, and life, in its hushed way, fell into the coma which is darkness, and those of us that are still awake are confronted with the choices we have made and the events we want to forget, but cannot. That's the trouble with memories, the painful ones won't go away, no matter what you try, they haunt you, like demons, and maybe that's what demons really are, they remind you of the evil, of the loss and of the sorrow, and then they drag you down until you don't feel like a man anymore and you take a bottle of Tylenol and give your little brother an ulcer and the city itself falls apart in reproach. Once you've been through something like that, once you've been through a hurricane, every time there's a good hard wind or a chilly rain you get that smell of death again, you get that panic somewhere in your heart, even though you don't show it.

"Baby," I said to Janus.

She didn't move.

"Baby!" I said louder. "Can you wake up for a minute? Can you please open your eyes?"

The skin on her face was so tight you could see her cheek bones, her lips were white, and the bottom of her jaw poked out and churned like a stray dog in the swamps rabid for a bone. Hearing me, she struggled a bit and then rolled over.

"Baby," I said, standing up. "I'm going to get us a place! It's magnificent! It's out on Lafayette! Rashad Philips is renting the place out, you remember him, right? Anyway, it's got this killer yard! There's a pathway up to the door and this cute little porch where we could all sit and talk."

I swear I could see her move.

"If I close my eyes," I said. "I can see us all there. You, me, and

Chubbs. We are laughing and you look so good Janus, you look so damn good. You are wearing one of those dresses with the poppies on it you used to wear. There's the peeled white paint of the deck, the mahogany door with the round black knocker, the porch swing held up by a rusty black chain, the winding dirt walkway leading up to the front stairs. There is something so perfect about it! Even the shape is like an old cottage that I remembered I'd seen in a storybook Dad read to me and Kirb. It was about a family of bears who were always getting into some kind of mischief, but somehow ended up learning a valuable lesson. At the end of the story, they would huddle up and eat a warm meal of porridge and rice. Then, because the little bears had been so good, they would sit down for a slice of razzleberry pie and ice cream. When the bears were tucked in, you would sail away through the round cottage window out into the forest. Then you would fly to the stream, that bubbling and somehow peaceful brook that ran along the bank with the patch of daffodils. I'm telling you that this house on Lafayette has that exact cottage window! I think that maybe I would plant some daffodils. Maybe I could tell our children the story of the bears. Maybe I won't even need the book, because we could sit in our own living room, looking out our own round window, and Kirb could walk our children out to the daffodils, out to the end of the story, out to the dream itself. You and I could watch from the porch, swing on the swing, laugh, and maybe even get a bit teary-eyed, even a bit sentimental, but it wouldn't take over the moment, the moment being so pure."

I let myself settle into it. I let my whole body move into that porch and it felt warm, like a hand on the middle on my wrist.

"There's even a place where Kirby can stay out on his own," I said. "It's this little guest cottage probably twenty yards off the main house, so if he wanted to come to see us, he could come anytime he wanted to. And we could go to that crafts store you love, and you can decorate it any way you want! As long as it's not a bunch of pink lace and doilies."

I laughed.

"Yep, my doll," I said. "We can all live together and we won't have to worry about Mama because she'll be nice and far away and we won't have to remember anything if we don't want to, we won't even have to remember Mama, we won't even have to go back into her dusty old house. We could even-"

I paused.

"We could even try to have another child. I know they wouldn't replace our boy, but we could start new. A whole new life!"

I walked over to Janus's dresser.

"I'm going to need some money though baby," I said. "Mama took everything I saved up for us. I've been saving for a while. I kept it all in a vent in me and Kirb's room, but Mama found it. She took it all to keep us there. I know she did. She did it to keep us close so we can take care of her while she drinks her years away, so we can clean up after her messes, and listen to her cry and scream like a madwoman, so we can coddle her like some grown up child. But Janus, I can promise you, I'll take your money, get us the place, and you can get out of here. I can work for all of us. I'll stay up with you as long as it takes until you get healthy again. I'll hold you until the pain goes away, until both our pain goes away, and it will be like we were baptized in magic waters, because everything that's hurt us will just melt away. We can even take you swimming if you want to, I know how much you love it."

I opened the first drawer, and it was empty.

Janus lifted her head a few inches off the pillow.

"I told you not to come here!" she said.

"Well, I know that" I said. "But you are my wife and I refuse to give up on you."

I opened the second drawer and the only thing in it was a used-up matchbook.

"I'm a whore and a junkie," she said. "I'm not your wife anymore. I don't want to be your wife. I want to be a whore and junkie."

I opened the third drawer and rifled through some unfolded shirts and underwear and at the bottom of the clothes was the framed picture of Adam we had kept on the mantle. It looked about five years older than it actually was. She must have picked it up the night of the hurricane when I had sent her to get the water. I turned away from it; it was making me feel queasy. I did not recognize it as my boy anymore. It felt like looking at one of those old photographs that are brown and white and how you get that eerie feeling because you are peering into something sacred in someone else's life.

"Don't say that about yourself Janus," I said, turning around to look at her feeble body.

"You are just lost. We all get lost. You and I have been to places that are so painful most people wouldn't understand, and I know all too well how phony it seems to be out in the world buying groceries or walking down the street when you're carrying around all that pain, and the only thing you really want to do is just scream until your throat won't work anymore. I know that. And I know that you know that, in your own way, in a way I can't even fully understand. But that's why I'm here, so we can get back on track together, so we can get our lives back the way they used to be, even better than that! And what kind of husband would I be if I just up and left you? We made promises to each other. We made a child together and we held that child and we loved that child, and we buried that child."

I put my hands through my hair and sighed.

"I'm not going to break my promises," I said. "I meant every word and no man of honor would leave his wife, especially when she needed him most."

"I've already broken my promises, ten times over," she said.

I pulled the pearls from my jacket pocket.

"Me and Kirb sold a vacuum today and we bought you a present."

I went over to her and put them in her hand.

"It's a present fit only for a princess," I said, "fit only for a classic beauty like you. You know who you remind me of? Audrey Hepburn! She had the kind of beauty that you can't give to someone with any damn makeup or clothes, it was just there. That's the kind of pretty you are, and my Audrey Hepburn deserves the best."

She opened her eyes and looked at them and put them under her pillow.

"There are real nice," she said. "Thank you."

And then she let her out a low cough and her hand dropped, and she fell back asleep.

"Don't go to sleep baby!" I called out. "Baby! I need to know where the money is. Where have you put the money?"

I looked in her pockets, nothing. I looked under the bed, nothing. I looked in her shoes, nothing.

"Goddamnit! Where is all the money?!" I screamed. "What have you done with it? How are we supposed to get you out of here? How are me and Kirb supposed to get out of Mama's without any goddamn money? Where is it?"

I slammed my fists on the bed.

"Where is it?!"

She groaned a bit but didn't show any more signs of living than she had the whole time we were there. I pulled the pearls from underneath her pillow and put them in my pocket and took Kirb by the arm before stomping out of The Geisha House and back onto the streets.

Chapter Nineteen

The night had settled in. It was deep and dark and hollow. I could feel its hollowness in the joints on my elbows as they swung passed my hips. It was that part of the night where sounds jump up out of their sleepy southern hammocks and buzz in your ears like mayflies. Where your eyes wander like lost children, and you *feel* the way you walk, every step you sense that what you don't know could be just around the corner. The streetlights offer temporary shelter. As you walk from streetlight to streetlight, you dip into the cinders and then cleanse yourself off in the dull yellow and you repeat this process until the lines of night blur, and what you are left with is no real impression of what you or anything else looks like. You have then, only the strong smell of the sea, like buckets of brine, crawling into the shadows and then getting brushed away by that waft of warm night wind that comes in waves as does the guttural cry of the gull.

I was still shaken from seeing Janus. Not only did she barely care that I gave her the necklace, but she also didn't have any money to help us. I thought to myself in that deep and dark and hollow night, that after what you have been dreaming for is good and lost and there is no way to get it back, not the way you wanted it, you have two choices: you can rush out into the nighttime streets and scream and cry and feel the weight of your loss in every follicle of hair on your arms and legs, or you can make a new dream, a dream not unlike the first, in that it soothes you like that old sweater your Grandma made you with the cowboys on it or a cup of hot cocoa with homemade whipped cream on a cool winter night. But what every dream has in common is that it takes you away, it takes you away from that velvet curtain in front you, it takes you away from loss and loneliness and it gives you something to get good and drunk on while you do those things that we all have to do, like walk home or clean up the yard or soap up your feet in the shower. And if you can dream just right, then you feel that these things don't take time from you, but that somehow you made your own time from them. I knew all this. I knew it just the same way I knew I shouldn't stay out late or eat too much salsa because it made my stomach like a boiling pot of water or even that I should move on from Janus, I should let her be, the way she had asked me, and I knew that we might all be happier then. But sometimes, you don't give a damn what's right, you just want to do, what you want to do, even if it's to think about how painful it all was and how in that damned universal scheme, you've been shafted.

I had been through it, been through horrible things and I deserved my happiness. And if I was mostly good and mostly kind and wanted what was mostly good and mostly kind for the people I loved, then why couldn't I get it? And what kind of person or God or universe would keep me from it?

Yes, it was all becoming clear. It was sinking in. The truth, with its hideous and stinking face, was smiling right at me. I knew then that I wasn't going to get the house on Lafayette. I knew I wasn't going to get Janus. I knew I wasn't going to get into medical school. I knew I wasn't going to stop being lonely. I knew I wasn't going to stop being afraid and sad, and I knew, with all certainty, that at that moment there wasn't anything I could do to fix it. So, knowing the helplessness of it all, I did the only thing anyone can do in that situation: I got good and mad. I got mad at myself for my hope. I got mad at Mama for taking so much from us. I got mad at Dad for dying. I got mad at Janus for leaving. I got mad at God for taking my son. I got mad at Nature for destroying our city. I got mad at Kirby for saving my life. My face got so hot that my neck got hot, and the sides of my arms got hot and my whole body boiled up in fury.

"Bastards," I said. "Goddamn bastards!"

And I was waiting for the steam to come out of my ears and the fire to come out spewing out of my mouth, when Kirb asked, very sweetly, "Can we go home now?"

And somehow that sweetness, that chubby red face, tired and innocent, well, it made me even hotter.

"If you call where we are going a home, yes," I cried out.

"Yes, we can go *home*," I said. "We can go home and watch Mama drink herself into a stupor and tell us how worthless we are, and we can go home and do the same thing we always do which is nothing. We can go home, and you can watch television and laugh while I try to hold together my sanity, so I can get us both up in the morning to go sell vacuums to rich people so we don't go starving in the streets. And after we've gone out and sold a couple of vacuums, maybe we can sit on the porch and stare out into the neighborhood and remember that we almost got there. Yes sir! We almost got out. We almost did something worth talking about, but too bad for us, because our dear and fine and beautiful darling of a mother stole our money. She stole our way out of all this.

And she didn't steal it because she was dying of cancer or to feed a sick child she saw in the newspapers, or even to buy herself a new car, she did it just so that we couldn't go anywhere, so that we would fold up into that damn nothing that she's been living with her whole life and our family has been drinking down with their milk at dinner for the past two hundred years! Yes, we can go home and do nothing, doesn't that sound great?"

Kirb contemplated the answer, while staring at the now limp purple iris he'd been carrying all day. He jiggled the flower gently as if to make it stand back up, as if when it did, all would be back to the way it had been. He studied it. It spoke in his weary fingers. "Why does that moment of love fade?" It asked. "Why does the dreaming stop?"

I put my hand on his shoulder, and he scowled at it, it was a smarmy annoyance in the face of his treasure. I took it off. The flower beamed, its rich color breathing heavily, defying its own questions. Kirb shook it again, and then again, and after it moved just a little bit towards being the way it once was, he looked up at me and said, "I'm hungry. Can you make me a grilled cheese sandwich?"

"Oh!" I answered, sarcastically, for I had expected him to say something profound. "You want a grilled cheese sandwich with your nothing? Well, then, by all means, yes, I'll make you a grilled cheese sandwich."

Kirb nodded and got comfortable again in his walk. When we had made it to the next block and were waiting at the crosswalk for that little person to pop up and tell us it was time to cross, Kirb looked over at the other side of the street and said, "I just thought we were getting our own place."

It was the manner in which he said it. It was how he pushed it out in that defeated way of his when he knew the music was over and the song was done. It made me hotter than ever. He didn't believe anymore. He had seen the inevitable nature of the truth before I could even recognize it myself and by God that made me mad.

I stopped. I stopped right in the middle of the street we were crossing and shook him. I wanted to shake that wisdom right off of his face until it dropped down and slithered away. I didn't want it to come back, not now, not ever.

"No!" I bellowed. "No, we aren't getting that place. We are stuck in the same goddamn house with the same goddamn twin beds and the same goddamn broken bathroom sink and we aren't never going to leave because that's the way it is and that's the way it's always going to be!"

"But you promised we were getting a place!" he yelled back, matching my tone. "You promised!"

I slapped him.

Helpless, Kirb's head bobbled back and forth while I pushed and pulled his arms, and as the fear and the sadness swelled in his tiny eyes, I shuddered. I had finally stepped too hard on the silk of the comb-footed spider web. My anger, the tool with which I used to protect my brother, was now being used against him. I had let the beast go unattended too long and he had caught me in his silky labyrinth. I was paralyzed by the venom, by my frustration at not being able to help Kirb, to help Janus, to help Mama, or Adam, or even myself. Now, the spider's neurotoxins had shot through my skin and hair and bones until it reached my central nervous system, and preventing the release of glutamate, caused my whole body paralysis. I was no longer in control if I ever had been at all. The anger overcame me. Then, relishing its every move, the brown widow took its long brown legs and wrapped me ever so delicately in a silky cocoon, so that I could watch while it's long and luminous back reached over me, fiercely and manically, and devoured the last of the dignity I had left. I hurt the one person I had sworn never to hurt. I had forever besmirched my family honor.

After the spider licked its furry feet, I took my hands off of Kirby and rushed him to the other side of the street. It was then that I felt the sticky sweet air hang heavy. I had created the beast. I had secretly fed him while he spun his web, and by lashing out at Kirb, I felt like I had destroyed everything. I had embraced that primal part of me where I am as much the spider as I am the man, and it was not graceful or pretty, it was that darker part of nature, the part that destroys. We know about it and so we try to understand it. And we sit around our dining tables with full bellies and drink coffee and wonder to ourselves how it is that we could hurt the ones we love, how we could destroy the very things we were working so hard to protect, because it doesn't follow logic, but we do it anyway and we keep doing it. We do it because it is in our nature to destroy, just as it is in our nature to create. We have such a hard time seeing the darker side as part of us, and so we end up repeating the same mistakes over and over again, because we refuse to see them. We blame the moment, as if the moment were our master. We say, "I was having a lot of stress" or "I got pushed just a little too far," and we fail to realize that there is something dark inside us all and until we confront it, we will never truly change. Destruction is the nature of the universe itself. There are supernovas and free-range predators and prairie fires and volcanoes. Nature isn't always this peaceful scene you imagine from some screen saver or weekend hike. Nature holds a terrible mystery. If we are said to come from nature, it is really our mystery, and if you look deep enough into the mystery, you too will see the spider, will gaze into its bloodless eyes, and you will know then, that it is you.

I pushed Kirb to pick up his stride. I wondered if someone had seen me slap him and in the same thought I worried if he was okay. You see, I didn't have the wisdom of looking back yet. I felt the shame of being caught as much as the guilt of what I had done. I looked around and the streets were empty. There were no sirens or laughter or bolts of lightning from the heavens, and yet, I still felt I needed to get away. Walking briskly on the hush of the sidewalk, I heard two lone sounds: the smacking of Kirby's lips and the throbbing of my heart. It had become an instrument of its own. It pealed in my chest like an old chapel bell ringing out my ribs. It beat to mock me, to remind me of the prison of my skin. It rang methodically under my chest, a strangled but efficient master, whose curved lips uttered but a single tone: Tick. Tick. Tick.

"You know what?" I asked, asking it as much to myself as I was to Kirby.

"We don't need that dusty old place on Lafayette," I said. "The siding is coming down and it's about a half a breath away from getting swallowed by a clinging ivy vine. And who wants to rent from somebody like Rashad Philips anyhow? He's a no-good swindler and we'd probably be sleeping in water the first time it rained."

I kept talking. I kept talking until I was caught again in that mad dream, spinning away into that narcotic of faith and wish that only imagination can fulfill. The more I talked, the more the idea became a part of the night air and the further me and Kirb got from the beast who had wounded us both.

"Could I might have my own room?" he asked.

"You're damn right you can!" I said. "We will find somewhere different, somewhere for you and me. Somewhere more rustic, more country. That place on Lafayette was way too much city for us boys. We need a place on the beach or in the swamps, a place where we can smell the honeysuckle and look for Hercules in the stars at night."

Kirb almost smiled, letting what I had done slide away, and then, frantic, he patted his pants and thrust his hands in his pocket and called out, "No! Oh no! Oh no!"

"What is it?" I asked.

"My flower! My flower!" he said.

"Oh! Chubbs! Just leave it," I said. "It's already worn down. That's what flowers do. It's in the road for crying out loud! Come on! We can get you another one tomorrow."

But it was too late. He had already run back into the street, and in a mania of hurried steps and reaching fingers, he chased the purple iris through the black stones of the road.

"My flower. My flower," he muttered as he searched the ground with his hands, as he bent down on his knees to pick it up.

"My flower! My flower!" He repeated triumphantly, as he held it up above his head like a trophy, staring into its petals with a childlike and genuine smile, having at last his treasure, which was the treasure of a boy, or so it seemed, the treasure of all boyhood in one way or another. I smiled too, because there was nothing else a man could do when he thought back on boyhood treasures and the love of his brother. I was smiling so deep and so real that I didn't see the light barreling toward him until it was too late, until my scream was muffled by what sounded like a baseball bat hitting the side of a steel shed, a sound so loud it ruptured the night, and what was left was a gaping hole, where all that could be heard was some backwater country song spinning eerily out of the cab of a light blue Ford pickup truck. The guitar whined as a phony southern drawl lamented some busted street in Arkansas and I stood aghast, stupefied.

All I could see was smoke rising from the truck's dented grill and its weak round headlights reaching out towards the moon.

I rushed to the front of the truck where Kirb was flat on his back. He was dirty. His right eye was swollen, blood was coming out both of his nostrils, and he was squinting in pain.

"Jesus! Chubbs!" I took his hand. "How do you feel?"

"It hurts Ernest. It hurts so bad."

I lifted up his head and let it settle in my palm.

"Where does it hurt buddy?" I said.

"Here," he said, and he pointed to his chest. Then, he pointed to his left leg, and said "here too." His leg was clearly broken. His shin was facing the other direction, and his ankle was twisted to match it.

I carefully pulled up his shirt and there was a large poppy bruise covering his torso from right below his neck all the way down to his belly button. The bruise was a red and purple mountain, rigid and deep, and his ribs were a pale yellow. I knew he must be bleeding internally and that we didn't have much time to get him to the hospital.

"I'm going to get this truck going," I said to him as I set his head down.

"P-" he choked. "P-promise me you won't leave me."

"I swear it," I said. "I would never leave you."

I opened the truck. In it, a tall elderly gentleman was hunched over the steering wheel, face on the dash, mouth open, tongue hanging over his bottom lip, blood on his teeth. There was a black cowboy hat that had fallen on the ground and his brown boots were muddied.

"Sir?" I said to him, not wanting particularly to touch him.

He didn't move and I knew. I knew even without checking his wrist that he would never drive this old truck or muddy his boots again. I reached around him to see if I could start it, but when I turned the key, the engine just puttered until it died out. I tried again, and then again, with the same result. I sighed deeply and shut the truck's door. But before

I could go check on Kirb a voice called out "Wh-at happened?" in that stout Southern timbre that you can only find in twilight rummaging through a back alley or sprawled out on a bus bench. I turned my head to see a time-worn woman of about sixty, a vagabond, a wino. She reeked of alcohol and sweat, and she waddled more than walked. She teetered over to us with her holey denim jacket and her green bottle clutched tightly against her breast.

"He got hit," I said. "Call an ambulance."

She hesitated.

"What are you waiting on lady?! We don't have much time!"

"The ambulances don't come down here much," she sniffled. "And when they do, it takes them a long time, because they only come out here to pick up somebody who's not coming back."

She looked down at her green bottle but thought better of it.

"Besides that," she said. "I don't have no phone."

"How far is the nearest hospital?" I asked. Feeling lost for the first time in my own city.

"It's about a mile and a half down this road," she said, pointing to the east.

"You find a phone and tell the ambulance I'm on my way," I said. "And check on that guy back there, he looks unconscious."

I didn't want to tell her the truth.

"Don't let him move if he says his neck or back is hurting him," I said.

"Y'all got a car?" she asked.

"Nope."

"Then why don't y'all use his car?"

"The front end is all smashed up," I said. "Can't you see the smoke? That thing won't drive and I ain't got time to try and fix it."

I picked Kirby up and held him like one might hold a giant baby, with one arm softly under his neck and the other under his knees.

"You sure you don't know anybody around here with a car?" I said.

"No sah."

She paused.

"But how you going to get him there then?" she said.

"Run," I said, and I took off without waiting to hear another word, using my long legs to make long strides as I galloped across sidewalk tiles and leaped over gutters, thrashing through the gloom with urgent and desperate gulps.

I was trying to hold Kirby in front of me so as not to bump him up and down, but I could tell that my efforts weren't saving him from it and with each movement of my legs, he winced. It felt like the storm, like the inescapable heat, like the loss of all direction.

"I'm scared," he said, and he said it in a voice I'd never heard.

There had always been, chiseled into his face, a determination born out of struggle, a resilient verse of triumph that lifted his high rosy cheeks and widened his smile. But now, the claws of frailty having burrowed their hooks, his face was fearful and so it wasn't his anymore. I knew I had to be strong, and I knew I couldn't let him see me upset.

It was the moon. That's what I focused on. On its silver bow. I ran toward it. It hummed to me with its light, with its torch that said, "Come closer. Come closer," and I ran with it, into it.

"Look at the moon," I told him. "Just keep looking at the moon and before you know it, we will be there."

"Mmm. Hmm," he said, and he watched it with me, struggling to keep his eyes open, and yet hypnotized by the grey-blue orb helping him cling to consciousness.

I stopped to call to a passer-by, but they bolted out of sight.

Houses were held together with aluminum rooftops and chicken wire and no lights were on anywhere. Cracks in caulk between doorways were sweating drops of anguish. I was sweating too. The knobby branches of prickly slash pine and the curved leaves of amber sweet gum moistened. I wasn't going to get any help, not here.

This part of the city was used to being hurt, it had been cut and murdered and raped for hundreds of years and so it wasn't concerned with a man getting hit by a truck, and it wasn't surprised by it either. It only wanted what it always wanted: to be left alone, to be left to heal. Everyone was so sick and hungry that no one could heal anyone else because you couldn't survive like that. Survival is old, old as biology, older than history and in the inner cities, in the places they don't put on the tourist maps, the scars and open wounds of America pulsate and thrive and are ignored. And maybe, all they need, is someone to look and see and say, "What ails you friend?" Like Percival said to the Grail King. Maybe then the soul can come back. Maybe then, the darkness will lift.

Kirb understood this. As I ran and rested, ran, and rested, he looked out over the housetops as he had once done during Hurricane Katrina and simply said, "Beautiful."

I'm still not sure why he said it at that moment or what he saw that inspired it, but the word felt unbreakable, new.

My arms and back strained and my legs were wobbling. I had never experienced so much pain in my entire life. I tried looking at the moon again, but it had stopped telling me to come closer, and it trembled as I ran, so I looked only forward. I willed forward. Ever forward. My knees knocked. I could not let the pain stop me. Kirb's mouth was open with the now blood-stained flower clutched tightly in his hand. In his eyes I found a strength I could not have imagined was possible. I pushed on.

Against all of my body's impulses, I moved.

"You stay with me Chubbs," I said.

"Okay," he mustered, and he sounded like a frightened child, and it was enough to break me, to break any man or woman with blood in their veins.

Broken or not, I couldn't stop. Not now. Ever forward.

Underneath the arms and on the tips of my elbows. Kirby was getting heavier. I used my knees to prop him up while I caught my breath.

The hospital appeared on the horizon like a white light of divine intervention. The parking lot was full, and two cars were outside, but there were no other sounds. Only the light. I had to move toward the light.

"Thank God," I said. "Thank God."

When we finally got to the hospital's emergency doors, I stumbled through them and collapsed onto my knees.

I screamed with the last of my strength, "Help! HEELPP!"

I looked around, but there was no movement of staff converging on us, no doctor screaming for a stretcher. Three or four people glanced at us briefly from the waiting area and went back to their magazines.

"You are going to be out of this soon, I promise," I said.

"Can we-" he coughed. "Can we watch a movie?"

"Any one you want," I said.

"Popcorn, candy, and drinks?" he said.

"You are damn right."

I chuckled.

"Popcorn, peanut M&M's, and all the Coke you can drink," I said.

He smiled, but behind it, I could tell he was in a lot of pain. Even bloodied on the emergency room floor, clutching at life, he could not afford pity, and neither would he tolerate it. Like most of us, if he stubbed his toe, he wanted you to ask if he was okay, but he was different than most of us when he felt you feeling sorry for him. If he even sensed there was some pity in you, especially about his disability, he pushed you away, laughed at you, jabbed at you with his snarky comments, to make you forget it all, to make you forget everything but the laughter. As if all of it to him were a game and that by taking it too seriously you had conceded your hand.

"I love you Chubbs," I said.

"I love you too princess," he said, and he smiled and coughed a harrowing cough and closed his eyes.

"Did I might die?" he asked.

"No, of course not," I said. "You are going to be just fine. Stay with me buddy! I promise, you are going to be just fine."

"I might not want to die," he said.

And as he took another breath, his body went limp and heavy in my arms.

I've heard people say that death is a peaceful experience, but the people that said that must have been trying to write some slick book or scene in a movie because they couldn't have been more wrong. It was as if a sledge hammer had suddenly came down from the ceiling and crashed into the floor, and that the vibrations had smacked my chest like a jolt from sticking your finger into a socket. I withdrew. I withdrew into that safe place, that angry place where I'd fortified a shield to protect me from the suffering I'd known. I withdrew so I didn't have to feel and without yelling or pounding my chest or tearing down the hospital, I lay there, holding his hand, waiting for his eyes to sink from this world to the next.

Chapter Twenty

He did not die, even though I had expected him to. He had suffered a subdural hematoma, a broken fibula, and a severely bruised hip. They were currently boring a hole in his head to evacuate the hematoma.

Mama didn't say anything. She didn't even move. I kept waiting for her voice, for her to say something, to cry out, to perform some liturgy to her now invisible God. We sat in the waiting room, and she scowled at me. Her lips trembled, but nothing came out. Mama was in a trance. She wasn't shocked or surprised, just there. It was like she was waiting for it.

She nodded her head, as if to say, "Yep, I knew something was coming," because that's all she could imagine, was tragedy, and for her the tragedy was always happening to Sally Larsen and it was never happening to anyone else.

And in the same way that the last few years had been slowed, that time had been walking with those heavy boots, in that moment time stopped. Nothing could speed it up. All of life's moments had been fossilized into this grotesque statue that used to be me. All the statue could do was sit and think about his brother, and wish his life would speed up, and do nothing to comfort his wayward mother.

There was a thought we all had that because of what we had lost, that there wasn't going to be anymore suffering, that people wouldn't betray each other, that death would wait awhile, would hold off until we were old and had lived. I guess it's because we think we have mastered death. We think because we have seen it, because someone we have known has died that it's over, but death keeps coming. It flows through life unafraid and without cause it murders fine men and women with equal monstrosity.

"Damn it all!" Mama started, husky and hot. "Everybody leaves me. Everybody gets up and walks out on me and flies away. Ain't nobody stay nowhere for too long. We are all running around looking for something and we don't right know what it is. We think we are so smart, but we don't know nothing. We can't even find one thing we are looking for our whole lives, because everybody leaves before you can figure out a damn thing. Even my Mama and Daddy didn't stay, they left before I could even tell them goodbye because, good Lord, I didn't stay with them either. I ran off with your father."

Mama finally cried, tears cascading down her chin. I went to comfort her, but she raised her arms and bore her breast so that her mad torrent would not stall.

"Then he left!" she said. "And my baby boy has left me, and I don't have nothing no more."

She swayed back and forth, conjuring up some spirit of loneliness and sorrow.

"Baka boolla hika goo!!! Don't nobody know what I mean when I say it anyhow. BALAAA!" she spouted. "I will walk and walk until I show life how haphazard I can be! I got the Lawd on my side and he will keep me from the beast, that fourth beast that comes in the fourth night of the fourth time of the fourth day. He might not keep people from leaving me, but at least he can keep me from the beast."

And she was spitting and flailing her arms and she pelted out. "Why should I be afraid? Why should I be in fear if I live in chance? Fate don't mean anything anyhow! Only the good Lawd knows what fate is. I can keep him if I want, and he won't leave because the Lawd is my LAWD!!! He ain't yours and he ain't nobody else's!"

She took a deep breath. Then, she wailed. My mother wailed so loud it hurt my ears. After she had given that wail everything she had to give, she bent over and wept some more. I watched her weeping and there was a part of me I had ferreted away from years ago that felt for her, that wanted to lie to her and tell her I was sorry she was in pain, but I couldn't, the statue could only watch his mother writhing in agony over her son.

Seth stood between Mama and the waiting room door. He was wearing a white shirt and white shorts and sweating like it was the middle of August. Mama brought her head up a bit and noticed Seth standing there and her eyes widened.

"BALALALAAAA!" she yelled. "Bakakalaka bushka bushka blleee goo haaa! You can't make me weep!" she screamed at him, as if he was a ghost haunting her anguish.

"I'll weep no more! I'll have no more of it! Crack your cheeks you damn winds. Blow!" she screamed. "BLOW!"

And she stomped through the room muttering and howling until I heard the waiting room door slam.

"Hello Seth," I said. "Sorry about Mama."

He sat down next to me and put his arm on my marble leg.

"What can a man or woman be, but what they are," he said and then he took in a deep breath. "This air is stagnant in here. You mind taking a walk?"

"That's fine," I said.

I was amazed I could even move, but it happened. I got up and walked through the lobby and sat down on a bench while Seth stood looking at the trees.

"There is a magic in this day," Seth said. "It don't take but a second to look at, but it's here. Isn't it girls?"

The trees tilted a bit and Seth smiled.

"I guess," I said.

"He has given us one hell of a story, hasn't he?"

"Excuse me?" I asked, feeling irritated. "A story?! That's all you think my brother is, is a goddamn story?"

I could feel my chest start to warm up.

"Everything's a story, if you think about it," Seth said.

He put his leg up on the step and I huffed a bit, frustrated not so much at what he was saying because I knew it was wise, but that he was right. And when you are suffering you don't want anybody to be right. You want to argue everything. If life isn't making any sense, then why should you let anybody make sense in it?

"You go into the doctor's office and tell him that your throat hurts," he continued. "He asks why, and you tell him the story. Them business types go to the water cooler and tell their stories about what they did for the weekend. Preacher tells stories about God and Jesus and Abraham. Movies are just expensive stories. Shoot, every time you go home, you tell your family the story of your day. We are all storytellers, Ernest. Some better than others, no doubt. And your story? Well, you tell your story more than any other story there is. Almost every time you open your mouth, you are telling a story to somebody. And no story ends! Each event gives way to the next and the next and the next. And so we are all one story, one long narrative, spoken and lived by different voices, by different sexes and ages and skins and on different continents and in different souls–this story, our story, it is forever. So, nothing ever really dies. And there can be no more powerful thing than this, than our story, because one story is as good to me or you as any other story. Details change sure, but our wants, our sufferings, our loves, they all howl and whisper together. And my story is my father's and his father's and even back to the beginning of time, just like yours or anybody else's. That must be why they call God a father in heaven because he was the first storyteller and in that way our lives are telling his story or her story or every story that's ever been told. So, the best storytellers are the best of all of us. Your brother Kirby is the finest storyteller I've ever known and I'm not exaggerating, because you know me, and I don't never say anything I don't mean."

"It just doesn't make sense," I said and kicked the ground.

"It just doesn't make sense," I repeated.

"Who said it would?" Seth said. "Life is full of it, plain and simple, and those of us that go through it are left to try and find meaning in the things we've known. It's early still, that stink. It's fresh in your mind and so you don't want to hear nothing, you only want to wallow in it. And you deserve to! But when you are ready to get up, remember this: the why don't matter, it's only the what that matters. What he means to you and what you are going to do now."

Here, he breathed in another deep breath, closing his eyes, and pleased with the scent of the outside air, he said "It isn't the world that makes beauty, it's beauty makes the world."

"What's the price?" I said, choking back my tears. "What's the price of this beauty?"

There came from Seth a slight chuckle, like one might do when a child asks them something simple.

"There is no price," he said. "Beauty is so much more than counting. We sure do like to count, don't we all? But while we are counting and counting and counting, how do we decide which is ahead and which is behind? We just is Ernest. We just is what we is. This is our journey. To be."

I blew out a stymied breath and let it hang there. I let it hang there so as not to let the air be anything but what I wanted it to be, which was dirty.

"What's the point of a journey that just brings you to death?" I said. "And then, what's the point of life since we are all headed there anyway? This!" I pointed to the ground. "This is where honor ends, where beauty ends. This is where the worms crawl through the skin and chew the bone."

I stood up and plodded on the great green grass, which seemed great because it was something living, something grand to stomp on.

"I mean, what is the point?" I kept on. "Why was I born in Louisiana? Why did my son die? Why did I become a vacuum salesman? Why is my goddamn wife running around with anybody that has twenty dollars in their pocket? And what the hell does it mean to me or anybody else? I'm seeing life now for what it really is! And that's a hell of lot better than putting on those rose-colored glasses and sitting down by a picture of a fire trying to get warm! Where's the honor in that? Where's the honor Seth?"

I looked at Seth, waiting for my words to shake him, to hurt him, because I wanted someone else to hurt, to know what hurt was, but my words didn't do what I wanted them to. Somehow, even my wrath made me more endearing to him.

"In any journey," he said, "you're bound to lose something, something you didn't account for. Nothing ever really turns out the way we got it in our heads. Nothing. You're the only man I know that still thinks of something like honor."

"Honor nowadays is only something you read about in a book," he said. "They might call honor truth or God even, but there's always an agenda behind it, someone getting at your pocketbook or trying to get a golden ticket to heaven or getting called a hero or getting pity or even love. There are people that think honor is something given to you, something that you earn from getting a medal on your chest, but you, you think of honor as by itself without God or country or praise. You are the judge of your own honor, and a formidable judge at that. You are one strange individual."

He scratched the side of his face and pulled a handkerchief from his jacket pocket to wipe his forehead.

"But" he said. "Honor is the one thing that makes us special because it allows us to do those things that aren't easy, that so many times go against our nature to do. It doesn't end because we make a mistake or even years of mistakes. It's still there, waiting. And real honor doesn't have to be told its honor. You know that. Kirby knows that."

And then, like ten thousand bricks on my shoulders, I realized I might never again hear Kirby's voice, touch his dry skin, hear his laugh or tickle his back when he was sad. Everything could be gone, and I wanted then to pull down the sun and bury it in the sand, to paint the sky red with war, to feel the ocean cry its tears, to taste the bitterness of loss in the air, but all I could do was stare dumbly at the cracked paint on the bench. And all I could hear was the wheezing of my throat. The in and out of my nose, sawing away into the evening like the back of an old wooden porch swing. I listened to the wheezing until I couldn't even hear it anymore.

I became the brown pelican again, rising and diving under the sea. The air dried my eyes and my mouth watered for a taste of fresh fish. The choppy blue water was ephemeral, something distant and cold and wanting, wanting so much that it could never be satisfied. Yes, the white wake wanted it all, but even that wasn't enough. It was barren and lethargic and wishing and wistful and plentiful. Could any of us be happy with the white wake charging toward us? With its still reflection following us into the land, into the glasses of water at lunch in the park, into the bathtub as we struggle to wash away the day's dirt, and even into the blood, even into the cells and the space between cells. It was a mirror, a mirror into all of us, but not the way we know mirrors to be, it was the mirror that nature intended, distorted as we are distorted, as we all really see each other, in fragments of light, intermittent beings only existing in

the canvas of a memory or two. A memory not of the clear-cut version
of our face in the bathroom mirror on the way to work, but a series of
constant reflections, like shifting kaleidoscopes, filled with laughter, and
suffering and sexuality and repulsion and tremors and passion and decay,
all of it moving and moving and moving. But, toward what?

I let my wings turn from it, watching the city return small on the
horizon, wondering if this would be my last flight. The city grew and
grew like a splinter inside a shell, bridges and towers like layer upon layer
of nacre, street signs and curling roadways rising and rising in my mind
until all of the trolleys and cruise ships and cafes and even the men and
women and children converged into one round obelisk, the eye of the
city, a splendid and shimmering pearl.

"What are you thinking?" Seth asked, washing away the silence.

It was such a simple question, but my mind couldn't say anything, so
I relied on my mouth.

"I never took the time." I said. "I never took the time to ask him
what he really expected out of life. I never asked him what he imagined
his future to be. I never asked him what he dreamed of in the curbed
places of the night. I never held his hands and looked into his eyes and
simply said, 'What do you want?'"

I cut it off there, mostly because I didn't want to cry when I spoke,
and I waited for the tears to ebb and continued.

"I only told him what *I* wanted for him and now the answers to those
questions may haunt me for the rest of my life."

There was no more for me to say. Now, there was simply the blank
stare, the statue curling back into its pose. Seth and the statue stared
together at the trees for a while. Seth even put his hand on the back of
the statue's head, but it didn't move.

"Well," Seth said with his voice toward leaving. "I better get going.
Let me know when he gets out of surgery."

"It should be sometime this afternoon," I said. "I'll call you."

He stood up as if he was going to walk away but didn't.

"You know, Ernest" he said, and he surveyed not the yard or the
neighborhood or even the skies as he was so wont to do, no it seemed
then as if he looked beyond even the skies themselves.

"Here," he told me, "Here in these streets, skidding on the surface of
the sidewalks and café windows and street lamps, he lives. And it don't
take but a walk down our street or down any street in this city for that
matter to see him. It will happen one day, when you have long forgotten
this conversation and you will be lost in that habit of the day-to-day
mulling around that we so love to do, that a cold breeze will blow off the
Atlantic and dress your cheek, sending a chill down the back of your neck
and up onto the top of your head. You will know then that it is him, that

he will always be here in New Orleans."

Then Seth tipped his hat to me and waved to the trees before walking very slowly and yet very joyfully down the sidewalk. I wanted to tell him thank you, to cry it out or maybe even to run toward him and kiss his cheek or to embrace him as the father I never had, but I couldn't move the statue. One of the great catastrophes in life is that we put off our gratitude until it's too late to give it.

Chapter Twenty-one

In the morning, the sun rose through the bottom of the hospital room window. The earth beneath it was black, burned through the night by the ashen sky and the looming shroud of what was to come. The hospital bed was covered in crimson, and as the doctor told me the news, his arms danced in the red glare while a sad tune sailed through the hallway speakers like the echo of a name across an empty courtyard.

Kirby was going to live. There was still a chance for brain damage, but it was slight. The doctor was relatively sure that Kirby's brain function would return to normal in time, but there were no guarantees. I would most likely have to face him again and that scared me, because I knew I would have to atone for what I had done.

Despite the trauma and the bandage on his head, Kirb still looked as young as ever. There were no scars or lines or wrinkles on his face and lying there in that light blue hospital gown, rouge circles of heat on his cheeks, he resembled a portly cherub. I sat with him, holding his limp hand. His breath moved slowly, efficiently. After a while, it was indistinguishable from the tempo of the lights and machines surrounding him.

I decided to take a break from the hospital.

A chill had come over the city and as I passed the sleepy houses, black and red with the morning sun, I felt cold. Nothing seemed real. Nearly killing your brother was one of those moments in life that transform you so much you wonder to yourself if any moment is real, if even you are real or if you are some dark fantasy birthed from a mythical creature or even a god and you exist only as long as they think you exist and when they are done imagining you: Poof! You will disappear into the vast expanse and all these mad imaginings will have only been a vision. You might want to say "dream," but cannot tell at these particular moments whether you are awake or asleep.

I took the 91 bus and got off at City Park Avenue. I walked until I could see the sign for the community college. I used to hike over with Kirb on aimless afternoons after the hurricane and sift through the thousands and thousands of waterlogged books that floated among grasses and garbage with sleek blue and green backs shining in the sun as legendary mast ships exploring treacherous waters.

The cemetery is behind the community college, so I marched through the parking lot and onto the dirt road and I could smell the draft of grilled burgers from the broiler across the street and it seemed out of place in Holt Cemetery, but not much feels in place there anyhow. It's a sad place and not just because people are buried there, it looks sad. A tall chain link fence, half with green slats and half just chain and a row of ramshackle houses surround the grounds. A few timid oak trees stand as guards over the single palm tree that's split in half, while a two-tracked dirt road winds itself through the sagging stones and wooden crosses.

Most of the gravestones were tilted and sunken. The ground was choked with tall weeds, and it seemed the perfect place for a snake to come creeping up on you when you were least expecting it.

"Gene Tilson" one of the stones said to me in its crude writing. There were no dates, just the name. I wondered if they were a boy or girl or man or woman and maybe they had a mama that didn't believe in mausoleums either.

Some of the graves had tiny white rocks in a rectangle over their bodies, some were covered with thick sticks, some had a blanket of brown leaves and others had tipped over flowerpots, cracked at their bases. Dead and rotted plants and squat roots climbed over wood chips and fallen crosses. There was no one stone or row of stones like most cemeteries. Each marker was unique. There was a blue steel cross next to a wooden arch with roses and vines painted on. There were white wood markers and white stone heaps punished by wind and flood. There was even one that looked like a road marker painted over and another that was just a board sticking out of the ground with someone's illegible handwriting on it. There was a basket with a doll and some animals coming out of what looked like Noah's ark, and it must have been built about the same time, because it was worn, and the black eyes of the bears stared right into your fear if you stared at them too long. One grave was protected by a wrought iron fence and chicken wire with a sign that said "Private Property." In another, a pink chair leaned over the fence and was tied to the ground by a purple ribbon.

Passed the sunken marble angel, I saw the grey teddy bear that Mama put outside of Adam's grave that still sits there guarding him over a gray marble stone that reads "A gift of life. A gift of love. A gift from God." And right next to him is Daddy's grave which simply says "Dr. Chester Larsen" in block letters over a long white stone and next to his is the prettiest of all three, a pink stone marker that says Sally Larsen with no dates.

I had then the desire to run and I imagined running away to some small Midwestern town, where my southern accent would seem exotic and I could be transported back to another time, a simpler time. I would create a new life there, with new people, and after a year or two they might stop asking where that new fella came from and what his story was, because they'd already know me by then, and I could leave the pain at The Geisha House and out on the water and underneath the earth of New Orleans.

I walked on, through the dirt and into the green grass. I could hear murmurs of unintelligible speech rising like a whirlpool from the center of the cemetery and shooting over the road through the mouths of eager talkers until all the noise came together in a single rumble. It sounded like a stern whisper, something like what you would imagine the early American colonists spoke in towns before they mounted against the English. "Revolution!" was their cry, but for secrecy they could not scream it and yet for passion's sake they could not merely whisper it, so it became both forceful and intimate. Yes, this whisper carried with it that same urgent tone, but it was "Kirby. Kirby! Kirby!! Kirby!!!" And they all seemed to be saying it at the same time as the beat of a single heart in a shallow wood. So beat on the word. So beat through the people.

I went to get good and lost like the old days, and as I ventured from the city, the noise got further and further away, until I was neck deep in that merciless southern silence. The silence that comes from going and going and going until you feel like you can't go anymore. It's when you get to the silence that you find out that time didn't give a damn, that it kept going too, and finally you are right here, in this moment, in the moment you should be, not the moment you wanted, but the one that you had been trying to avoid. Yes, even the leaves stopped, the mosquitoes, flies, dogs, cats, bats, lights -all were quiet.

I came upon a lonely road by the water, dirt tracks and oil smell. You can find about a hundred of those little dirt roads along the banks of the Mississippi without even trying. What used to be a house was there. Its roof had been caved in and the middle sucked out. The glass on the windows was fractured and the pieces of wood and brick were scattered across the bank and into the water. An old porch swing was the only thing left still standing and it was tilted toward the ground. The house had been white, but most of it was either grey or black now, and you couldn't see the foundation because the house had moved over it.

There is that blackness lying underneath the things we build. We build those things to get away from it, but it's inescapable. There will always be the chasm, the void, the gap between us all. I felt it underneath the legendary Walker's Oak, and it chased me down at the New Orleans Radiology clinic, what I hadn't counted on is it would swallow Janus and that Kirb would defiantly spit in front of it the petals of a flower. And yet he did not stop it. What are we supposed to do then? What can we say amidst the vast abysmal chasm? I knew that it would never leave. I would feel it in every song. I would think about it every time I looked at the moon.

I drank in a good pint of Mississippi river air and stared into the pain like it was a map underneath the hair follicles of my skin. It pulsated in me, a creature crawling through my nervous system.

"I could get another place and-"

The old devices no longer worked if they ever had at all. I could not spin a new story. I could not fathom a new life. I had spent so much of my life living for me, for what I wanted for my life. For what I wanted for Kirb, for what I wanted for Janus, for what I wanted for Adam, even for what I wanted for Mama, but I never spent enough time living for what *they* wanted. That moment of triumph when all the things I had imagined would come to pass would *never* come, and knowing that, I pitied myself. I wanted to tear up my hair by its roots in fistfuls and throw it on the ground and watch it blow away. But I could not concede, not yet, or all the gut-wrenching sorrow, all the loss, all the tears and heartache and suffering would be for naught.

To make the suffering matter, I was going to have to learn to shelter the will of other people, not just my own. This must be the charge of every true man or woman that lives: to live and love for others. It was the honorable thing to do. "To help other people," Dr. Plum had said. It was what made you feel better and even if it wasn't, it's what an Englishman would do, what an American would do, what a southern man would do, what a New Orleanian would do. How would I do it? That I didn't know. I did know it would be on my own.

A fierce western wind jumped up and grazed the bottom of my throat.

Day had not yet set in, and I wished that it was coming, but the city was trapped in that long stretch of morning where nothing much seems to happen except the rising of the sun and occasionally the sound of the husky horn of a ship moving out of harbor. The grass was tufted and the ground hard. There were no footprints or insects or animals, only the quiet warble of the murky water as it shifted sand and fish out to the Gulf of Mexico.

Poking out of the water was a half broken and burnt tree, split sideways from lightning, its fallen limbs drooped into the river and yet you could see fresh white bark sticking out like a bone. I bent over and touched its living parts and it felt smooth and cool. I ran my hand across it until I hit the ash and some of it came off onto my thumb.

The darkness came again. The chasm confronted me. I wanted to step into that darkness. I wanted the pain of it to make me forget the pain I had. I could walk into the water and see the bottom. There could be peace there.

Something occurred to me.

I'd be running right back to that imaginary place, that home where Janus, Kirb, Adam, and me were together. It wasn't real. It would never be real. I would be inseparable from the pain then, the pain that comes off bricks and hides in the shadows of the deep dark night. I would be the lunacy of Mama. I would be my grandmother in the garage, three sheets to the wind, poisoning my grandfather with fumes. Yes, I'd be Julius too. I'd be whole sad parts of my city that drowned, not in a single day or week like the hurricane had drowned so many, but I would drowned a long and terrible death over many years.

I rubbed the ash against my fingers. It was soft. At that moment I knew I must become something more than I was or more than my family had been, or I'd evaporate into the dark alleys of the city, stumbling around with a flask, weeping and gnashing my teeth, and wringing my hands, and crying for the dead, following that time-honored lifetime funeral procession, that dream that one never wakes from. I fought off my biology and my history and my impulses.

But there was something still burning in my pocket. I pulled the pearls out. I looked down at them, just as white as when I had given them to Janus, but their luster was gone. "I will always live in the melody of your heart," she had said when she put her hand on my heart with our baby boy growing healthy inside her. It hurt to think of it, to think of what I once had and could never have again.

"I will always live in the melody of your heart," I said out loud while I looked into, not the muddy white of the pearls, not the past, not the pain, not the ash, but, somehow, hope.

I looked into hope. Hope for something that I did not know. Hope for her and hope for me and hope for Mama. It had to be there somewhere. Hope in a truthful way, not the hope of the house on Lafayette, but the hope of Kirby's flower. A flower! A wistful creature in the age of logic and numbers and technology. It has no logical purpose. Its purpose is simply to be beautiful, to be stark, to be the fool for all our purposeful mechanisms. It did not come from our desire for it to be there, it simply is. And now that I think about it, maybe we came from flowers. Birthed from fields and fields of purple irises that said to one another that they needed a purposeful device to give them meaning, so their desire created mankind. I didn't know that it was true, but I didn't know that it wasn't. I mean, who can sit here and tell you that they know everything, that they know why a clock ticks instead of sings or why a city sleeps when it should be awake or why flowers can't be the seat of all creation or why any damn thing is the way it is?

We make our own truth. We are the clockmakers, and the city gets up when we get up. I know that now, as sure as I've known anything else I've ever known, and what truth is, you decide. The way I figure it, we can see life as a dream, or we can choose to see it as something else, something more gloomy, something like truth, and we can scratch our heads and dive into our books and say we know what truth is. But if you have lived in the world long enough, and you have known death, you understand that life is more than a dream and more than something gloomy, more than truth even, and then you can see life for what it really is, which is a moment, a moment and no more, and that's all it can ever be. That's where hope is. Not the imaginary hope that's manufactured by our minds, but the hope we were meant to find. And what a moment is for me is different for you and different for a brown pelican and different for a boat. A moment can be sixty seconds if you let it, but it can also be a whole day, or even a lifetime of days. I guess the most you can hope for is to say that you lived and that you lived beyond the knowledge of what most people consider life.

This is what I submitted to the chasm: "I will always live in the melody of your heart."

I said it again. I said it slower and even slower, and even slower, until it was just words, until it was just vibrations coming up my throat and out of my mouth, throttling my lips.

It was then that I fed the pearls to the city, watching them drop like grains of sand slipping through the fingers of an hourglass.

Looking into the deep brown of the Mississippi, it heaved like a man's chest, water churning up our collective histories just long enough to let them back out with a sigh.

I understood the river then. It shoulders all things. It claps against the shore because it cannot stop, it must continue on and on and on, through sunrises and hurricanes and billowing clouds overhead.